D1462244

TAMING THE COWBOY

CAROLYNE AARSEN

CHAPTER 1

"*R*ace you to your ranch," Trent called out, flashing Elliot a grin, his horse prancing in a circle, obviously as eager to go as his owner was.

Elliot shook his head, holding his horse back, thinking of the terrain they had to cross yet to get home. "Kane would shoot me if I showed up with a broken leg just before his wedding."

"Some saddle bronc rider you are, Elliot." Trent laughed, pushing his hat tighter down on his head as if in preparation for the race he hoped to run. "Afraid of some buck brush and a wooden bridge?"

Elliot held his friend's challenging look, still holding his horse back. Sancho was picking up on Trent's eagerness to get going, and Elliot was struggling to hold him in.

The sun was shining and a light summer breeze whispered through the trees edging the river below them. A perfect day for a ride, which was why he was out here. When Elliot woke up this morning the cabin he was staying in with Mason, his future brother-in-law, was empty, as was the main ranch house.

His brother Kane had left a note telling him that he and their father hoped to be back by noon, and if he was up before that, could he at least clean up after himself. Kane's fiancée was expecting company later on today.

The note put Elliot's hackles up. Though Kane said frequently that their relationship was okay, that he had forgiven Elliot for keeping himself apart from the family so long, Kane clearly didn't think his little brother was responsible. So Elliot skipped breakfast thereby skipping making a mess, got his horse saddled, and headed to Trent's place to go riding. Trent had a couple of days off and was happy to head out with him.

They were on their way back and had taken a shortcut, which led to the ranch.

Now they had to cross the river, and Trent wanted to race.

"I'm not afraid, just trying to be responsible." Elliot put heavy emphasis on the last word, struggling with the feeling that his brother and father still didn't seem to think he was.

Trouble was, more often than not he agreed with them.

"And as a cop, I'm surprised you're not more responsible yourself," Elliot added.

"I'm not on the clock," Trent returned with a grin. "I get to be reckless. When I'm back in uniform, I'll be all citizen of the year again. So you can stay behind and be responsible or you can show me if you still got it, Meacher."

Before Elliot could correct him, tell him he didn't go by his birth name anymore, Trent turned his prancing horse around, gave it a nudge in the ribs, and, with a spray of dirt, he was off. Elliot held his horse back a moment, watching his friend, then gave in to the challenge and let his own horse go.

The wind flying past his face, the thundering hooves, combined to create an exhilaration he hadn't felt in some time. A freedom he had missed.

Trent rounded a corner, but Elliot pulled his horse back and made a split second decision to take a shortcut. Plunging through the brush, he avoided slapping willow bushes, his horse gamely charging ahead down the bank and into the river, water spraying up behind his horse's hooves. Elliot glanced sidelong to see where Trent was, then heard an ear-piercing scream.

He yanked his attention back to the water in time to see a woman closer to the opposite bank perched precariously on a rock a third of the way into the river. He glimpsed dark blonde hair pulled up into a tight bun, brown eyes wide with shock, a suit jacket, and a narrow skirt and bare feet.

And he was a headed right for her.

Elliot pulled hard on the reins, hoping Sancho wouldn't slip on the rocks or ram into the woman, who was now splashing through the water, trying to get to the bank, tottering, struggling to catch her balance.

Sancho pulled back, ears up, eyes wide, and slammed to a halt, his feet scrabbling on the river rocks, trying to find his footing. Elliot held his seat against the sudden stop, giving his horse enough leeway to get his feet under him and still hold him back.

And then the woman, still trying to get away, took a wrong step and fell into the river, face first.

Elliot got his horse calmed and quickly dismounted, wading through the water to get to her. She was pushing herself up in the shallow water as he approached, water streaming down her face. She tried to get to her feet, but the slippery rocks prevented her getting a decent foothold.

"Sorry about that," he said, holding his hand out to her as she struggled to stand. "I didn't see you."

She glared at him, ignoring his outstretched hand. "You weren't even on the trail. What were you doing crashing through the bushes?"

"I was taking a shortcut," he said with a shrug and a grin. Up close she was prettier than his initial glimpse of her had shown him, despite being soaking wet, water dripping down her face, which made her mascara run. Thick, spiky lashes fringed her brown eyes, and he caught a faint sprinkling of freckles over

3

her nose and cheeks. The suit jacket and skirt set off her trim figure.

"You didn't need to come charging through here," she snapped.

For a moment Elliot was tempted to tell her he had more right to go charging on his horse wherever he pleased than she did to get upset about said charging.

Then her eyes widened, and she spun around, her head shifting from side to side. "Where is it?" she called out, panicked.

"Where's what?"

"My camera." She flailed around in the water, now on her hands and knees. "I lost my camera."

Elliot flashed on a vague memory of her crouched down holding something in her hand before she made a dash for the riverbank.

He searched with her, and then he saw it. A large, black, wavering blob, lying on the riverbed. He bent over and fished it out just as she grabbed it from him.

"I hope it's okay," was all he could say.

She turned it over in her hand, the distress on her face clearly showing him it wasn't.

"All my pictures," she wailed, brushing ineffectually at the water dripping off the camera. "Ruined. No thanks to you."

"Look, I was just out for a ride," he said. "You were the one wading through a creek on someone else's property," he couldn't resist adding.

Despite the humor of the situation her anger created a responding anger in him. She had no right to accuse him of ruining her camera.

She shot him a glare. "The fence was down. I didn't think anyone would care."

They wouldn't, but she was still trespassing. Not that he was pushing that point. He didn't care either. Technically, it was his

4

brother and father's land. He was just visiting and following through on a promise to help his brother Kane with his wedding while waiting out an injury.

And once his arm healed up completely, he'd be gone again. The rodeo was calling, and this year was his year.

But for now he was faced with a sopping wet woman. And despite her anger, Zach, his foster father, had taught him to always be polite and considerate, even to trespassers wearing clothes more suited to corporate Calgary than rural Rockyview.

"Do you need a ride to town or wherever you're staying?" he asked.

She looked up at him and shook her head. Then her gaze darted past him. And once again she was scrambling awkwardly backwards, eyes wide, mouth open as if to scream again.

What was wrong with her now?

"Your horse. Get him away." The way she was flailing to maintain her footing while moving away from him would have been comical if not for the terror in her voice.

He frowned, glancing back at Sancho, who had finally joined them, nudging Elliot with his head, looking for attention.

The angry woman was at the riverbank, grabbing at roots with one hand, her camera dangling from the other. She clawed her way up the dirt, falling a couple of times, her narrow skirt hindering her, then shot another panicked glance over her shoulder.

"Stay away," she called out. "Just stay away."

Elliot could only stare at her, unable to process the idea that anyone could be afraid of Sancho.

"He's okay. He won't do anything," he said, catching the reins in his hand and walking toward her.

"Just stay away," she called out, making it to the top of the bank. "You've done enough for one day."

As far as Elliot was concerned he hadn't done anything more than go for a ride on his own land.

"But you're all wet. Let me help you out."

"I'm not made of salt. I'll survive."

"What's your name? Where are you staying?"

"None of your business," she called back.

"I could pay for the camera," he said.

But all he got in return was a dismissive wave of her hand over her shoulder as she stumbled through the tangle of willows and brush on the edge of the river.

He wanted to follow to make sure she was okay. She might not be made of salt, but if she had arrived here by car, it was a hike to get to the road and, even though it was summer, she could easily be chilled by the time she got there. Besides, he didn't know how she would navigate the field in bare feet. He hoped she had her shoes somewhere close.

Then Sancho whinnied and Elliot turned to see Trent splashing down the river toward him.

"Hey man, what's up? I heard a scream. Thought something happened to you," Trent called out as he approached.

"Not me. I took a shortcut and scared some girl taking pictures. She was standing in the river. In a skirt of all things."

"What was she doing here? You know her?"

"Don't have a clue. Never seen her before in my life."

"Was she cute?"

He would say more pretty than cute. But he shrugged. It didn't matter. He doubted he would see her again.

"So, we going back to my place?" Trent asked.

Elliot looked back at the spot on the bank where the mystery woman had clambered up. Then he shook his head. "You go on home. I got something I need to do." Though the woman didn't want his help, he was still concerned about her. He wanted to make sure she got safely to wherever it was she was headed.

"I can help," Trent said.

"I doubt it." Elliot glanced over at his friend's horse that was even larger than his and thought of the woman's terror at the sight of Sancho, one of the quietest horses on Tall Timber Ranch. "I'll be okay."

"Suit yourself. Whatever." Trent paused a moment as if to give Elliot a chance to change his mind. Then, with a wave, he turned his horse and headed back to the opening in the trees further down the river.

Elliot waited until he was gone, then led his horse to the bank, water squishing inside his boots.

He was tempted to pull his boots off, hating the feel of wet socks, but he knew it would be impossible to remove them now. So he got on his horse and followed the disturbed willows, checking for the mystery woman's footprints in the dirt.

He kept his distance, remembering her panic, hoping she hadn't hurt herself.

ᕙ◯ᕗ

Were those hoofbeats behind her?

Kinsley stopped, shivering as she stood in the shade of a large aspen tree, water still dripping down her face. She shot a panicked glance over her shoulder. Her heart was still pounding from her encounter with the crazy cowboy and his horse.

But it didn't sound like he was following.

She retrieved her shoes and slipped them on, thankful she hadn't tried to wear them in the creek. The heels would have given her even more trouble.

A gust of wind created another shiver, and she thrashed through the rest of the willow trees and out into the open field and the blessed warmth of the sun.

She paused a moment, rubbing her arms that were rough with goose bumps. As she did, her camera bumped her arm.

With a sigh of dismay she slid it off her shoulder and looked it over again. The guy who sold her the camera assured her it

7

could withstand water, but she was sure he meant from rain and not from getting doused in a rushing river.

And she'd had such gorgeous shots of the sun filtering through the trees, sparkling off the water and splashing over the large, rough rocks. She tried to turn it on, but nothing. Hopefully the SD card would be okay. Hopefully. She had a months' worth of pictures on it she hadn't saved onto her computer yet.

Dumb cowboy, scaring her like that.

She fought down a shiver of fear at the memory of his horse coming so close to her. She'd thought she was over that fear by now.

But she could still feel the terror clawing up her throat when that cowboy came toward her leading that huge, lumbering beast. Those huge nostrils and those buggy eyes…

She shivered again, memories and fears slithering into her mind. It didn't help that her hip was aching now, a reminder of that horrible day.

The fact that this good-looking cowboy had mesmerizing eyes and casual hair that framed a masculine and attractive face didn't help her confusion. She didn't like how he made her heart beat a little faster.

Didn't like how he got to see her all awkward and stumbling. Of course, if she had thought things through and put on some running shoes, she might have been sturdier on her feet.

The muffled sound of footsteps behind her made her spin around, her eyes flicking over the moving branches of the willows. Did that guy and his horse follow her? She took a few quick steps backward, almost stumbling in the thick grass of the field.

Her cheeks flamed at the memory of floundering in the river, first getting balance then getting her camera. The cowboy must have thought she was a complete fool.

Another sound behind her sent her heart into overdrive. Was that a horse snort? But she saw nothing.

Relax, she told herself. *Why would he follow you?*

Because you were trespassing?

She couldn't imagine that being here would cause any problems. There were no cows in the field, and there had been a huge gap in the fence she walked through. It had been a hot long drive, and she wanted a break. When she crossed over the river and followed it for a few miles, she knew she wanted to stop.

It was only supposed to be a moment to enjoy the outdoors. Then she saw a bird on a branch and pulled her camera out to take a picture. The sound of the river lured her on through the field. Once she got to the river and saw the sun and the play of its rays through the leaves on the water she needed to capture the shot, and the best way was to go right into the river. The rocks looked flat and safe and the water was shallow. So she took her heels off and went barefoot. It was a good idea.

Until that cowboy came crashing through the underbrush scaring the living daylights out of her, potentially ruining her camera, and making her even more embarrassed. She wasn't sure which emotion made her feel the worst.

She took another look at her camera, wanting to take it apart and see if anything was damaged, but she told herself to leave it alone. When she got to the ranch she could look it over more carefully.

The sun had warmed the inside of her vehicle, and the heat that had been oppressive half an hour ago was now welcome. She set her camera on the seat beside her then rubbed her chilled hands together. She would be glad to get out of these wet clothes. So much for making that good first impression she always prided herself on.

Even though Faith was her friend, Kinsley was determined to treat this wedding with the same thoroughness and attention to detail she did with all the previous weddings she had planned.

And now she would show up at the ranch looking like she had lost a water fight.

As she started her car she shot another sidelong glance to the willows, just as the cowboy she had run into came walking out of the bush leading his horse. She'd been right. He had been following her. But why?

Her instinct was to turn the car on and take off, but the cowboy stopped on the edge of the field, watching her.

She wasn't getting out of the car and approaching him to find out what he wanted. Not while he was still leading that beast. So she started her car and without a backward glance drove away.

She turned the fan down, and when she was around the first corner, she pulled to the side of the road to check the map on her phone again.

Though she and Faith had been friends through college, she had never come with her to her home in Rockyview. Kinsley never had much time off. Her reality was she needed every spare moment for either studying or for working to pay for said studying and, of course, the physiotherapy sessions.

Though they drifted apart they kept in touch via Facebook and Instagram. There were a few years, after Faith and Kane broke up, that Faith drifted away, but in the past year she and Kinsley had reconnected.

When Faith found out Kinsley had worked for several years as a wedding planner she contacted her via Facebook. This was a perfect opportunity. Though Kinsley no longer worked for the company she had been at for eight years, she was hoping to partner up with another company. A very prestigious company. When she told Jill, her potential employer about the wedding, Jill had encouraged her to go solo. This would give Kinsley a chance to show Jill what she could do. So this wedding was essentially a job interview and trial run mixed into one.

She got her bearings then drove on, hoping her clothes would be dry by the time she got to the ranch.

Fifteen minutes later she pulled up in front of a large ranch house with an impressive veranda that covered arched double doors leading inside. Stone pillars supported an entrance framed with heavy timbers. Brightly colored pots of flowers crowded against the pillars. Flowering shrubs nestled against the aged wood of the house, creating a welcoming appeal. A curved walkway led from the space she had parked in to the front door. This was also edged with flowering plants and shrubs.

And behind all this rose the mountains, majestic and rugged, snow icing their peaks, white against the blue of the sky.

What a setting for a wedding, Kinsley thought, getting out of her car, trying to take it all in.

An open grove of trees stood to one side of the house. A path wound through it, edged with more flowering shrubs and flower beds. On the other side of the house an expanse of lawn stretched toward yet another grove of trees.

Kinsley's imagination went into overdrive. The ceremony could be to the left with an arch that framed the mountains. The house looked large enough to hold a post-ceremony tea if Faith and Kane were sticking to the number of guests on their list.

Then Kinsley heard her name being called. Faith Howard, soon to be Faith Tye, came hurrying around the side of the house, her arms open wide, her smile as bright as the sun that streamed out of the sky.

Kinsley came around the car to greet her old friend. "Hey, Faith."

Then Faith stopped, frowning at her. Kinsley realized how she must look. Her hair still wet but, thankfully, still up in a bun.

"Don't hug me," she warned as Faith came close. "I'm soaking."

"I see that. You better come into the house and get changed."

"My suitcase is in the car."

"I'll get it for you."

Kinsley waved off her offer and got it herself, then grabbed her camera and her laptop bag as well. She could only hope the pictures would be okay. She wasn't sure about the camera.

But despite her protestations, Faith took her camera and laptop.

To her surprise they didn't go through the front door. Instead they followed another sidewalk around to the side of the house, Kinsley dripping water as she went. Faith frowned at her. "So what happened?"

"I fell in the river," Kinsley said, her cheeks warming with embarrassment as Faith opened a set of French doors leading into an entrance. As Kinsley spoke she realized that there was a good chance the fence she had crossed was on Tye land. Faith's future husband's land.

"The river? How? Are you okay? Did you hurt your leg again?"

"I was taking pictures," Kinsley said, ignoring the last question. Her hip was throbbing now and her leg was twitching. She prayed it wouldn't start spasming again.

"Pictures?"

"The scenery here is gorgeous," she said. "The fence I went through was broken, so I didn't think there were any cows in that field. I mean, I might not have gone through if the fence wasn't down—"

Faith waved her hand back and forth as if erasing her concerns. "It's okay. No one cares. You should get out of those wet clothes right away though. You can tell me the rest of the story when you're dry. I'll show you where you'll be staying."

"You know I could have stayed at a hotel in town." Kinsley stopped in the entrance, set her suitcase down and tried to toe off her shoes. But her wet foot created suction, so she balanced on one foot, bracing herself with a hand on a wall to pull them off.

"Let me help," Faith said.

"No. I'm fine." Kinsley wiggled the first shoe off her foot then struggled with the second.

"Seriously, girl. Stop being so stubborn."

"I'm not stubborn," Kinsley grunted, still working on the unyielding shoe. "I'm just not letting any bride-to-be of mine help me pull off shoes."

Finally, with a squelch and a trickle of water dripping onto the tiled floor, Kinsley freed her foot.

Faith grinned, and Kinsley could almost hear the question reverberating through Faith's mind.

"Leg is fine, by the way," Kinsley said before her friend could ask too many questions.

Fine was a broad term that, she hoped, would keep Faith off the topic for a little while.

"So you'll be okay with sleeping upstairs? Tricia and the twins are staying in the house, but they're downstairs—"

Kinsley waved off her objections. "It'll be fine. I don't want you to change anything for me."

She could manage the stairs as long as she didn't have an audience.

"Okay then. I'll take you upstairs so you can change. I'm curious how this trespassing story will unfold." Faith ambled through a large kitchen, and Kinsley glimpsed warm oak cabinets, a large granite island and aluminum appliances, and then a small table with chairs snugged around it tucked into a bay window full of flowering plants. It looked welcoming and cozy, and for a moment Kinsley paused to take it in, missing her parents' home back in Prince Edward Island. Their house was probably an eighth of the size of this place, but it also had a bay window with a table and chairs as well as the plants her mother loved.

But Faith was already passing through the adjoining family room and into the main foyer. Kinsley quickened her awkward pace to catch up, thankful her fall hadn't caused a flare-up of the muscle spasms that could debilitate her.

"And here we have the great hall," Faith said with a wave of her hand, indicating the huge entryway they were passing through. "Grace Tye had a vision of light and openness, and this huge entrance was her dream. Zach, of course, did whatever she wanted."

"It's stunning." Light spilled from the windows framing the heavy double doors as well as from the multiple windows in the vaulted ceiling above them.

"Yeah, but the family seldom uses it. We always use the side door I brought you through."

Kinsley was looking at the play of light in the room but Faith was already headed up the stairs.

She moved to catch up, wishing she had time to inspect the pictures hanging on the stairwell. She caught glimpses of pictures of a girl posed with a horse, another one of her riding that same horse, racing around a barrel, hair flying behind her, pink cowboy hat anchored on her head. Tricia, she guessed. There were others of three boys astride horses as well, another action photo of a cowboy on a bucking bronc. She would have liked to check out the family photos but Faith was well ahead of her, looking back to make sure she was okay.

"I'm coming," Kinsley said, shifting her weight as she worked her way up the stairs. Thankfully the pain was easing.

She followed Faith down another long, wide hallway with doors leading off to other rooms.

Faith stopped at the fourth door. "I put you up here," she said, "so you could have your own space away from the noise of the house. Kane's room is on the main floor. Elliot and Mason, Tricia's fiancée, live in one of the cabins on the property. We've had to do all kinds of rearranging as people come and go."

14

In their many phone calls, Faith had mentioned her future sister-in-law, Tricia, and how she was training horses on the ranch with her fiancé, Mason.

"There's a desk in the room but you can also use this room for an office if you want," Faith said, indicating another door beside the one she was opening. "And this is where you'll be staying. It used to be Tricia's room, so it's a little girly."

Kinsley halted in the doorway.

She could only stare at the large, light-filled room with its pink carpet, two bay windows draped with white gauze curtains, and four-poster bed covered with a white duvet, pink pillows scattered on its cover.

"I can't go in there," Kinsley said, glancing down at her still-wet clothes.

"Well, I can," Faith said, walking into the room and dropping Kinsley's laptop and camera bag on the desk situated in one corner of the large room. Then she came back for the suitcase, but Kinsley grabbed it before she could pick it up. "There's an en suite bathroom, so you can change in there," Faith said flicking a thumb over her shoulder at a door in one wall of the room.

En suite bathroom? Just for her? How big was this house?

"So go change, have a shower, and we can swap coming-to-the-Tye-ranch-soaking-wet stories," Faith said with a smile.

"What are you talking about?"

"Change first, Miss Janas," Faith said, shaking her finger at her. "Stories later. I'll be downstairs."

Kinsley waited until Faith left before dragging her suitcase to the bathroom, leaving damp, uneven footprints on the carpet. The bathroom was huge, and she had more than enough space to lay out her suitcase and find dry clothes. She wrapped a towel around her head hoping it would soak up some of the water while she changed. Though she had packed blue jeans, she preferred to keep up her professional image, so she changed into another suit. She would wait until tonight for a shower. She didn't want to keep Faith waiting.

As she shook out her wet clothes she looked around for a place to hang them. A claw-footed bathtub large enough to swim in seemed a likely place. So she draped the skirt and blazer over the edge thinking they might dry enough she could flip them over tonight. Hopefully the river water didn't damage the wool and she could take them into town to get them dry-cleaned. She'd packed three other suits, so she should be okay for now.

She eased out a cramp in her thigh, grimacing as she stretched. She held it until it released then pulled in a breath. Her physiotherapist kept promising the spasms would ease with steady therapy—something Kinsley never seemed to have time for.

She walked into the bedroom and brought her camera back to the bathroom with her, turning it over in her hand, not sure what she was looking for or what she could do, struggling with a sense of dismay.

She pulled the SD card out, grabbed a fluffy facecloth off the shelf piled high with white towels, and set it out on the counter beside the sink. Then she set the card on it, hoping and, yes, praying that it would be okay. She'd been so busy the past few weeks she hadn't had time to download the multitude of pictures from it onto her computer. She'd hoped she could do some of that while she was here. Faith had assured her the wedding would be simple, so she wouldn't be working on it twenty-four seven. She would have time to wander around and take pictures.

Kinsley was excited about the idea. She so wanted to spend time working on her photography, a dream of hers since she picked up her first camera when she was ten. She had always hoped to make a career out of it. But it was difficult to get a foothold, and bills didn't get paid on their own.

She had to be practical, so she'd taken a job at a wedding shop. Her life took an interesting turn when she'd met Drake. He and his mother had a wedding planning business, and he asked her to come on board. To work her way into a partnership with him and his mother. They fell in love, got engaged, and she started planning her wedding. She also took a business degree to apply to the business. But Drake kept putting off the wedding, saying that he didn't want to get married until they were full partners in the business, which wouldn't happen until his mother quit.

But his mother wouldn't quit, and Drake couldn't commit.

When she overheard a painful conversation between Drake and his mother, Kinsley knew neither the wedding nor the partnership was happening. She gave Drake back his engagement ring and deleted her dream-wedding Pinterest board.

She got a job working at a bank. Not optimal, but it paid the bills. And then she met Jill, a client of the bank, who was looking to expand her wedding planning business. She wanted to give Kinsley a chance, but she needed Kinsley to apprentice, so to speak. So when Kinsley was approached by Faith to plan her wedding, she jumped on it.

This wedding was a chance to prove to her future partner what she was capable of.

Kinsley wiped her camera down, slipped the lens off, and set everything on another towel hoping and praying that there had been no permanent damage. This was her backup camera, but still. It cost enough, and she didn't want to have to replace it yet. There was no way she could afford to buy another camera, let alone the lenses she wanted.

She toweled her hair, ran a brush through the tangled and wet strands, then pulled it all back in a tight bun, slipped her feet into a pair of flats, and avoided looking in the mirror. It was fine. It was all fine.

She grabbed her laptop and made her way back down the stairs and through the hall to the kitchen.

"You're back quick," Faith said as she added a plate of cookies to the tray she had put together.

"Yes. The shower will have to wait till tonight." She could see Faith's frown as she looked at her suit.

"Did you pack any casual clothes?" Faith asked.

"Some, but I'm here on business so that's how I want to dress."

Faith grinned. "Haven't changed much, have you?"

"As one of my favorite photographers said, 'Fashion is the armor to survive the reality of everyday life'"

Faith gave her a sympathetic look and Kinsley realized how her words sounded.

"And how have you been doing since you broke up with Drake?" Faith asked, pouring boiling water into a coffee press.

"I'm doing just fine. Forging ahead and putting all my energy into my potential career. And speaking of, I know you'll probably want to get to work as soon as possible."

"First some coffee and catch up. Then wedding plans."

Kinsley knew her friend wouldn't let her off the hook, so with a sigh she followed Faith past the cozy little table and chairs through a set of sliding glass doors and out onto a veranda covered with a pergola. Pots of bright petunias and lobelia hung from the upper railing, and huge planters spilling with other flowers Kinsley didn't recognize filled the corners of the veranda.

"Just sit here," Faith said, indicating a large wicker chair filled with cushions. She set the tray on a glass-covered table and pulled it closer to her own chair. She handed Kinsley a mug then sat down with a satisfied sigh. "So. How did you get so wet?"

"Nothing like getting directly to the point." Kinsley chuckled, setting her laptop on the table. She took a sip of the delightfully hot coffee. "You said something about sharing stories about coming to the Tye ranch wet. Why don't you start, since you got here first."

Faith laughed and tossed her brown hair back. "I was hitch-hiking with my guitar in the rain. Sick as a dog with food poisoning. Kane and his dad became my own personal heroes, picked me up, and I ended up here." She shrugged one slender shoulder. "And the rest is, as you might say, history, or the reason we are getting married now."

Kinsley couldn't help a touch of envy despite being gratified her friend had found happiness. During the year they lived together while Faith studied law, pursuing her music on the side, and Kinsley studied for her business admin degree, they'd shared everything. Kinsley found out that Faith loved Kane to distraction, but she didn't want to become a lawyer as her grandfather and Kane, her then fiancé, wanted her to. Faith found out that Kinsley was struggling with her own fiancé's lack of commitment. Kinsley encouraged Faith to follow her heart and Faith told Kinsley to follow her head.

And now Faith had found her place in life while Kinsley was still trying to get her feet under her. In more ways than one.

"I'm glad you followed my advice," Kinsley said with a grin.

"And you followed mine?" Faith prodded.

Kinsley stared down at her bare hand. It had been over a year since she broke up with Drake and it still felt strange, to not be wearing the square-cut diamond that had graced her finger for six years. "It was good advice. It just took me longer to figure it out, that's all."

"I know it sounds cliché, but better to be single and content than miserable and married."

"That's what my mom told me too," Kinsley said with a melancholy smile. "Which is funny, because she doesn't know the first thing about being married and miserable. She and Dad are the happiest married couple I know."

"You're blessed to have that legacy," Faith said.

"And speaking of family, how are you and your grandfather getting along?"

"We still have our moments, but he's coming around. I've been helping him out with clerical work at his office, so that has made it easier. He's glad I've got a job working as a teacher this fall." Faith took a sip of her coffee. "So tell me how you came to the Tye ranch soaking wet."

"My story has more to do with geography than meteorology."

Faith frowned.

"Wrong place. Wrong time," Kinsley said, settling back in the chair. "I'd been driving through this amazing country and I desperately wanted to capture it. I had driven across this river a couple of times, so when I got close again, I stopped and walked out to take pictures. The water wasn't super deep close to the bank and I saw a perfect shot I wanted to capture, so I took my shoes off and walked over to the river to take a picture. Or more precisely, into the river to get the shot I wanted."

"And you fell?" Faith sounded skeptical. "'Cause of your leg?"

"Not at all, which is ironic. I got the living daylights scared out of me by some idiot who came charging down the opposite river bank on a horse and almost bowled me over. Completely irresponsible."

"No way." Faith shook her head. "Do you know who it was?"

"Actually, that idiot would be me."

CHAPTER 2

"So this is where you ended up," Elliot said, trying to mask his surprise and shock at discovering that the woman he had frightened was now having coffee with his future sister-in-law.

And not only that, was complaining to her about him.

The woman whirled around, staring at him, clearly as surprised and dismayed as he was. "You again?"

Not exactly the reaction he had expected, but maybe understandable given the circumstances. She had no idea he was staying here.

"I could ask you the same question."

She stared at him as if trying to figure out if he was kidding or serious, then looked away.

He had followed her far enough to make sure she got to her car, but he didn't know where she was going. If he had known she was ending up here, he'd—

You'd what? Been a little nicer to her?

She started it. And she was the one who freaked out at his horse. As if Sancho would do anything to anyone.

"So you're saying Elliot is the one who made you fall into the creek," Faith said to the woman, fighting down a grin.

"I didn't make her fall into the creek," Elliot protested, defending himself. Bad enough that this girl blamed him for ruining her camera. He didn't need to feel like he had been the instigator.

"Well, you sure didn't help," the woman returned.

Elliot could only stare at her. Who did she think she was?

"I'm sorry, where are my manners?" Faith asked, fluttering her hands as if to diffuse the situation. "Kinsley, this is Elliot Tye. And Elliot, this is Kinsley Janas. She's the wedding planner."

Ah, that's who she thought she was. Or rather that's who she actually was. The woman Kane wanted him to say hello to, be nice and helpful to.

He was in deep trouble now.

"You'll be seeing a lot more of her the next couple of weeks," Faith said, sounding as if this would be a good thing.

"Guess I didn't know what I was in for when I offered to help." Too late he realized how that came out, and before he could correct or apologize, the wedding planner—aka Kinsley Janas—leveled him an arch look that, in any other circumstance might be considered flirtatious but in this case was more conde-scending. Like she wasn't too crazy about him either.

Didn't matter. He didn't care.

"I might not need your help," she returned.

Seems she could give as good as she got.

Clearly they had not hit it off right. Any other time Elliot would have tried to make nice, turned on the charm that usually eased any potential tension, but he had also heard a few things about Kinsley the wedding planner that had made him decide to keep his distance even before their disastrous first meeting. She was a workaholic and a career person. Very focused and intense.

And thanks to their run-in at the creek, terrified of horses.

Certainly not his type on any level. Besides, he had to stay on track. Right now he was the closest he had ever gotten to a Canadian Finals Rodeo championship in years and he wasn't going to let any girl blow it for him.

"Actually, that's my designated position," he corrected. "Helper."

He had promised his brother Kane that he would do what he could to help Kinsley and Faith with the wedding because Kane was too busy with the haying to help as much as he'd like.

And because of the guilt that dogged Elliot, he'd agreed.

"Will you two be okay?" Faith asked, sounding concerned.

"Of course," Elliot put in, not wanting to make Faith uncomfortable. "I'll be on my best behavior," he promised.

Faith gave him a cautious smile and Elliot winked at her.

"So are you home for supper or are you going out?" Faith asked.

Elliot glanced over at Kinsley, who was still looking at him as if waiting for another apology.

"I figured on you being here," Faith added.

She gave him a bright smile, but he could see from the angle of her eyebrows and the tilt of her head that she expected him to stay.

"I promised Trent I would work with him at his arena tonight but I suppose I can cancel."

"Nice of you to do that," Faith said, giving him a tight smile.

Which immediately made him feel even guiltier. He had come back to the ranch to absolve some of that guilt. And apparently that meant helping Faith work with this uptight woman.

He held her gaze a moment then his cell phone buzzed. "Oh. That's Kane," he said, holding up his phone as if to verify his ducking out. "I gotta go."

He glanced over at Kinsley and caught her knowing look. Like he had manufactured his own getaway. Which he kind of

23

had. Kane's text was just a reminder to say hi to Miss Kinsley Janas and make nice.

Too late, brother, he thought, pocketing his phone.

"I just want the wedding to go well," Faith said. "Especially because Kinsley has to do so much in such a short time."

"It will all work out perfectly." Kinsley lifted her chin and tossing another glance Elliot's way as if daring him to challenge her.

"Picture perfect," he said. He would have asked her about her camera but the atmosphere was a little dicey right now, so he tugged at the brim of his hat, turned, and left.

Well, that didn't go well. But whatever. He shouldn't care.

It was just he wasn't used to being so totally shut down.

❧❦☙

"So do you and Kinsley have the wedding all planned?" Kane asked as he layered a piece of cheese on the hamburger he had just placed on his bun.

"In one afternoon?" Faith laughed, flashing Kinsley a wide smile.

"I'm good," Kinsley returned, smiling at the groom-to-be. "But I'm not that good."

"We were just catching up," Faith said. "That's why I wanted her to stay here at the ranch. So we wouldn't be constantly talking about the wedding and would have time to talk about other things."

"I thought you only had three weeks to plan the wedding," Elliot said, frowning at his future sister-in-law. "I'm thinking you should do more than just catch up."

"Things will come together." As she spoke Kinsley realized how she sounded. Uptight and little bit snotty.

She couldn't help it. She knew she should be more adult about the situation. It was just that Elliot made her feel uncom-

24

fortable. Part of it was her own disability combined with her unwilling attraction to him.

It also didn't help that she knew him as the man who had come between Faith and Kane the first time they broke up. Nor did it help he had terrified her and potentially ruined her camera.

All in all not the best first impression.

"Do you think you'll get it all done on time?" Zach, Kane and Elliot's father, asked.

"I'm sure we can," Kinsley said with a little more confidence than she felt. So much was riding on this wedding. If it wasn't that this could be her opening into a new partnership, she could be more relaxed about it all.

She gave Zach a quick smile then turned her attention to the massive burger Kane had made for her, trying to figure out how to eat it and still maintain some semblance of dignity.

Faith had decreed they should have a barbecue on the patio in honor of Kinsley's arrival. But it made for difficult eating, balancing the plate on her lap and juggling utensils, not to mention keeping her hair tamed. Because she'd had to put it up wet, she hadn't anchored it properly. Now strands of it blew around her face.

"I know what I'd really like," Faith said, shooting Kane a quick smile. "I was hoping to hold the wedding service and the reception here, on the ranch."

"Are you stuck on having your wedding outdoors?" Kinsley asked, wiping her mouth with her napkin.

"You've never done one before?"

"I have done several, but they've all come with a measure of stress about the weather and backup plans." Kinsley vividly remembered one of the last outdoor weddings she had worked on. The forecast had been good, but without warning the rain had come bucketing down.

And they'd had to make on-the-fly changes, which had

25

created even more tension between her and her future mother-in-law and boss. Sally Hansen had never cared for Kinsley, and it seemed she took any opportunity to put her down.

Well, she won in the end, Kinsley thought bitterly, taking another bite of her burger.

"It won't be a large wedding," Faith said.

"We could put up a tent," Elliot suggested. "That could be a good backup plan."

"Only if the wind doesn't blow," Kinsley said after she swallowed.

"We could be all pessimistic about it, or you could assume that the weather will be bright and sunny." Elliot flashed her a tight smile, and she guessed he was picking up on her feelings about him. She wished she could just act normally around this guy. It didn't help that he exuded charm or that his long, wavy hair, in need of a cut, gave him a rakish appeal. Nor did it help that her hip was throbbing, probably a result of her fall this afternoon in the river. Her very embarrassing fall.

Right in front of Elliot.

"I never like assuming with weddings." She took one more bite then wiped her mouth and set the rest of her hamburger aside.

"So you don't think we should have a wedding outside?" Faith asked. The stricken look on her face made Kinsley realize how harsh she'd sounded.

"I think we should do whatever you want to do," Kinsley said firmly. She wiped her hands and gave Faith a broad smile. "If you want to have your wedding outside then I'll make it happen. But I still want to make sure you're okay with a backup plan. I want this to be as perfect as you do."

"Okay. I think we can do that," Faith said. "All my life all I've ever wanted was an outside wedding. But I might have another favor to ask."

"What would that be?"

Faith wobbled her hand back and forth. "I've been having some hassle with the photographer I booked. I haven't heard from him for a while. So I was wondering if you could find someone for me. Just as a backup. You have connections to lots of photographers, I'm sure."

"I do, but I know for a fact they're all booked up."

Faith wrinkled her nose then sighed. "That's what I figured."

"You've got a camera," Elliot said to her. "You could take pictures."

Faith's dejection immediately flew away. "Yes. Genius, Elliot." She turned to Kinsley again. "You can be my backup plan."

Kinsley held up her hand. "Honey. Sorry. I will have my hands full getting everything going. There's no way."

"What if I don't hear back from the photographer in the next few days?"

"You will. I doubt he's that busy in a town like Rockyview."

"Actually, he kind of is. Though I was talking to a lady who came into Grandfather's office yesterday and she said she had him booked for an engagement shoot and he hasn't gotten back to her either." Faith gave her a pitiful look. "Please? Just as another option so I won't be freaking out about it."

"I'm not a professional photographer," Kinsley protested. "I just do it as a hobby."

"I've seen your hobby pictures," Faith said with an indulgent smile, ignoring her reluctance. "They are just as good if not better than many professional photographers. You have a real good eye. And I told you, I want to keep this wedding simple."

Kinsley felt everyone looking at her and wasn't sure what to say. In her experience simple and outdoors didn't belong together. There were always details that needed tending to and last minute glitches that needed supervision and the weather always hung over the day like a looming question mark.

And now she might be snapping photographs as well? What

would Jill think if that would happen? This was her first "solo" wedding, and if she wanted to prove to her potential partner she was capable, it had to work.

"I know it will make you busy," Faith said, leaning forward as if getting close to her would make Kinsley change her mind. "But we'll pay you whatever we would pay a professional photographer. And you could use it in your portfolio."

Despite her resistance, Faith's words hearkened to the old yearnings Kinsley had about her photography. The desire to do more than just snap pictures and spend hours editing them in Lightroom for her own pleasure. The desire to bring them out into the world. To use her dream in other ways.

"Don't worry about the photographer," she said, reminding herself to be practical, forcing the dreams aside. "I can talk to him too."

She could see Faith marshaling her arguments, just as she always did when they were in school. And Kinsley knew if she let her, her friend would talk her into it.

But Kane laid his hand on his fiancée's shoulder, pulling her back. "We can leave that for now," he said. "We've got a few other things to plan first. Like Kinsley said, I'm sure he'll get back to you."

He gave Kinsley a smile, and she was thankful for his intervention.

"For now, we need to discuss the venue", she said. "I know you want the wedding outside, but did you book a hall? As a backup plan?"

"No. I didn't."

"Okay. We'll have to take care of that right away," Kinsley said, making a mental note. "Give me a list, and I'll make some calls."

"Kind of late to book those now anyway," Elliot put in. "This late in the year they're all taken, even in a hick town like Rockyview."

Kinsley frowned at him. "I never said that."

He flashed a charming grin. "Nope, you sure didn't, but I did."

Which made her wonder if he assumed that was how she viewed the town.

"Just have it outside," Elliot continued. "With a tent."

If the halls were all booked up, would the tent company be as well?

She cut that thought off. First make the call. Then worry if it doesn't work out.

"Okay then. If you want the wedding outside, I think we should look into booking a tent like Elliot suggested." Kinsley wasn't going to look at him, but out of the corner of her eye she caught his smug smile. "It will make it a little more complicated for the caterer, so we need to talk about that next."

"Did you ask Kinsley about the horses?" Kane asked, leaning back and slipping his arm over Faith's shoulder.

"Horses? What about horses?" Kinsley couldn't help the shiver snaking down her spine.

"That's right. How could I have forgotten?" Faith snapped her fingers. "I want to come to the ceremony in a horse-drawn buggy," Faith said, her eyes turning dreamy. "That's another dream I've always had."

Kinsley's heart began a heavy pounding as her thoughts slipped back to this afternoon and how close Elliot had brought his horse to her.

She clenched her hands to stop their trembling, reminding herself that she didn't have to ride in the carriage.

"And like you said, you'll have your hands full with all the details, so I was hoping that you and Elliot would be able to work together on this," Faith said glancing from Elliot to Kinsley. "He could help you with all of the, well, technical planning and arranging."

"I don't know—"

"Horses and I—"

Elliot and Kinsley protested at the same time.

He went first. "I said I would help. I didn't think that would mean planning and arranging. I'll be gone most of the weekends till then."

"You'll find the time," Kane said. "It's not like you're busy on the ranch."

"Not out of any choice of mine."

Kinsley frowned at the sharp tone in Elliot's and Kane's voices. She hoped what had happened between Elliot and Faith in the past wouldn't cause more problems in the family. Weddings were tense enough as it is. She didn't need drama in the middle of the preparations.

"Kinsley doesn't know the ranch or community like you do," Kane put in. "I think you could help her out with the horses as well."

Kinsley swallowed her trepidation and shot a quick glance at Elliot. He looked about as pleased with the idea as she felt.

"I guess I could." Elliot folded his arms over his broad chest, chewing on his lower lip. He looked over at her and she could see from the concern on his face that he was remembering her reaction to his horse. "I'm sure we can figure something out."

"Okay. That's good." Faith looked relieved, smiling at them. "I'm so excited about coming in with the horses and the buggy."

Later. Deal with the horses later. Maybe she could steer Faith in another direction.

Unbidden came old memories, old pain, and terror. The dark and harrowing memory of being pinned beneath that huge horse, the sound of his panicked whinnying and thrashing legs grinding her even deeper into the rocks.

She swallowed and swallowed, sending up a prayer for strength. God had pulled her through that time. She needed to trust that He would help her now.

CHAPTER 3

"*W*here's Faith?"

Kinsley walked into the dining room, a clipboard tucked under her arm, glancing around, looking puzzled.

Elliot looked up from the rodeo stats he was reading on his iPad and stifled a sigh when he saw what she wore.

Another day, another fancy suit. Clipboard in one hand and oversize purse in the other.

"She had to go to the school to talk to the principal about the class she'll be teaching this fall," he said. "She said she'd be back in about an hour, so she asked if you and I could scout out locations for the tent and the service." Elliot couldn't help a quick glance at Kinsley's feet. Thankfully she was wearing sensible shoes this time. "Ballet flats" Denise had called them when she was educating him about the various shoe-types available to women. The lesson had made him glad his choices narrowed down to his black cowboy boots or his brown cowboy boots.

"She wants you and I to do it alone? Shouldn't we wait for Faith?" Wasn't hard to tell that Kinsley was as excited about the idea of their working together as he was.

"No. You never know with her these days. She isn't as time

conscious as she used to be." Elliot got up from the table. "I don't know what you want for breakfast. There's sausages and pancakes in the warming pans, fruit and yogurt in the fridge, and bread and a toaster on the sideboard."

"Wow. Lots of choices." Kinsley set her purse down on a chair, the clipboard on the table. "Yeah. Faith said you like big breakfasts, so she came early to make it for you." "She came back from her place in town just to make breakfast?" "Yeah, lucky for us, we were allowed to have some." Elliot gave her a cautious smile. "Faith likes people to feel at home here. Which is good because soon this will be her home."

Kinsley looked around, her hands folded together in front of her like she was waiting for something to happen. "Has everyone else eaten already?"

"Yep. Zach and Kane are riding fence."

Kinsley shot him a puzzled look. "So you don't need to help them?"

Her question was innocent, but it hit a sore spot with deadly accuracy. "You don't need more than two people for that." He tried to sound casual about it. He knew exactly why he wasn't involved.

He had been chasing a CFR championship for so long now, he had drifted too far both from the ranch and his family. Any job he took on was simply a side-hustle to make money to hit another rodeo. Because of this, he was gone a lot and had left his father and brother on their own for so long he felt he had no right to be part of the ranch.

And taking off with Faith over two years ago had only added to the tension between him and Kane.

"They don't really need me," he said hoping he sounded more unconcerned than he felt. Since coming to the ranch, Mason often helped Kane, but he and Tricia wouldn't be back for a couple of days. They were visiting the father of Tricia's first husband, Roger Bouche, down in Sweet Creek.

"But your father is getting kind of old," Kinsley pressed. "And you're part of the family, aren't you?"

She sounded genuinely puzzled, but it would take too many hours to explain to her the drive that kept him on the road, the remorse that had kept him away from Tall Timber, and the ghost he was trying to exorcise from his life.

"Zach is like an old bull. He just keeps going. Besides, I've got my own plans."

"Faith said you're a saddle bronc rider. I've never met anyone who does rodeo. So, where do you go with that? What kind of future does that have?"

Her question caught at the reality he'd managed to avoid for most of his career. A reality that hit him with a thud every time he landed wrong on the arena floor, every time he wrenched yet another body part on a rank bronc. It was a young man's game, and he wasn't getting younger.

"A short future. The pension plan sucks and the job security is sketchy." He gave her another grin. "It's hard to explain to someone who doesn't know rodeo..." He let his sentence drift off as he caught himself thinking about the same future she referred to. Then he shrugged. "It's a challenge. A kind of thrill."

His reasons sounded lame, even to him, but he wasn't about to share his concerns about his future with her. He'd been doing this too long, and he was too close to doubt his focus now.

"I guess I wouldn't understand," was her bland response.

"I'll just be outside," he said, walking away from the table before she could ask any more pointed questions.

He scraped the crumbs off his plate into the sink as he had been taught, yanked open the dishwasher, and set the plate and his mug inside. As he closed it, he looked out the window to the fields beyond the house. Somewhere out there Kane and his father were riding, out in the wide open spaces, sky above, earth below, wind in their faces.

He put on his boots and headed out, his thoughts chasing

him, remembering the days he and his other foster brother, Lucas, would be with them. The four of them on horseback, working together. Then coming back to the ranch where their foster mother, Grace, would be making dinner and Tricia would be working with one of her barrel-racing horses or hanging out with Drew, her on-and-off boyfriend.

They would sit down at the table all together. A family.

Lucas was the first to leave, signing up for the armed forces as soon as he finished high school, as he always said he would. Kane, Elliot, and Tricia stayed at the ranch. Rodeo was a big part of their lives at that time. Tricia with her barrel racing and Kane and Elliot with their team roping and saddle bronc riding.

Then Grace died of a massive heart attack and the family fell apart. Zach, full of grief over the loss of his beloved wife, retreated into himself. Kane, engaged to Faith at that time, grew morose and withdrawn. Elliot just went crazy. He had never known a mother before coming to the Tye household. Grace was a calming influence, a loving counterpoint to the vicious anger of his biological father. Her death was a body blow that made him lose his focus. His equilibrium.

He and Tricia started partying hard. When Tricia and Drew got pregnant, Elliot went with them to the courthouse as a witness to their quickie marriage. On the way back, Drew was driving, drunk. One wrong turn of the wheel, and the car went end over end. Elliot only remembered waking up in the hospital a few days later with bruised ribs and a broken arm. Drew was dead, and Tricia was gone.

His life got darker, more restless. The rodeo season was done, and he was angry and bored. He started hanging out with Faith the weekends when Kane was too busy on the ranch to go out with her. When Faith talked about ditching her future as a lawyer in her grandfather's firm, Elliot encouraged her to follow her dreams of playing guitar full-time. To that end he introduced her to a friend of his who had his own band and was looking for someone with Faith's talent. Kane and Faith fought, Elliot took Faith's side. And when he and Faith left together, Kane presumed the worst. He cut himself off from any contact with Elliot, blaming him for Faith's choices. Choices that sent her down a road leading nowhere.

Elliot clenched his fists, thinking about his own choices and the situation he had put Kane and Zach in.

He suspected that if he wanted, they would find a place for him on the ranch. But he didn't feel he had a right to lay a claim to that.

Elliot got to the corrals and wanted to check on his horse before Kinsley came out. Sancho stood dozing in the sun, his eyelids barely lifting as Elliot came near him.

"Hey buddy, I think we'll use you in the wedding. You and Seamus. You're the quietest animals we've got on the place." Elliot ran his fingers through Sancho's tangled mane, then patted him on the neck. "But that's for another time. For now we need to find a place to have this infernal wedding."

He walked back to the fence. Then, just to make sure his arm was still in good shape, vaulted over the rails. Perfect landing. He flexed his hand, satisfied.

He shoved his hands in his pockets, walking across the yard. Birds sang, and a gentle breeze wafted the bugs away. Above him the sky hung like an unbroken bowl of blue from horizon to horizon. A gentle peace wafted over him as he looked over the yard.

There was the barn he and Kane had helped build when they were only teenagers. There were the fences he and his dad had put up the summer that Kane had spent sick in bed, fighting a viral infection that the doctors couldn't diagnose. The tack shed he, Lucas, and Kane had built as a surprise for Tricia. The barn they used to play in when they were all getting along.

He frowned as he saw one of the barn doors hanging askew

on its hinges. He should fix that before Tricia, Mason, and the twins came back from their trip to see their grandfather.

The door of the house opened, and Kinsley stepped out carrying her clipboard. Could she look any more uptight and businesslike? He waved to her, and she came walking over.

"So where do you think we should start?" she asked, looking askance at the horses in the corral.

Yeah, we'll be dealing with them later, Elliot thought.

"Let's first figure out where to put the tent." Elliot strode past the corrals to the large open space on one side of the house. "I'm still not convinced the weather will cooperate," he said. "June tends to be our rainy month."

"I'm glad we can agree on that. The weather not cooperating, that is. I read that on the internet."

"You checked it out?"

"Also part of my planning process," she said. "I did some more research, and considering the size of the guest list and the fact that Faith wants a dance floor, we'll need a thirty-two hundred square-foot tent. Unfortunately that will take up most of the space in this yard."

Kinsley was writing something. A plan of the yard, Elliot noticed. "Looks like you been doing other planning too," he said.

"It's my job to be pro-active and on top of things. I did this last night," she said. And there it was again. That cool, collected tone.

"Well, I think no matter what, we should hold the reception in the tent." Elliot dropped his hands on his hips, glancing up at the sky as if checking to see what the weather might hold.

"Sounds like a good idea to me. But if I know Faith, she will want to have everything outside. So I'll have to make sure that I can manage her and her expectations."

"Manage her? That sounds more like you're planning a hostile takeover than a wedding."

She flashed him an annoyed look, and he guessed she didn't like his sense of humor.

"This is my job, and I am a professional. I've had to deal with dozens of starry-eyed brides who needed a dose of reality. I try to find a balance between what they want and what will work."

"How many of these weddings have you done?"

"More than you can count."

"I dunno. Math may have not been my best subject in school, but I can count pretty high." She sounded a little prickly, and he knew he should leave it alone. But something about her attitude toward the whole situation made him want to needle her. Just a little.

"I've been involved in over fifty weddings."

"Fifty? That explains the dispassionate attitude."

"What you mean, dispassionate?"

"Like I said, you're so businesslike. This is supposed to be the happiest day of any girl's life, but I guess to you it's just a job."

"It's what I've done for the last eight years. I've learned how to handle brides and their dreams. So, yes. In a way it is just a job." She made another note on her clipboard and gave him a cool look that clearly said, *Mind your own business.*

"I just thought because she's your friend, and she seems to really like you, that you might be more emotionally invested in this. This is a happily ever after moment. I thought girls lapped this stuff up."

And just like that, her face grew hard. Remote. "First of all, it's chauvinistic to think all a girl wants is to get married."

"Don't you?"

She bit her lip and turned away from him. "That's none of your business."

Guess he'd stepped over some invisible line and been slapped back.

"And second of all, happily-ever-after only belongs in fairy tales." Her tone was so cool it made him shiver.

"A cynical wedding planner. That's rather an oxymoron, don't you think?" he asked, unable to let it go.

"Not really. I've planned enough weddings that didn't...well..."

Her sentence drifted off and he wondered what she was going to say. But he guessed from the way her lips were pressed together he wasn't getting an answer.

But as she moved ahead of him, he frowned.

She was limping.

"Hey, are you okay?" he asked, guilt washing over him. "Did you get hurt when you fell yesterday?"

She paused, her head lowered, but she gave an emphatic shake of her head. "No."

Elliot waited, wondering if she would say anything more but she wrote something on her clipboard, her movements hard and jagged.

"So we agree on putting the tent here?" she asked, turning around but keeping her eyes down, her lips in a thin line.

Guess that topic was closed, which made him feel even guiltier about her spill. But though he wasn't the most avid reader, he was fluent in body language. This girl was saying loud and clear, *Back. Off.*

Okay. Back to business then. "If Faith sticks with the list she and Kane wrote up and doesn't decide to invite everyone she ever met while she toured and everyone in Rockyview, we can easily fit a tent here that can seat one hundred and fifty people."

This netted him a nod. "We might have to go with seating for one hundred and sixty, just to give us wiggle room," she said.

"But she's only inviting a hundred and twenty."

Kinsley tapped her pen some more, looking distracted. "I know. But when I planned my wedding—"

She stopped, and Elliot's ears perked up. "I didn't know you were married."

"I'm not."

"Oh. I'm sorry. That must be difficult."

Kinsley waved off his apology. "I'm not divorced. I just never...well...never got past planning the wedding." Her pencil tapped faster as if she was still dealing with the emotions of that. She shot him a look and in her eyes he caught a glimpse of pain and sorrow but as quickly as it came it left.

Oh boy, he wasn't hitting it out of the park here. This girl was one huge bundle of conflicted emotions.

"So we'll put up the tent here," she said, her voice brisk and businesslike, shutting that topic down. "Let's see where you thought of doing the ceremony."

He followed a few steps behind her as she strode away, her previous comment igniting his curiosity, as did the hitch in her step.

She certainly was a mystery. It seemed every moment with her he made yet another misstep and raised more questions.

Not that he was about to ask her anything. She wore that suit like armor, and her prickly attitude was enough to put him off.

But in spite of that, he couldn't forget that brief moment of vulnerability.

$$\backsim\hspace{-0.3em}\curvearrowright\hspace{-0.3em}\backsim$$

"So what's on tap for today?" Kinsley asked, finishing her coffee and looking over at Faith. This morning she'd gotten up earlier than yesterday, determined not to look like a slacker.

She had hoped to have eaten and be working in her room before everyone got up.

Kinsley prided herself on her work ethic, but how was she to know the Tye family kept such early hours? As a result, she was now eating with the entire family, something she'd hoped to avoid.

"Just give me a minute," Faith said, then looked back at her laptop she had sitting on the table beside her, her fingers flying over the keyboard.

Kane and his father were talking about the hay they had to cut today and fixing one of the balers. Elliot sat beside Kane, buttering his toast, not participating in the conversation. Yesterday he had said they didn't need him. Guess they didn't today either, which surprised her. She'd have thought he would be more involved in the ranch.

"Well, that's perfect," Faith announced, turning to Kane, her smile wide. "Fred Den Engelson is delivering the buggy today. Will you be around to help unload it when it comes?"

Kinsley stifled a beat of nervousness at the mention of the buggy.

You don't have to drive it. You don't have to have anything to do with the horses. Let it go.

Kane looked over at Faith with a rueful smile and shook his head. "Sorry, honey. Dad and I have to get the baler going as soon as possible. We need to finish getting this hay up before the wedding."

"I thought you were going to wait until Mason was back. He helped you the last time."

"He won't be back for a couple of days, and the hay is dry now. What with Joe quitting on us, we don't have much of a choice."

Faith made a face but then with a shrug turned to Elliot. "So, guess you'll be helping when the buggy comes."

"I guess that's my job these days." Elliot's voice clearly held a note of reluctance.

"Have you decided which horses to use?" Kane asked him.

"I think Sancho and Seaumus would be our best choices," Elliot said.

"Are you sure? Seamus hasn't been handled for years."

"I checked with Mason and Tricia. They told me they did

some work with Seamus. He's good. Besides, Tricia used to ride him. If anyone would know him, she would."

Kane scratched his chin with his forefinger as if thinking.

"Look, if you want me to help with this wedding you're going to have to trust my judgment," Elliot said, his voice holding a hard edge that startled Kinsley.

"Of course. Sorry." Kane gave him a half-hearted smile, but Elliot didn't seem mollified.

"Kinsley, I heard you went to Carmen's place yesterday evening to talk to her about catering," Zach said, seemingly eager to change the subject to something safer. "How did that go?"

"It went well." Kinsley wiped her mouth with a napkin and laid it on her lap, stifling her concerns about that particular situation. When she'd gotten to Carmen's, something was burning in the microwave, something else was boiling on the stove, and Carmen was on the phone. "She insisted on letting me try samples of the appetizers she hoped to serve."

"You're going with Carmen?" Elliot asked. "Why not Kerry who runs Mug Shots? She's a lot of fun, makes great food and has been around forever."

"And she's booked until forever too. Carmen said she wants to shift more into catering from running the coffee shop. I thought I would give her a chance." Then Faith stopped, giving Elliot a sly look. "Will that be a problem?"

Elliot gave a quick shake of his head. "No. Of course not. Me and Carmen are good."

Kinsley sensed there was something else going on, and as she caught Kane's smirk and Faith's teasing look, she guessed what it was.

"Old girlfriend?" she asked him.

"Ages ago. High school romance." He shrugged, as if to show it didn't matter anymore.

"Apparently she was the only girl to break Elliot's heart," Faith put in with an exaggerated sigh of sympathy.

"I think we can do without this trip down memory lane." Elliot leaned back in his chair, his arms folded across his chest.

But he was grinning.

"You could try again, you know," Faith teased.

"I thought Carmen was dating some school teacher named Brent," Kane said. "At least that's what Joe said before he figured he couldn't stick around to watch his own hopes for Carmen's affections die."

"Brent is a perfect match for Carmen," Faith put in. "I'll be working with him at school this coming year."

"Dietrich Bogal is on the school board. He's pretty happy with this Brent guy," Zach said, looking up from the magazine he'd ducked into.

"Dietrich would be happy with anyone who has half a brain and a pulse," Kane snorted.

"Including me?" Faith returned, her hand on her heart as if he'd wounded her.

"Well, you know, I didn't mean..." Kane sputtered.

"Oh to have the ability to think before one speaks," Elliot said with a wry grin.

"I forgive you for now," Faith said to Kane, flicking her dark hair back over her shoulder, adding a grin. "Though help with the dishes after supper wouldn't hurt."

Zach and Elliot laughed at that, and Kinsley sat back, smiling at the give and take. It reminded her so much of her own family that it created an ache of homesickness. It had been too long since she'd sat at a table with her parents, brother, and sisters. Though they called each other regularly, it wasn't the same as being with them.

"And I think we've left Kinsley marooned long enough," Faith said, turning back to her friend. "So. Carmen. What did you think of the food she served you?"

Though it was fun watching the family interaction, Kinsley was glad to get back to the business at hand.

"What she gave me was very tasty and unique."

Faith had said that she wanted heavy appetizers and barbecued ribs for her dinner, so when Kinsley arrived at Carmen's trailer she had half expected mini sausages in dough and meatballs. Instead she'd been served cranberry chicken salad on apple slices, chocolate dipped oranges, and smoked salmon and cream cheese cucumber bites.

Faith was beaming as she sat back. "She's a fantastic cook. And it helps that she's just starting out with her catering business. Tricia said she's willing to help Carmen, which is great because her, I can boss around."

"Good luck with Tricia," Kane said, wiping up the last of his egg with his toast. "I don't think anyone has ever been able to boss her around."

"Tricia has changed a lot," Elliot said, an edge to his voice.

Kane shot him a frown and shrugged. "I was just making a joke."

"Tricia is turning her life around, and I think we should encourage her," Elliot added, still sounding upset.

"And I think we can stop there," Zach said, his voice stern. "We have a guest, and we shouldn't make her feel awkward by bringing up family struggles."

Kinda late for that, Kinsley thought.

"I sense you're not totally sold on Carmen though," Faith said looking at Kinsley. "Don't you think she can do a good job?"

"I think she's a great cook and baker—" She paused, wondering how to phrase the next sentence.

"But..."

"But I would be lying if I didn't say I had concerns." Kinsley took a steadying breath and sat back in her chair. "She doesn't have a lot of experience, and her facilities aren't extensive. If I'm doing this wedding, you know I need to be completely honest with you. And I have to say I have a few concerns about someone like Carmen taking this wedding on. Appetizers are actually more work than a straight-up dinner. They require a lot of ingredients and perfect timing to make sure the hot stays hot and the cold stays cold. Especially if you want to do this outside."

"But she'll be doing everything here. In the house." Kinsley heard a note of doubt enter Faith's voice.

"If your future sister-in-law, Tricia, is an experienced cook, that would help a lot."

Kane snorted, and Kinsley saw Faith shoot him a warning look.

"Are you sure Tricia should help," Zach asked, not helping Kinsley's concerns one iota. "She's got the kids and the horses—"

"I think Tricia knows what she can and can't do," Elliot said. "And Carmen is enough of a perfectionist that she'll do an amazing job."

Kinsley knew from Faith that Elliot and Tricia had always been extra close, so she shouldn't be surprised at his defense of her. She had to confess to a niggle of jealousy at his defense of his old girlfriend though.

However, this wedding was more than a favor for an old friend.

Though she had never been the point person on a wedding plan, she knew how one small thing could cause huge problems. If Carmen didn't come through, if Tricia wasn't capable, if she didn't deliver the food on time, if she didn't make enough, it would be a reflection on Kinsley as the planner. And that would make it harder for Jill to consider taking her on.

"I don't want to state the obvious here, but it is my wedding." Faith added a smile to her comment as if to soften what might be perceived as a judgment of Kinsley. "And I'd like to give

Carmen the chance. I know she wants to sell her coffee shop and do more catering. This is an opportunity to show people what she can do."

Kinsley returned her friend's smile, curbing her doubts. "Of course it's your wedding. So if you want Carmen as your caterer with Tricia helping her, then that's what we'll go with."

She couldn't help a quick glance at Elliot as if to gauge his reaction to her comment. He gave her a tight nod, and she wondered why she cared what he thought.

"So the next things we need to deal with are the flowers, the minister, and the music." Faith looked around the table. But Kane and his father were pushing their chairs back and getting to their feet.

"Don't you want to be involved in this?" Faith asked, a hurt note in her voice.

Kane gave her an abashed look and a weak shrug. "You know I don't know much about this kind of stuff," he said. "I could give you advice but it wouldn't be much help. And right now I need to get as much of that hay up before the rain they're forecasting for this afternoon comes down. If you want to leave things until tonight I can go over some stuff with you."

Faith waved off his offer. "No. I understand. I'm marrying a rancher, and there are some things that can't wait. Serves me right for wanting a July wedding." She gave Kinsley an apologetic smile. "And I guess, deep down, that's why I hired you."

"Well, if you guys don't need me," Elliot said, getting up as well. "I'm heading over to Trent's place. He's got some horses he needs bucked out."

"But I need you to help me with the buggy and the horses this afternoon," Faith protested. "We have to get them ready to go. We only have a few weeks, and I want to make sure they don't spook."

"I'm still not comfortable with you using Seamus," Kane said turning to Elliot. "Maybe you should harness him up with Sancho and do some basic groundwork today."

Elliot sucked in, what sounded like, a frustrated sigh. "Okay. I can do that."

"When Mason comes back, he can help you." Kane gave his brother a smile, but Kinsley could tell Elliot wasn't happy about the situation.

"That's perfect," Faith said. "Before you do that though, Elliot, can you help me and Kinsley figure out how to set out the chairs and the arch for the church service on the yard?"

"I think we can figure it out on our own," Kinsley said, not sure she wanted to work with Elliot in the mood he seemed to be in right now. "Especially if Elliot has to work with the horses."

"It won't take that long."

Faith flashed her a quick smile, and Kinsley knew any more protests would draw attention.

Quite frankly she would prefer not to have to work with Elliot this much. Yesterday as they walked around the yard consulting about what to put where, she had a hard time not being attracted to him. Elliot was a completely different kind of man than any she had ever met. He was an unabashed flirt, and there was a rawness to him and an earthiness that was both appealing, and yet, intimidating.

It also didn't help that she had almost spilled her most well-kept secret in front of him. She had come close to making a fool of herself, and there was no way she was letting that happen again.

CHAPTER 4

*E*lliot pounded a stake into the soft grass. As he straightened, he glanced over at Kinsley and Faith who were standing around, doing nothing more than talking.

"Elliot, we need your expert opinion," Faith called out. "Kinsley thinks we could put the arch here."

Elliot set his measuring tape and stakes aside and walked over to join them. He looked at the horizon and shook his head. "If the wedding service is at five o'clock, the sun will end up right in everyone's eyes."

"But the arch will frame the mountains so perfectly," Kinsley said, sounding put out.

"Yes, it will, but the wedding guests won't be able to see much of the bride and groom and neither will the photographer."

Faith's phone rang and with an apologetic look at Kinsley and Elliot, she held it up. "Sorry. It's my grandfather. I've got to take this."

She scurried away, leaving Elliot with Kinsley, who had her arms folded over her chest. Definitely on the defensive.

"According to the tables the sun won't go down until ten," Kinsley protested.

"Doesn't matter. That time of day the sun will still shine directly in our guests' faces. But I can see you still don't believe me."

Her only answer was a shrug.

"Okay. At five this afternoon you and I are coming out here, and we'll sit down right there." He pointed to where Kinsley had pegged a ribbon in the grass for the chairs. "And you can get blinded by the sun."

Kinsley held his gaze then eased out a tight smile. "You sound angry."

Elliot blinked, realizing that she was right. "I'm sorry. I guess I am. I have a hard time with people asking me my opinion and then arguing with it." And an even harder time hanging around the ranch while his dad and brother worked, delegating him to this job. The last time he was here it had been a short visit after his win at the rodeo. Even though his family had congratulated him on his high score he still felt as if he had fallen short of their expectations.

"I apologize. It's just I so badly wanted the arch to be where we planned." She turned to look again. "Can't you picture it? The mountains, the arch, your brother and Faith standing in front of that amazing setting."

"It is amazing. You're right." He gave her a careful smile. "Look, I know we didn't get off on the right foot, figuratively and literally speaking, but from the way things are shaping up, we'll be working together a lot. We may as well make the best of the situation. It would make things easier for both of us."

She was quiet a moment then gave him a half smile. "I suppose you're right."

"We can make this work on a temporary basis. Once the wedding is over, you can go back to the city and your wedding planning career and find fame and fortune, and I can go back to the rodeo and find, well, something."

Kinsley chuckled, and Elliot was glad he had extended the olive branch. "Is that what you're looking for? Something?" she asked. "Sounds rather vague for a dream you've been chasing for years."

"I see Faith has been talking about me."

To his surprise she blushed. "Just chitchat."

"Actually, what I'm chasing is a buckle, a saddle, and my name being announced in the Michener Center as the new Canadian Saddle Bronc Champ."

"So what do you have to do to get that?"

"Win. Win. And win again. Every ride, every go-round, every rodeo."

"That's a lot of pressure." Now her smile was polite, and he could tell she wasn't that interested. "I hope you get there."

"Me too."

"And then what?" she asked. "What do you do after you've hit your goal, achieved your dream? Would you come back to the ranch? Come here?"

At one time that was the plan. Settle down at Tall Timber. Find someone.

"I don't think there's a place for me here," he said, then realized that he sounded like he was feeling sorry for himself. "And that's because of my own choices."

"What are you two talking about?" Faith asked, breaking into the conversation.

"Elliot and I are deciding where to put the arch and he thinks if we place it where you and I want it the sun will be in the wedding guests' eyes during the ceremony."

"But I really like it there."

"I do too," Kinsley said. "But Elliot has a point. No one will see you and Kane at all."

"What if we have the wedding ceremony earlier in the day?"

"You've already printed the invitations with the time on them," Kinsley reminded her.

Faith pursed her lips, and Elliot could tell she was already figuring out how to change things. "We've only invited a hundred and fifty people. We could call them and tell them we've changed the time."

Elliot wanted to smack his forehead. This was classic Faith. Changing plans midstream. She had grown up a lot in the past couple of years, life had hit her hard enough, but he could see there were still parts of her that hadn't changed at all. She was still the eternal optimist that figured things would work out just because she thought they should.

"That's way too much effort, and you don't have time for doing all that," Kinsley said, thankfully being the voice of reason. Elliot was already picturing himself hunched over the phone making countless mind-numbing calls. "Nor do you want the stress of keeping track of who you've been able to get ahold of. You're still waiting for RSVP's for about half of the people. You don't want to confuse them now."

Faith looked over to Elliot as if appealing to him would help.

"Kinsley is right. Leave everything the way it is," Elliot said. "We'll figure something else out with the arch. Something you'll be happy with. You have to trust that Kinsley knows what she's doing."

Faith looked back and forth at the two of them. Then, as if realizing she was outnumbered, she blew out a sigh. "I understand. It's just that I had this vision."

"Don't we all," Kinsley said with a wry note, and once again Elliot wondered about her "almost wedding" and what happened to her. Part of him wanted to find out, but he doubted he would get much out of her. He sensed she kept things close to herself, which piqued his curiosity.

And why do you care? She's just here for the wedding, and you're just here for the penance.

Elliot pulled himself back to the job at hand, pushing any curiosity about Kinsley and her past into the back of his mind. Right now he had to get through the next month and then he was off, free as a bird. On the road, living out his own dreams.

Just the way he had always planned.

ᕦ◯ᕤ

"That's the buggy?" Kinsley stared open-mouthed with dismay at the large, wooden, wheeled contraption that Elliot and the driver were unloading from a flatbed trailer pulled by a pickup truck.

It was Thursday, the clock was ticking, and now this.

"Isn't it beautiful?" Faith released a happy sigh, her hands pressed over her heart.

"It's…rustic," was all Kinsley could manage.

She should have asked Faith for pictures of said "buggy." She had imagined large metal wheels and a delicate gleaming black body with upholstered seats. Like the buggies she'd seen in *Emma, Sense and Sensibility,* and both versions of *Pride and Prejudice.*

She was a closet Jane Austen fan. Read all the books. Saw all the movies.

But this buggy was less Jane Austen and more *Little House on the Prairie.* A very rough and rugged *Little House on the Prairie.* The wood was vintage, for lack of a better word. The wheels had at one time been white but were now peeling, leaving most of the wood exposed. The sides of the box were uneven and one board in the back was missing.

She had no idea how Faith would climb up into the seat.

And that seat. Really? An old car seat with ripped upholstery in a faded shade of aqua?

"You don't like it?" Faith asked.

Guess she hadn't hid her dismay well enough.

"It has a certain appeal." To someone, no doubt.

But Faith was looking at it as if she were Cinderella and the fellow with the pickup and trailer had just delivered her a transformed pumpkin. "It needs work," she admitted. "But I think it will be great once that's done."

And Kinsley's heart dropped just a little further. Now, on top of the plans and the organization, she had to make sure this wagon was up to snuff?

Faith turned to Elliot. "So, do you think you can get this looking all spiffy by the wedding?"

Elliot looked about as excited as Kinsley. "When am I supposed to do this, between working with the horses, helping Kinsley, and my own rodeo schedule?"

"You have time during the week," Faith said with a note of confidence that Kinsley could tell Elliot didn't feel. "And I'll get Kane to help you when he's done with the hay."

Kinsley somehow doubted that Kane would have much time to do any restoration work. Not the way he was talking. But she could see from the dreamy look on Faith's face that she would have to find a way to work with her vision. Then Faith turned to Kinsley. "So what do we need to do next?"

Kinsley pulled out her phone. She had given up on the clipboard a while back. With Faith things seemed to be in perpetual flux, so she'd put everything in a document on her phone. She tapped the screen now, then frowned as her agenda came up.

"We need to talk about flowers. Where you're getting them and who is in charge of arranging them here at the ranch. And what exactly you want. And then we need to discuss music and—"

"I had a great idea for the flowers," Faith said, interrupting her, looking all excited. "The local greenhouse is having a big sale on all the plants they couldn't sell last month. I thought we could load up a bunch of those and bring them here. Because we're doing this outside, we can just use the pots the flowers come in."

And once again Kinsley had to switch her thinking. She had been imagining the usual formal floral arrangements and bouquets from a florist shop, not leftovers and rejects from a local greenhouse.

"You're giving me that funny look again," Faith was saying.

"I'm sorry. I don't mean to do that." Kinsley gave her a quick smile. "It's just something…different, and I have to wrap my head around that."

"That's what I want for this wedding," Faith said. "I want different. I want homey and easy to organize."

This wedding would be homey, but easy to organize was fading with each new curveball Faith threw at her.

The truck delivering the buggy started up and drove away as Elliot came to join them.

"What are your plans for the day?" Faith asked him.

"Well, I was going to connect with Trent."

"When?"

"Tonight."

"Excellent." Faith smiled at him. "Can you get your truck and do a small chore for me right now?"

Elliot nodded slowly, as if he was unsure of what Faith wanted now, and Kinsley wondered how "small" the chore would be if it required a truck.

"I thought you and Kinsley could go to the nursery and pick up some pots of flowers for me."

"Me and Kinsley?" he said, not sounding too thrilled about the idea.

"You're not coming?" Kinsley asked Faith, not sure she wanted to spend an entire afternoon with Elliot when he didn't seem to want to be around her either.

Faith shook her head. "No. My grandfather needs me to stop by his office before I go for my dress fitting."

"Wedding dress fitting?"

"Yeah." Faith shot her a bemused glance as if wondering what other possible dress she would be talking about.

"Shouldn't I come along for that?" Kinsley, once again, fought her frustration. Faith was throwing wedding stuff at her left and right and she couldn't seem to get her bearings.

"No. I thought I had to take care of that. Besides, I'm getting a local seamstress to make it."

Oh dear. In-laws and ex-girlfriends of the best man catering, old wagons, homemade dresses, leftover flowers. How would this all turn out?

"Would you mind sending me a photo of the dress?" Kinsley asked, pushing down a beat of panic. "Just so I can get an idea of where you're going in terms of style?"

"Sure. No problem." Faith glanced at her phone again. "My grandfather is getting antsy. I should go." She looked from Elliot to Kinsley. "So, you two will take care of picking up the plants from the greenhouse?"

"I still think you should come along," Kinsley said.

"That's okay. I trust your taste."

Taste wasn't her concern as much as selection. "And what about your bouquet? And the ones for the bridesmaids?"

Faith pulled her mouth to one side, as if thinking, and for a panicky moment Kinsley imagined herself wandering through fields of daisies gathering flowers for the bouquets and boutonnieres.

"Why don't I meet you at Carmen's in town?" she asked. "Elliot can drop you off there after you get the plants, we can go talk to the Mia Verbeek, the florist, and I can bring you back here."

"Or I could just take my car." Kinsley figured she could make quick work of picking out the plants and then she and Elliot could go their separate ways.

"No. Then you'd have to follow Elliot and find your way

there..." Faith scrunched up her face. "Just go with Elliot. That'll work best."

Kinsley wanted to protest once more but figured that would only draw attention to her reluctance to be with Elliot.

"Okay. We can do this." She gave Elliot a tight smile and was rewarded with a lackadaisical shrug.

She wasn't sure why Faith thought the two of them working together was a good idea. So far, she wasn't impressed and, she guessed, neither was Elliot.

CHAPTER 5

Be mature. Be responsible.

Elliot repeated the words to himself as he turned on the radio in his truck.

Kinsley sat on the seat beside him, her manicured hands tapping away on her phone. Today she was back to heels, which surprised him. It hadn't been hard to see the faint hitch in her step as she tried to navigate the lawn the other day.

"So what are you working on now?" he asked, curiosity getting the better of him.

"Just trying to plan out the actual service. I'm hoping to meet with the pastor in the next couple days, but he hasn't been answering my emails or phone calls."

"So who is the pastor at the church right now?"

"You don't know?" Kinsley shot him a puzzled look.

He answered her question with a shrug. "Haven't been for a while. Not exactly living the kind of life that God would approve of."

"And what kind of life is that?"

He wasn't sure how to answer her. Wasn't sure she would

want to be faced with the reality of his choices. Wasn't sure he wanted to look at it that closely himself.

"Just haven't been to church for a long time. And rodeo life doesn't lend itself to a strong spiritual experience." He neglected to add the fact that cowboy church was offered every weekend and that one of his fellow competitors had often encouraged him to come.

"I'm sure God would love to see you again," Kinsley said. Her reply surprised him.

"I take it you go to church regularly?"

"I need to. I need the strength I get from being around fellow believers, from worshiping, to get through the week. I'm always thankful to be reminded of God's love."

He glanced at her, surprised at the look of quiet peace in her expression. How sincere she sounded.

"Well I haven't had a lot of reminders of that, have I?" he said, unable to keep the bitter tone out of his voice as he turned his attention back to his driving.

"What do you mean?"

"All that talk about God as a loving father, kinda hard to jive with what my life's been like." As soon as the words left his lips, he wished he hadn't said them. But something about her quiet questions seemed to draw the words out of him.

"And what's your life been like?"

He gave her a cynical smile. "You really missed your calling. Are you sure you shouldn't be a reporter?"

"What do you mean by that?"

"And there you go again, answering a question with a question."

"Actually that's part of my job. I need to ask a lot of questions to find out where brides want to go with their wedding."

"Well I'm sure you're fantastic at that."

"I can be." But her sigh and the way she bit her lip seemed to show otherwise.

"You seem unsure."

"I just wish…the wagon…and…" She lifted her hand as if to stop anything further she might have to say.

"We didn't have to work with the horses?" he finished for her.

Another sigh and then a quick nod. "I once planned a wedding for a woman who insisted on having her dog pull her niece in a wagon down the aisle. It didn't turn out well. And horses are a lot bigger."

"And based on our initial meeting, you seem afraid of them."

She pressed her lips together and folded her hands on her lap, her knuckles white with tension.

He waited, the only sound in the truck the muted twang of country music from the radio.

"Yes. I am," she said finally.

"Why?"

Another beat of silence.

"I'm taking a chance and guessing that your limp has something to do with it?" he asked.

"That is none of your business," she snapped, rounding on him, her eyes flashing. "You have no right…" She let the sentence trail off, looking ahead, her chin up, her position defiant.

Guess he was right.

He knew he shouldn't have pushed, but he was trying to find out more about her. Especially seeing that Faith was determined to use the horses. He didn't want to deal with any issues that might arise with Kinsley.

"I'm sorry," he said. "I wasn't trying to pry. Just…well… wanting to get to know you better."

She gave him a wry look. "And why would you want to do that? I'm no one special." Her voice held a self-deprecating tone that surprised him and, if he were honest, bothered him.

"We'll be spending the next couple of weeks together. Just

thought it might ease some tension between us. I know you're not too crazy about hanging out with me and, once again, I apologize for almost running you over with my horse and ruining your camera."

"Actually, it's fine. It's water resistant, as the salesman told me it would be. Besides, it's not the only camera I brought along."

"Well, that's good to know. I'd hate to think I'd have to replace it."

"From the way Faith talks about how much you make, the cost of my camera wouldn't put much of a dent in your earnings."

"I do okay compared to my competitors. A win at the CFR would bring me in some serious money." He shot her a grin. "Almost as much as you make."

"I do okay as well," she returned with a wry smile. "Don't know if I need serious money as much as a steady job."

"And what would that steady job look like?" He slowed down as he came to the outskirts of town, looking out for the sign for the greenhouse.

"Doesn't matter."

"I'm truly interested," he said, shooting her another glance as he turned off the main road into town.

She hesitated a moment as if unsure of herself.

"Really," he added, puzzled at her reticence.

"Okay. I'd like to be full partners in a wedding planning business. Faith's wedding is my first solo project, and if it goes well, I'll have a shot at that partnership."

"Ahh, I see. So there's a lot at stake for you with this wedding."

"Yes. And I'm still concerned about the horses, regardless of how I feel about them. Animals in a wedding, no matter how large or small, are problematic."

"I have to admit I see your point," Elliot agreed. "I know our horses, and they're well-trained, but we'd have to run them through their paces a few times before they're comfortable. And that buggy isn't ready to use yet."

"So you agree we shouldn't use the horses?" She sounded relieved.

"I didn't say that. And if you're angling for a partnership, just think how having something like a horse-drawn buggy in a wedding would look on your résumé."

"I'm thinking of what having a bride break her neck in a runaway wagon would look like on my résumé."

Her candor made him laugh.

"You don't have to go to disaster mode right away," he said, still chuckling.

"It's part of my job. Imagine the worst thing that can happen and then try to prevent that."

Elliot understood her reasoning, but he knew Faith wouldn't budge. He just had to get Kinsley on board with the whole idea.

"I'm guessing this is the greenhouse?" Kinsley asked as Elliot pulled into a parking lot by a group of clear Quonset huts.

"She's smart, and good-looking," Elliot said with a grin.

He got out of the truck and sauntered around to her side, reaching for the door handle just as she opened it herself.

"You don't have to help me out," she snapped, reverting immediately to the old Kinsley.

"Actually, I was going to open the door for you," Elliot said disappointed at her sudden defensiveness. "Just like my mother taught me to."

"I'm sorry," she said. "I shouldn't have made that assumption."

She got out of the truck, but it took her a while. Elliot pretended to be checking his phone while she did, guessing she didn't like him watching how awkward it was for her. And as she did, he realized why she had pushed to take her car.

"So do you have any idea of what Faith is looking for?" Elliot asked, letting Kinsley go ahead of him, slowing his pace to match hers.

"That's why she hired me," Kinsley said, glancing around at the buckets overflowing with colorful flowers. "I'm the one that's supposed to have the ideas."

"Lead the way then," Elliot said.

Once inside the greenhouse Kinsley slipped into professional mode. She pulled her phone out of her large purse, swiped the screen, and glanced at some notes she had made.

They walked up and down a few of the aisles, all of them so full of flowers Elliot wondered if the owner had sold anything yet this year.

"Can I help you?" Adelle Rosychuk, the owner of the greenhouse, joined them. Elliot remembered her from the days he did attend church.

Kinsley tapped her phone against her chin as if considering her question. She paused a moment, then pointed at a wooden planter filled with blue and white flowers.

"Do you have another one of those?"

"Yes, I do. I have two more. You'll need to trim the petunias down, but they're still good."

"Excellent. We'll take all of them."

Kinsley pointed out a few more buckets, asked a few more questions, and Elliot just followed them. It was interesting watching Kinsley work. Her defensiveness had dropped away, and she was very much in charge of the situation. And she seemed to know exactly what she wanted.

An hour later Elliot, Adelle, and a few staff members had loaded up all the flowerpots and planters Kinsley had chosen. They filled up the back of his truck.

"This looks like way more than we need," Elliot said as he covered them with a tarp to prevent them getting damaged on the way home.

"You'll be surprised once we set them out in the yard. It won't look like near as many."

"I guess you're the expert." He tied up the tarp, snugging the straps and glancing up at the low-hanging clouds. Kane wouldn't be thrilled with the coming storm. "We need to get going if we want to meet Faith on time. And, if it's okay with you, I'll be the gentleman my mother raised me to be."

Her response was a quick smile. One of the first genuine ones he'd seen from her yet.

He opened the door and had to resist the urge to hold out his hand to help her into the truck. She slung her purse over her shoulder and, to his surprise, got in the truck with no trouble.

"I'm not so helpless after all," Kinsley said, her voice holding a sardonic tone, as if she noticed his surprise.

"I would be if I wore that skirt and those shoes," was his reply, choosing to avoid the obvious.

Her expression softened at his comment. "It's all part of the uniform."

"If you say so. I prefer blue jeans and plaid shirts myself."

"Why am I not surprised," she returned, taking in his shirt and faded denims.

He laughed, closed her door, and made his way around the truck. Somehow, he felt as if he had passed some kind of unknown test.

As he started the engine, he glanced her way and was surprised to see her looking directly at him. Their eyes held a moment longer than necessary and, to his consternation, he felt a slow lift of his heart.

Her expression grew serious, and she was the first to break the connection.

Elliot spun the steering wheel, frustrated with the emotions she raised in him.

Emotions he had no room—or time—for.

Elliot parked on the main street of town, walked around the truck and, before she could stop him, once again held the truck door open for her. And once again Kinsley was strangely touched by the polite gesture. She knew it was simply habit, and despite her initial annoyance with Elliot's behavior, she couldn't help the tiny thrill his actions gave her.

Not to mention the look they had shared in the truck.

She shook off unwelcome distraction and walked into the coffeehouse, determined to be more discreet and self-disciplined.

Sure, he was good-looking. Tall, broad shouldered, and confident. Sure, he had a way of looking at you as if you were special, but she could not allow herself to be sidetracked by a charming man again.

"Good afternoon, Kinsley. Nice to see you again. What can I get for you?"

As she was greeted by Carmen who, at one time, had dated the man behind her, she was reminded once again why she had to be careful. Carmen was petite, brunette, and absolutely adorable with large brown eyes and a smile you couldn't help return. Plus, she was a genuinely sweet and kind person.

"I'll have a black slow roast coffee and whatever you recommend for a snack," Kinsley said.

"I'd try the lemon cookies." Elliot, who had come up beside her, rubbed his stomach. "A recipe handed down from Carmen's mother, who is as fantastic a cook and baker as she is. And almost as good-looking."

Carmen rolled her eyes. "Oh, you old smoothie," she said. "But yeah, the lemon cookies are good. Elliot's favorite. Sweet and sour at the same time."

"Nice," was all Elliot said.

Kinsley thought of the comments Zach and Kane had made about Carmen and Elliot. How they had dated at one time.

But Elliot seemed comfortable around her.

"So I hear you're dating some guy named Brent?" Elliot asked, leaning on the counter and giving her a lazy smile.

"Well, I wouldn't say that, exactly."

"Oh, look at her blush," Elliot teased.

Carmen shot him a warning look, but Kinsley saw the humor in her dark brown eyes.

"I'm happy for you, sweetie," Elliot said, no trace of rancor in his voice. "You deserve someone who'll stick around and take care of you. Does he have decent parents?"

Carmen's expression softened. "He does. He comes from a good family. You know, you do too."

"Yeah. I guess."

Which made Kinsley sense there was history behind that comment.

Carmen turned to Kinsley. "Sorry about the chitchat. I'll get your order together." She glanced at Elliot again. "I'm guessing you'll have the same as Kinsley."

"Seems we share a love of slow roast coffee and lemon cookies." Elliot looked over at Kinsley with a smile. He pulled out his wallet. "I got this."

She felt she should protest but figured this was a small thing to give in on. "Thanks."

Elliot looked surprised. "You're not arguing with me?"

"I'm not that independent that I would turn up a chance to save myself some money." Kinsley grinned at him.

Elliot laughed at that, the sound a lot softer than before.

And once again it gave her a funny little thrill.

When Carmen gave her the coffee and the cookie wrapped up in a parchment paper bag, she gave Kinsley a sly little look. Kinsley wondered what she meant by it.

A few other people were sitting at the mismatched tables in

the café. Some nodded at Elliot as he passed, said a quick hello, and gave Kinsley a puzzled look as if trying to figure out the connection between the two of them.

She agreed that they couldn't look more disparate. Elliot in his cowboy hat, plaid shirt, faded jeans and worn boots and she in her tailored suit and high heels.

Country boy, city girl.

Elliot found an empty spot, pulled off his hat, and set it on the table. He looked like he was about to pull the chair out for her. Though she beat him to it, his attempt made her feel oddly pampered. Cared for.

Something she hadn't experienced in a long time.

As soon as they sat down, the door burst open and Faith rushed into the coffeeshop, looking flustered.

Her eyes fell on them and she hurried over, yanked the empty chair away from the table, and dropped into it, her phone in her hand. "Sorry I'm late. It took longer at Mrs. Boyko's than I thought. But while I was there, I got a text from the teacher I'm taking over for. I need to talk with her, but she can only meet me today. I know I said I would go check out the flowers, but I have to do this now." Faith gave them an apologetic shrug after her rush of explanations. "I feel like I've been such a doofus the past couple of weeks. I'm not usually this unorganized."

Kinsley knew that. When they were in college together, Faith was the one who was focused and always got her work done.

"Wedding jitters," Kinsley said, absolving her with a smile and a lift of her hand. "It's pretty common."

"I know, but I hate being so scattered. I feel like I've got too many balls in the air. My upcoming job, my wedding, trying to get ready to move into the house." She rubbed her forehead with her forefinger, then her phone binged again. She blew out a breath in exasperation as she looked down at it. "I'm sorry, I gotta go."

"Did you see the flowers we picked up?" Elliot asked, sounding peeved with his future sister-in-law. "The ones you insisted we get because they were so cheap?"

"No. I didn't. I'm sorry."

"Will you at least look at them when we get back to the ranch?" Elliot urged.

"I'm hoping this meeting will only take an hour. That'll give me lots of time to check out the flowers. We can even figure out where to put them once I'm there."

Kinsley flipped through her phone, checking her weather app. "If it doesn't rain," she said, feeling a niggle of concern.

"The forecast is just for scattered showers. I doubt we'll get hit with that so close to the mountains."

"Okay." Kinsley wasn't as optimistic as Faith was but then, what did she know about local topography and meteorology?

Faith shoved her chair back and gave Kinsley a quick hug. "See you back at the ranch. Thanks again for picking up the flowers."

She waved at Elliot and with a clamor of the bells on the café door, Faith was gone.

"Okay, I guess we're on our own again," Elliot said, tossing back his coffee. He glanced out the large-paned windows overlooking the patio and made a face. "And it's starting to rain just like your forecast said. We should get going. I don't want to unload those flowers in the rain."

Kinsley agreed. She set her uneaten cookie aside, finished her coffee, and stood. Unfortunately she moved a little too quickly. Her heel caught on one of the chairs and, to her embarrassment, she teetered.

Elliot was right there, his hand on her arm, steadying her. "You okay?" he asked, concern etching his features. His hand was warm, his face inches from hers. She could see the gold flecks in his hazel eyes, the faint stubble shading his rugged jaw.

Too handsome for his own good and too attractive to ignore.

As soon as she jerked away from him she knew she had overreacted. But not for the reasons he expressed when his smile faded and his eyes narrowed.

"Sorry. I didn't mean you to think—"

"I just...just caught my heel, that's all." She wished she didn't care, but his visible retreat bothered her. "Thanks though," she offered.

He returned her comment with a vague smile. She was thinking he might say more when the bell above the door jangled again and a tall young woman walked in, paused, then called Elliot's name.

"Hey, mister, I heard you were back." She strode over and without a moment's hesitation wrapped her arms around Elliot in a hug, her leather purse swinging against him.

"Denise. Hey." Elliot returned her hug, grinning as he did so.

Another old girlfriend? She seemed his type, Kinsley thought. Denise's hair hung loose, her curls flowing down the denim vest she wore over a plain white shirt. Her faded and torn blue jeans and scuffed and worn cowboy boots completed the look of country girl comfortable in her own skin.

"So I'm guessing you're in town for Kane and Faith's wedding." Denise still had her hand on Elliot's shoulder in a proprietary and natural manner.

"Yeah. I'm helping Kinsley here. My future sister-in-law's wedding planner." Elliot gave Kinsley a sheepish look as he took a step away.

Denise turned to Kinsley, her smile shifting just a little, her eyes narrowing as she took Kinsley in.

Trust me, I'm no threat, Kinsley wanted to say as she held her hand out to the beautiful woman. "Hello. Nice to meet you," she said instead.

Denise gave her hand a perfunctory shake, still looking at her. "So, a wedding planner. Kind of lah-de-dah, no? I didn't think Faith was like that." Though Denise was still smiling, her voice held a faint note of disparagement.

"It's easier for her," Elliot put in before Kinsley could say anything. "Faith's busy with getting ready for her job and helping out her grandfather. Besides, Kinsley is an old friend of Faith's and offered to help."

"Good of you," Denise said, still looking at Kinsley.

"That's me. Kindness personified," Kinsley couldn't help but retort. Denise's jealous look was annoying and, frankly, a waste of energy.

"If you need any help, I don't mind pitching in. I helped both my sisters with their weddings," Denise said, her smile shifting again.

"Thanks for the offer," Kinsley said. "I'll keep it in mind."

"As for you," Denise said, turning her attention back to Elliot and tapping one perfectly manicured finger on his chest, "Don't be such a stranger. We don't live that far away. Stop by sometime. We could go out for a ride like we used to."

"We'll see," Elliot said, slipping one hand in his back pocket, his grin widening. "Those were good times, for sure."

"They sure were." She held his gaze a beat longer than necessary, as if recalling those very good times, then pulled a pen and notebook out of her purse and jotted something down. She tore off the sheet and held it out to Elliot. "That's my new cell phone number. Give me a jingle. I've got the next week off. It would be fun to reconnect."

Elliot took the paper, glanced at it, then slipped it into his pocket. "It was great seeing you again, but Kinsley and I have to get going."

His simple connecting of their names gave her an obscure niggle of pleasure.

Which she stifled. What did it matter to her that this stunning woman wanted to reconnect with Elliot?

And yet, as he walked ahead of her and held the door open,

she couldn't help a quick glance his way, pleased to see him smiling down at her and not looking back at Denise.

Rain splattered down, harder now, making the sidewalk wet, and she forced herself to take her time. She didn't want to slip in front of Elliot and, even worse, in front of Denise, who was watching them through a window of the café.

Elliot paid no attention to Denise and opened the door of the truck for Kinsley.

Just before she got in she looked at him again. "I'm sorry I overreacted. Back there when I stumbled. I knew you were just trying to help. But I was okay."

A slow smile crawled across his lips as his eyes crinkled, rain dripping off his hat. A smile that only increased her awareness of him. "You're right. I shouldn't have jumped in. I thought you were going to fall."

"I...I tend to get a bit touchy at times," she said. "About my balance and, well..." She let the sentence trail off.

"Your limp," he finished for her.

She startled at the bold pronouncement, her cheeks warming with embarrassment.

"I've had to struggle along a couple of times myself," he added. "One broken leg, one sprained ankle."

Part of her felt like she should take issue with his comment. A one-time injury wasn't the same thing as a lifelong disability. But when she chanced a look his way she caught gentle understanding in his deep hazel eyes.

"I know it's not the same but, well..." He let the sentence drift off and added a shrug. His words combined with his killer smile eased her protestations.

This time he allowed her to get into the truck on her own and he didn't help her even though he could see she was struggling. As she settled into the seat, she shot a quick glance down the street at the coffeehouse. But to her relief she couldn't see

69

Denise anymore. The difference between them couldn't be more pronounced.

Denise, easy and comfortable with Elliot. Obviously comfortable with horses as well. She looked and dressed the part of a girl from a ranching background.

And she didn't limp.

Kinsley pushed the unwelcome thoughts out of her mind. Denise shouldn't matter to her.

She set her purse on the seat and pulled her phone out to check her schedule as Elliot drove.

She shivered a moment, her clothes damp from the rain, which grew louder and harder despite Faith's optimistic forecast.

"I'll turn the heat up," Elliot said.

She gave him a nod of thanks, glancing behind her at the truck bed. "I hope the flowers survive the rain."

"The tarp I covered them with should help." Elliot looked back at the load then gave her a quick smile. "I don't want to have to go back to the greenhouse again."

"It wasn't that bad, was it?"

Elliot shrugged and flicked on the windshield wipers. The rain was coming in hard drops, falling with heavy splats on the truck window. "Actually, no. I used to go with my mom every spring." He shot a glance her way. "By my mom, I mean Grace Tye."

"I assumed that," she said.

Faith had said little to her about Elliot's past, other than they had brought him into the family as a foster child. "That's kind of neat that she took you along."

"She was a great mother." The hitch in his voice was so small she might have missed it had she not been watching him. Had she not caught the way his jaw clenched and chin lifted.

"I'm sorry about her death."

Elliot shrugged, as if erasing the flash of pain she had seen.

"It was a tough time for the family. Things kind of went off the rails for a while." The truck slid on the now-muddy road but Elliot corrected, slowing down.

"I understand that was when Tricia and Drew got married?" Kinsley asked. And when Elliot and Faith had run off together, though Faith had repeatedly assured Kinsley that nothing had happened between them. However, she heard from Faith it had caused estrangement and tension between Kane and Elliot.

Elliot released a harsh laugh. "If you want to call it a marriage." He turned off the radio, still looking ahead. The windshield wipers were slapping in double time, as the rain had become a torrent.

His terse comment ignited her curiosity. "What do you mean?" she asked, knowing she was prying yet unable to keep her questions at bay.

The increasing bad weather was making her nervous, and she wanted to talk about something, anything, rather than focus on the roads that were now like grease.

"We got into an accident on the way back from their elopement. I think she and Drew were legally hitched for about forty-six minutes."

"Forty-six minutes?"

"Drew died in the accident."

"Oh, I'm so sorry." This was news to her. She knew Tricia was a single mother, she just didn't know the entire family dynamics and history. "That's so sad. That's a lot of sorrow for your family."

"Yeah, well, Drew wasn't the best boyfriend material, and he wouldn't have been a great husband or father either." Elliot pulled his hand over his jaw and then flashed her another signature grin. "But now Tricia has met Mason, who is a way better guy than Drew ever was."

"And now Tricia and Mason are engaged."

Elliot nodded, still grinning. "If you do a good job with this wedding, maybe Tricia will hire you to plan hers."

"I think we'll take it one wedding at a time," she said, but couldn't keep herself from returning his smile despite the tension now gripping her neck. She hoped the rain quit by the time they got back. "However, all these celebrations, this must be such a happy time for your family."

This created another beat of heavy silence as his smile faded. She wondered if she'd overstepped. Said something insensitive. Then she realized they had just been talking about Grace, his mother. He was probably thinking about her as well.

Should she speak and risk making another mistake?

She was about to apologize when Elliot yelled, slammed on the brakes, and spun the steering wheel. She glimpsed a deer as the truck spun sideways then bounced over a rut in the road. She bit down a scream as the truck jolted again, Elliot fighting to regain control on the slick and muddy road.

The truck spun, bounced once more, and then crashed into a tree.

CHAPTER 6

*T*he truck rocked to a halt.

Elliot clung to the steering wheel, dazed by the sudden impact. His mind twisted back to that horrible moment almost three years ago. Broken glass, screaming, agony.

He blinked, dragging himself back to the present. His chest ached from the jolt on the now-deployed airbags, the dashboard was lit up, steam poured from the hood of the truck, but he didn't think he was injured. To his surprise, his hat was still anchored to his head.

The window beside him was shattered as was the back window. The windshield was a maze of stars and cracks.

Kinsley.

He spun sideways, pain shooting through his body at the sudden movement.

Kinsley sat slumped in her seat, her head to one side.

Elliot fumbled for his seat belt, suddenly desperate.

"Kinsley, Kinsley, talk to me," he pleaded, lunging across the seat toward her.

She slowly lifted her head, looking at him. A small trail of blood trickled from a scratch on her temple. Elliot's heart thundered in his chest with a mixture of relief and concern.

She was alive, but hurt.

"What happened?" Her voice was strong, which allayed his concerns.

"Don't move," he said, touching her forehead, his fingers gently probing. He touched her neck, his eyes on her face the entire time. "Does this hurt?" he asked.

She shook her head, then groaned. "That was a mistake."

"Do you feel okay? Are you dizzy? Do you feel nauseated? Like you want to throw up?" He fired the questions one after the other, watching, waiting, anxiety thrumming through him. He'd helped enough of his fellow bronc riders off the arena floor to know what to ask, what to look for in case of a head injury.

"Just my head hurts," she said, touching her forehead again. "I'm not dizzy."

Elliot's hand still rested on her shoulder, his eyes still held hers.

He hardly dared believe that nothing had happened to either of them. The last accident—

He shut his eyes, erasing the image. He had to focus on the now.

"I'm so sorry. I thought I had control."

"It's not your fault," she said, giving him a pained smile. "We'll blame it on the deer."

That may well be, but Elliot still felt as if he should have done something. Anything.

The truck was still running, the lights pointing at an awkward angle, lighting up the glistening trees. Rain still pounded down, coming in through the side windows now.

"We can't stay here," Elliot said, shifting to one side to pull his phone out of his pocket. He glanced at it and his heart dropped at the blank screen. It was dead. He looked around for his charge cord, but then realized he had brought it into the house yesterday but had forgotten to charge it.

"I can't phone for help," Elliot said, feeling stupid and useless.

Kinsley unbuckled her seat belt, wincing as she did, then bent over looking at the floor of the truck. She frowned and glanced hurriedly around. "I've got my phone in my purse, but I don't see it. My purse, that is."

Elliot couldn't see anything that resembled the large, pink bag she carried everywhere. He lifted the deployed airbag in front of her just in case, but nothing.

"It must've flown out of the truck on impact."

"It has everything in it," Kinsley cried out. "My wallet, my phone, my papers."

Ignoring the throb in his chest, Elliot shifted, trying to get a better look around the cab of the truck. Unfortunately he still couldn't find the purse.

Kinsley shivered, and Elliot realized the longer they stayed here, the colder and wetter they would get. But what were their options?

He looked behind him, thinking.

"We need to get somewhere dry. There's a house about a half mile down the road," he said. "It's abandoned, but I'm sure I can break in."

"What about my purse?"

"You stay here, I'll have a look outside." Elliot tried to open the door, but it was jammed shut. "Can you open your door?"

She tried, but hers was stuck as well. Elliot bit his lip, thinking. He had no choice but to climb through the window beside him. He checked, but no glass shards remained on the frame. As he maneuvered his way out, the pain in his chest made him wince. His hat came off, but he grabbed it, clamping it down on his head again.

The ground was spongy beneath his feet, and he grabbed the

side of the truck bed to make his way up the side of the truck. The rain made it hard to see, and he squinted as he glanced around, looking for Kinsley's purse. He made his way around the entire truck, still nothing.

So they couldn't use her phone either.

He tried to open her door from the outside, yanking on it, but it didn't budge.

Rain streamed down his back, pouring off his hat.

They had to get moving. The steam from the truck was making him nervous.

"You'll need to climb out my window," he called.

She bit her lip, looking apprehensive.

"I'll help you," he assured her.

She nodded, shifting to the other side of the truck as he worked his way back to the driver's side window again.

"Just come out head first." He held out his arms. "I'll help you."

Kinsley hesitated a moment, looking from him to the broken windows. The seats were wet, the dashboard was wet, and it would get worse as the wind picked up.

Then with a shrug she leaned out, stretching her arms to him. He held her as she wiggled her way out of the truck. But at the last moment, as her full weight came on him, he was thrown off balance. He caught her, falling back against a tree, holding her close.

For a moment their faces were inches from each other, moisture spiking her thick eyelashes. He shifted, still holding her, suddenly aware of the slenderness of her body, her warmth. His breath caught a moment as he saw a sudden spark in her eyes. Then she blinked and looked away and that brief moment of connection was gone.

"We've got to get going." He swallowed down his reaction and gently moved away from her.

"Just follow me," he said, walking back along the side of the truck.

He got to the back of the truck and saw that Kinsley was struggling. Should he help her? Would she be insulted?

"Just hang on to the frame to help you along," he called out to encourage her.

Her narrow skirt and high heels were hampering her progress, but he waited, getting wetter by the moment.

Finally she made her way to where he was, but this time he didn't even hesitate. He caught her by the arm, supporting her, as he helped her up the steep incline to the road.

She accepted his support, but when they got to the road she jerked her arm back.

"I'm sorry. I was just trying to help," he said.

Kinsley swiped the moisture away from her face. "So where do we go?"

"Just down the road here. I'll lead the way." Elliot glanced once again at her high heels, wondering how she was going to manage the muddy road.

And when she started walking, the hitch in her step was even more obvious. She hunched her shoulders against the rain, wrapping her arms around herself as she walked. It would be a long, slow haul.

He caught up to her and pulled his coat off. He draped it over her shoulders and was given a grateful look. Then to finish it off, he dropped his hat on her head.

"You'll get soaked," she protested.

Elliot shrugged as he sidestepped a huge puddle. "As you so wisely once said, 'I'm not made of salt.'"

Kinsley chuckled and looked like she about to say something more when she stumbled over a rut on the road. She cried out as her ankle twisted.

Elliot caught her before she fell, holding her up as her face twisted in pain.

"I'm sorry, I turned my ankle," she gasped.

Elliot wasn't surprised. Her high heels looked dangerous on flat surfaces, let alone a rutted gravel road in the rain.

But this meant it would take them forever to get to the house. And the rain wasn't letting up. Rainstorms this close to the mountain always dropped the air temperature. Hypothermia was a real concern.

"You won't like this, but you'll need my help." Elliot stopped, his arm still around her.

"But you're helping me now," she said through gritted teeth.

"You can't keep walking like this," Elliot insisted. "You'll do some real damage to your ankle, and we'll both be freezing by the time we get to that house."

As if to underline his point, she started shivering.

"Sorry, girl, you'll have to climb on my back so I can carry you piggyback."

She looked horrified and tried to take another step, stumbling again. She stopped, pulling Elliot's coat closer around herself, squinting through the driving rain. She bit her lip, then glared at him.

"I don't like this at all," she complained.

"Protest acknowledged. Swallow your pride, put your arms through the sleeves of my coat, and I'll help you up."

Her narrow skirt was a hindrance, but as he hitched her up, he heard a tear. Guess that skirt was a write-off.

Thankfully she wasn't heavy, and with her on his back, he immediately felt a little warmer.

He shifted her again, lowered his head into the rain, and continued walking, hoping the house was as close as he estimated.

Kinsley clung to Elliot's neck, the driving rain more of a concern than her feelings of self-consciousness. Elliot's coat was warm and his hat protected her. She felt bad that she wore them instead of Elliot, but really, that was the least of her worries right now.

Her ankle throbbed, and her hip hurt, but she rode out the pain. She had no choice. She couldn't walk, and they had to get to shelter.

"How much longer?" Kinsley asked, her mouth close to Elliot's ear.

"One step at a time," he grunted, stepping around another puddle.

"You sound like my physiotherapist," Kinsley muttered through lips growing numb with the cold.

"Actually, I sound like mine."

"You have a physiotherapist too?"

Elliot nodded. Kinsley couldn't see his face, and she guessed he needed all his breath for the walk. So she kept quiet, hung on, and endured.

His back was warm, and to her surprise, she stopped shivering. But her hip was throbbing even more now, keeping time with the pulse of pain in her ankle. Her legs were wet and her feet, in their ineffectual high heels, freezing.

Please, Lord, let us get there soon, she prayed, her head now tucked against Elliot's, trying to garner what precious heat from his body she could.

"Hang in there, honey," Elliot said, breathless, breaking into her thoughts. "Just a few more yards."

Kinsley was too miserable to protest his endearment.

She could tell Elliot was getting tired. His breathing grew heavier, and his steps slower.

"Let me down, I think I can walk from here," she said, feeling guilty and too aware of how he held her and how close they were.

"Not a chance," he grunted, stopping to give her another

shift, moving her a little farther up his back. His arms held her legs just a little tighter.

He was strong. She could feel his muscles moving under her arms. She doubted Drake could ever have carried her this long let alone this far.

And then, finally, through the rain she saw a driveway with a mailbox at the end. A few minutes later, Elliot was trudging up some wooden steps and onto a dry porch. A pair of metal chairs sat by the front door. Elliot walked over, gently slipped her off his back, and helped her onto one of the chairs. It was freezing as well, but at least she could sit.

Shivering in earnest now, Kinsley clutched Elliot's coat close. To her surprise, he knelt down and picked up her ankle, touching it as carefully as he had touched her neck, gently probing. She winced, and he gave her an apologetic smile. He grabbed the other chair, dragged it across the porch, lifted her foot, and placed it there.

"You'll be okay for a little while?" he asked.

Kinsley shot him a look of dismay. "Where are you going?"

"I need to break into the house." Elliot wiped the moisture off his face. "I helped build it, so I know how to get in."

Then to her surprise, he touched her cheek with his fingertips. As if to reassure her.

"We'll be okay," he said. "Once we get inside."

Kinsley nodded, resisting the urge to grab his hand.

"You better take your hat," she said, tugging it off her head.

"Keep it. It will keep your head warm." His smile flashed at her, and then he vaulted over the porch railing and jogged around the side of the house.

As she sat in the gathering dark, rain spattering down, her thoughts spun. She didn't like being by herself in the rain, and being alone, soaking wet, and in pain made it even harder. Would anyone miss them, and if they did, would they come looking for them? How would they get warm in a house that looked uninhabited? Would this do even more damage to her aching hip?

An old memory flashed into her mind. Another time when she was alone and wet, afraid, pinned under a flailing horse, pain and fear flooding her as she waited. And waited.

She pressed her hands to her eyes, willing the pictures away. *That's done. It's over.*

Please, Lord, she prayed again, rubbing her aching hip, wincing at the pain in her ankle. *Please, Lord,* she begged, sending up another plea, fighting down her guilt.

As a young girl she used to pray all the time. After her accident and dealing with months of physio and pain, she struggled with her faith in God. Especially after enduring the taunts of some of her classmates about her limp. Crooked Kinsley they called her.

And stop.

Kinsley clenched her fists, shaking off the thoughts. That was long ago. She was a successful woman now, on track to becoming a partner in a flourishing business.

If this wedding goes well.

Kinsley groaned again, thinking of the plants in the back of Elliot's truck. They couldn't have survived the crash. They'd have to get more, which was too bad. There weren't many decent pots left at the nursery.

She shivered again, her present distress overtaking thoughts about the wedding. A gust of wind swirled around the house, blasting rain on her back. She wanted to get up, but her hip was aching and her foot throbbing.

Where was Elliot?

Then, finally lights flicked on, the door beside her opened, and Elliot stood in the doorway, framed by a gentle glow of light coming from inside the house.

He knelt down beside her, gently lifting her foot off the

other chair. He fitted his hands under her arms and helped her up.

"We'll be okay," he assured her. "Someone will come looking for us. Or someone will drive by and see the truck and let Kane or Zach know what happened."

Kinsley let his words wash over her. Right now her focus was on getting inside the house. She tried to take a step when Elliot caught her by the arm, stopping her.

"Hold up, honey. You'll do more damage to that foot if you try to walk." He slipped his arm around her waist, holding her close to his side. "Walk with me."

She had no strength to protest, and she knew doing so would be foolish. So once again she let him help her along, trying not to be self-conscious about the rip in her skirt. She needed to get out of the cold and wet.

They stepped into the entrance of the house and Elliot closed the door behind her. "There's not much for furniture in here but we'll make do," he said looking around the large, open space they had stepped into. A stone fireplace, flanked by two large floor-to-ceiling windows took up one wall with a cracked leather couch sitting in lonely isolation in front of it. The floor was bare plywood—no carpet or flooring anywhere. One lone lamp supplied a feeble light.

"Here, let's sit you on that couch. There's electricity but the furnace isn't hooked up yet. But I can build a fire."

Kinsley wanted to protest. She was far too aware of the rip in the back of her skirt, but if she walked slowly, maybe he wouldn't notice.

So she let him take her to the couch. When she got there she tried to sit down slowly but her hip gave way and a hot surge of pain seared her ankle, so she plopped ungracefully down, her entire body shaking with cold. Elliot lifted her legs and shifted her sideways so she could keep her ankle elevated. "I think we can take these off," he said, flicking a finger at her heels.

"Probably," she admitted, knowing full well what he thought of her shoes, now caked with mud. And, she had to admit, right about now, they did seem foolish. He pulled them off and set them aside, the simple gesture oddly intimate.

"You're freezing," he murmured, grabbing her hands as if to warm them. "I'll get that fire going."

"With what?"

"There's a stack of wood outside. Tanner and I cut that up when we cleared the yard. Hang in there, I'll be back." He gave her a crooked smile that made her heart skip, then, once again, left her alone.

Moments later he returned with an armload of firewood and an ax.

"Are you going to chop that in here?" she asked, aghast at his boldness.

"It's just plywood flooring, and I'll be careful. It's too wet to make kindling outside. Besides, this will all be covered once Tanner puts flooring down. If that ever happens."

"Why hasn't it?"

"He doesn't live here anymore. He stops by maybe once every half year to visit his grandma down the road, but for the rest, he stays up north. Working."

"What does he do?" Kinsley asked, sensing there was more to this story.

"Something in the oil fields." Elliot shrugged as he dropped the firewood on the floor with a heavy clatter. "After losing his wife and kid he was gutted. He needed to get out of town so he left and stayed away. I just know he got Kane his job after he and Faith…after Faith joined the band."

She wanted to ask after Tanner, but Elliot's momentary hesitation after mentioning Faith caught her attention more.

"Which was a mistake with some bad repercussions," he added.

"Are you talking about her breakup with Kane?"

Elliot swung the ax, neatly cleaving a log. He set it aside, then chopped another one, frowning as he worked, as if it required his entire focus.

"Yeah. I wish I'd had nothing to do with that." He stopped abruptly as he grabbed another log and chopped it. Harder than before. He snatched one up and, with rapid cuts, broke it down into much smaller pieces for kindling. One of the pieces he feathered with his jackknife, frowning as he worked, intent on the job, not adding to his previous comments.

With quick, efficient movements, he had the kindling set up. He pulled a lighter out of his pocket, flicked it on, and in a few moments, the welcome crackle of wood burning filled the room. Elliot got up and fiddled with, what she assumed, was the damper. The entire time his mouth was set in a grim line and a frown darkened his eyes. Smoke eased up the chimney, and the fire grew.

"I'm sorry if I stepped out of line with my comment about Faith and Kane," she said.

The warmth from the flames was reaching the couch, and she took Elliot's wet coat off and rubbed her arms, shivering again, thankful for the heat.

He shook his head then turned to her, still squatted in front of the now-blazing fire. "It wasn't you. It was me. I know Kane is happy now, and that he and Faith are good. Obviously, they're getting married, but I still feel like he resents me being around because I took off with her after their fight."

"If he's concerned about you and Faith, he has nothing to worry about. She's head over heels in love with him."

"I know that," Elliot said with a wry smile. "She always has been. Truth is, Faith and I didn't leave town 'together,' the way Kane seemed to think." He made air quotes with his fingers. "The guy in the band I introduced her to was a friend of mine. They were looking for someone to sing and play guitar. Faith did both and wanted so badly to play music. Wanted to give herself some space from the pressure her grandfather and Kane were putting on her to become a lawyer. Something she had no joy in. When she left with the band they were following the rodeo circuit, so I went along for the ride. I knew Kane was angry with me and blamed me for Faith leaving, so I didn't come back to the ranch."

"Does Kane know about you and Faith not being a couple?"

"I'm sure Faith told him," Elliot said, pushing himself to his feet. He laid his coat on the remaining stack of wood, close to the fire. Then he walked over to the couch and picked up her hands, rubbing them between his. "You seem to be warming up a little."

"Once my clothes dry, I'll be nice and toasty," she said with a smile. "How about you? Are you warming up?"

"Yeah. I am," he said.

He seemed only too willing to move on to another topic of conversation, but Kinsley couldn't forget the note of bitterness in his voice as he spoke of Faith's decision and his brother's reaction.

"You said you think Kane resents you being around," Kinsley pressed. "Have the two of you talked about it?"

Elliot shrugged then started unbuttoning his shirt. "It's been busy since I came back," he said.

Kinsley swallowed, trying not to stare as Elliot stripped off his shirt. Thankfully he was wearing a T-shirt underneath it. Not that that helped much. The sleeves were tight around his bulky arms, emphasizing his biceps. The damp shirt clung to his broad chest, showing her the defined muscles she'd been clinging to as he carried her.

She couldn't help but compare him to Drake, who was slender and shorter than Elliot. Who always wore a suit and kept his hair perfectly clipped.

Elliot's hair, however, was a tangle of waves curling past his neck and falling over his broad forehead. He looked exactly like the cowboy he was.

"Why don't you give me your suit jacket?" he asked. "I can dry it and my shirt at the same time."

She wasn't so sure she wanted to take her coat off. Her shirt underneath was damp, and the thin silk would probably cling to every part of her body.

"You'll warm up faster if you take it off," he said, sensing her hesitation.

This was sensible advice and made her self-consciousness seem silly. She shrugged her jacket off, and he helped her, his rough hands scraping over the fine fabric of her shirt.

"Sorry," he apologized. "I hope I didn't snag anything with my callouses. And I'm also sorry about your ripped skirt."

Kinsley couldn't stop the blush that crept up her neck, warming her rain-cooled cheeks. "I guess I was hoping you wouldn't notice."

"I probably should have kept quiet. Kane and Lucas always say I run off at the mouth too much." He shrugged. "But I felt it give way when I carried you. I felt bad for you because I know how you like your suits."

He took her jacket and his shirt and draped them over a broken wooden chair that he dragged closer to the fire.

"Like I said, I like to look professional."

"Why? You think you can't look professional in blue jeans? I mean, I do," he said with a teasing smile, waving at his own jeans. "My office clothes."

Which made her laugh.

"Each profession has its own dress code, I guess," she replied.

"And your dress code is tailored suits. Have you always liked to dress so…" He waved his hand at her jacket. "Like that?" He'd hesitated, which made her wonder what he was really going to say.

"Actually, no. I grew up wearing sweat pants and the loose,

sloppy clothes my mother chose. Once I started working in the wedding planning business, I bought a suit." Not that it made much difference to Drake's mother. She'd always made Kinsley feel that she was lacking.

Elliot flashed her a puzzled look. "I can't imagine you in sweats."

"I even had matching warm-up jackets." Easier to wear in a wheelchair, her mother would say. "So you can see, I've always liked suits. Just wore a different kind then," she added in a breezy tone she hoped would stop his line of questioning.

He chuckled at that.

The light of the fire silhouetted his figure, drawing her attention. He was exactly the kind of guy she would have been attracted to in high school. If someone like him would ever have given Crooked Kinsley the time of day.

"So do you think Kane would listen to you if you talked to him?" she asked, returning to a safer topic. At least safer for her. "If you found out how he feels?"

"So instead of talking about your fashion choices we're going back to my life choices?" Elliot shot her a wry look as he got up. "This really matters to you, doesn't it?"

Kinsley shrugged off his question. "I have an ulterior motive. This wedding is important to me, and I want things to go off without a hitch. Underlying tension doesn't look good in family wedding photos." She added a smile of her own, hoping he would think she was teasing him.

She was, just a bit. But she came from such a close family, it bothered her to see other families at odds. As a wedding planner she often had to deal with the emotions of distrustful in-laws, ex-husbands and wives, and extended families. From some of the things Faith had said, the Tye family had had their difficulties, but they had always been close. And the fact that the sons had come from such disparate backgrounds and still created a family with Tricia, Zach and Grace was a testament to the love they had shared and been given.

Elliot tunneled his fingers through his hair, rearranging its messy waves. Then he turned his shirt around, shaking it to dry it.

"I guess that's a good enough reason," Elliot agreed. "I just don't know how to introduce the topic."

"You could just start."

He looked at her, a slow smile lighting his face. "So I should walk up to Kane some day and say something like, 'Kane, I know Faith and I took off together, but it wasn't what you thought it was.' Would that work?"

Again Kinsley caught a hint of bitterness.

"It's a start. But I'm wondering if he doesn't know that already. I'm sure he and Faith have talked about it."

"If he already knows, why should I talk to him then?"

His question seemed legitimate, and part of Kinsley was telling her to let it go. It wasn't any of her business. But there was something about Elliot that called to her. Something hidden beneath that posturing and strength that she had never seen in Drake. A hint of vulnerability, which he tried hard to hide.

"Maybe it would be good to get it out in the open between the two of you."

Elliot didn't respond to that. Instead he pulled his phone out of his jeans pocket. He looked at it in disgust. "Still dead." As if he expected it to charge while he was carrying it. He dropped the phone back into his pocket, checking his shirt again.

"Well, this will have to do," he said, walking over to her. He bent down and lifted her ankle.

"What are you doing?"

"We need to wrap this so it doesn't swell. I didn't want to do it with the shirt so wet. It's not completely dry, but the fact that it's damp will make it cool, which will also help keep the swelling down."

"You think of everything, don't you?" she said with a shaky laugh as he adjusted the shirt, wrapping it around her ankle. "You've obviously done this before." She was dismayed at the breathless tone of her voice. It seemed rather intimate, having a man tend to her, hold her leg, wrap his shirt around it.

"Once or twice," he said, tying the sleeves of his shirt together and easing her leg back onto the couch. "Us cowboys know how to take care of each other. Though a tensor bandage would be easier to work with."

"Thanks. That helps a lot." Though her hip was still aching, the pressure felt good on her ankle.

"What about your hip?"

Could he read her mind?

"It'll be okay," she said, glancing away. She didn't want his pity. She'd seen enough of that in her life.

"So, what happened? To your hip?"

His straightforward question was unexpected, surprising, and not entirely welcome. Then again, this was Elliot. From what she'd seen of him, he preferred to get to the point.

"If you don't want to talk about it, I get it, but seeing as how you were giving me all this relationship advice..." He flashed her a teasing smile as if to say he hadn't really minded.

"I guess fair is fair," she conceded, unable to stay self-conscious in front of someone who was so direct. "I actually injured it riding a horse."

"Really?" He pursed his lips, nodding. "Well, that explains a lot." He got up and tossed another couple of logs on the fire then returned to the couch. He lifted both her feet this time and set them on his lap, checking the pressure of his shirt.

Kinsley swallowed down her reaction. He was just being kind. There wasn't enough room on the couch for her to stretch out, and it wasn't right of her to take up the whole space and make him sit on the floor.

But the feel of his legs under her feet, the casual way he rested his hand on her lower leg, was more intimate than she liked. He had done this many times before, she guessed, reminding herself that this was nothing special to him. Just a guy trying to get comfortable while sitting with a girl in front of a fire. No big deal.

She drew in a slow breath, trying to steady her pounding heart, annoyed at the reaction he created in her.

Her brain reminded her he wasn't her type. At all.

Take care of you, she reminded herself. *Don't get pulled into other people's lives.*

"So how old were you when you got hurt?" Elliot asked, obviously not content with the bits of information she had given him.

"I was fourteen." She kept her tone matter of fact. Just a simple retelling of an old story.

"How did it happen?"

He wasn't letting this go either.

"I'd been out riding a few times before with my friend," she said, keeping her tone light. Conversational. "We used to get together every Saturday and go riding on her farm. I was never comfortable, but her horses were old, stable. Easy to ride. That day she had a cousin over who wanted to join us. So I was switched to a younger horse I was unfamiliar with. Cousins get priority, you know," she said, slanting him a self-deprecating smile. "My friend and her cousin decided they wanted to race, and I didn't think I should. I didn't trust my horse. It was raining, like now," she said, waving her hand, trying to sound casual. No big deal. "I held him back, trying to keep him to a walk while my friend and her cousin galloped away from me. But my horse went crazy being separated from the others. I couldn't control him. He took off. We got to a muddy spot on the trail and he slipped and panicked. He lost his footing, I couldn't get my foot out of the stirrups fast enough, and when he fell over, he pinned me underneath." She stopped there, fighting an unwelcome surge of fear. She clenched her fists, restraining the memories. Keeping them at bay.

"So how long were you pinned underneath him?"

"I'm not sure. By the time they noticed I wasn't behind them, they were already back at the farm. It was raining hard, and they took a while to find me. They had to put the horse down because he broke his leg. Thankfully they didn't treat me the same way." She released a harsh laugh.

"So what was the prognosis? For you?"

"My pelvis was broken, as was my femur. So it was a good thing they found me when they did."

"You could've died." The anger in his voice surprised her. "A broken femur? That's ridiculous dangerous."

"You're right," she said, smiling at his adjective.

"So I'm guessing it required a long hospital stay and a lot of therapy."

The fingers of the hand resting on her leg, made gentle circles, as if trying to assure her.

The movements sent gentle shivers up and down her spine. She wished he would stop. It was doing nothing for her equilibrium. She was feeling vulnerable right now. Thankfully his face was devoid of pity.

"It did. I spent months at a rehab hospital in Edmonton. The staff was fantastic and encouraging but—"

"Things weren't the same as before," he said, his voice matter-of-fact.

"Not exactly. The doctor told me I was fortunate to walk at all."

"Well, there's that," Elliot said, nodding his head as if in agreement.

She couldn't help a flash of annoyance, as if he, like everyone else she had worked with at the hospital, assumed she should be content. That she should be thankful.

"Don't get me wrong, I was glad I could be walking eventually. But it's hard when you're a teenage girl, to come back to school in a wheelchair. And then, when you finally can walk, you've got a permanent limp."

"What about your friend and her family? Did your parents sue them?"

She shot him a puzzled frown. "No. Not at all. It wasn't their fault."

"It kinda was. It was their horse. Your parents never talked about that? Never threatened to do anything?"

Another memory returned. Her sitting in her wheelchair, sobbing that she might not be able to walk again. Her parents kindly and gently reassuring her that she should be content with what she had. She knew they meant well and were trying to support her. But their lack of outrage, their lack of desire for justice for her, had bothered her for a while.

"They said it wasn't the Christian thing to do."

"That might well be, but parents are supposed to look out for their kids. They're supposed to fight for them."

The way his eyes narrowed, the hint of anger in his voice, puzzled her and raised further questions about his own life. "Did the Tye family not look out for you?"

His gaze shot to her, his eyes dark with tamped anger. "I never said that."

She held her hands up as if to defend herself. "I'm sorry. It was just… The way you're talking…" She let her voice trail off, not sure anymore of her conversational footing.

He removed his hand from her leg and rubbed his forehead. "No. I'm sorry. I wasn't talking about Mom and Zach. I was talking about…well… My biological dad."

He lifted her legs, stood, and laid them back down on the couch. He grabbed some more logs, setting them carefully on the fire. His movements seemed deliberate. As if he was holding himself in, holding back.

"Is he still alive?"

Elliot gave a tight nod. "Yeah. Very much so."

"So, are you in contact with him?"

Elliot poked the fire with another stick, his features hard, set. Again Kinsley caught undercurrents of a deep and unre-solved anger.

"Not out of any choice of mine. I wish he was out of my life. Completely."

CHAPTER 7

*E*lliot wished she would quit poking and prodding. He didn't want to talk about Dennis.

"I'm sorry for prying. I think I hit a nerve," Kinsley said, her voice quiet through the snap of the fire.

Elliot took a deep breath and fought down the usual bitterness and anger his father could create. He forced himself to smile. Something Grace had taught him.

Make yourself smile and be happy. Often feelings will follow actions.

Her calm voice smoothed the edges of his emotions. And when he forced the smile, the tension gripping his shoulders eased.

"Dennis has a way of doing that," he joked, deepening his smile as he looked back at her.

The firelight cast a gentle glow over her features, enhancing her cheekbones, making her dark eyes even more mysterious, highlighting the sheen of hair that had escaped from the severe bun she always wore.

Yet the faint frown between her arched brows seemed to suggest his forced humor hadn't fooled her.

"Was it because of him you ended up at the Tye family?"

"Yeah. Not exactly a candidate for Father of the Year."

"What was he like when you were with him?"

Elliot turned back to the fire, giving it another poke. He wished she would let it go but, other than Grace and Zach, she was the first person who seemed interested in his relationship with his biological father. Previous girlfriends seldom asked him about Dennis. Most of them knew who his father was and preferred to avoid him.

"Mean. Nasty. Vindictive. Had a wicked left hook." Elliot tried to keep his tone light. As if he were simply describing a character in a book. Someone who would make a delicious villain you could dislike and not feel guilty about.

For a moment the only sound in the room was the murmur of the wind outside, the rain ticking at the windows, and the snap and crackle of the fire. Kinsley had obviously been rendered silent by his comment.

Just as well. Talking about Dennis drained him.

"I'm so sorry to hear that," she finally said. "That must have been difficult."

Guess they weren't finished with this.

"Well...that's how I ended up with the Tye family off and on."

"What do you mean off and on?"

Trust her not to miss that slip.

Elliot sat down by the fire, preferring to keep his distance from her. She was too pretty, too appealing, and sitting with her on the couch had been a mistake. She was becoming a distraction he couldn't afford to indulge in and one, he knew, Kane would warn him off of.

And Kane would be right.

So he rested his back against the rough-hewn stones. Stones he and Tanner had heaved and dug out of the riverbed and brought here.

"I'm not sure. It was like I'd be with the Tyes for half a year and then Social Services would take me back. Dad always told me it was 'cause the Tye family didn't want me anymore. But that didn't make sense, because as soon as things went south with him, I'd end up back at the Tye ranch." He rested his wrists on his upraised knees, looking at his hands. One of his fingers was crooked from the time Dennis grabbed it and twisted it, breaking it. He blinked, trying to erase the memory.

She said nothing, but her posture, the tilt of her head, showed she was listening. Intently. Something about her made him want to tell her more. To unload.

"The third time I landed back with Zach and Mom as a permanent ward." He tried another smile, but knew it failed. "Never got adopted, but I spent my best years there."

Kinsley held his gaze, her expression serious but, thankfully, not pitying. "I hope you found happiness with the Tye family."

This time his smile was genuine. "I did. We had a lot of fun together, me, Lucas, Kane, and Tricia. Zach encouraged me in my dreams to become a saddle bronc rider. He bought me my first saddle and helped me get lessons. He and Mom put a lot of miles on driving us from rodeo to rodeo."

"Did Kane and Lucas ride rodeo too?"

"Lucas quit in high school. He was always afraid of hurting himself. He knew fairly early on that he wanted to join the military. And he wanted nothing to jeopardize that. His biological dad was military. He always had a dream of being like him." Elliot released a harsh laugh. "We weren't biological brothers, but we were both trying to compete with our fathers. Except Lucas's father was a really good guy."

"You tried to compete with your father?"

"Forget I said anything," Elliot said. Again, he was frustrated with how easily he shared information with this woman. She had a quiet way about her, an unexpected way of holding your gaze, as if completely interested in everything you might have to say. Maybe it was part of her job, but at the same time he sensed listening and caring came naturally to her.

"I'm sorry," Kinsley said. "Again, I'm prying too much."

"It's okay," Elliot said shrugging off her objections. "I try to avoid Dennis as much as possible though he calls me every time I compete. To give me tips." Too late he realized how that came out. Bitter. Angry. She would pounce on that.

But thankfully she kept quiet, the hiss and snap of the fire in the fireplace filling the silence.

Elliot wanted to say more but knew it would only make him move to places he promised himself he would never go again. He glanced over at her, taking another approach.

"I'm sorry to hear about your leg. I guess I should be more tactful."

To his surprise she gave him a broad smile. "Actually, it's kind of refreshing to have someone ask me point blank, instead of trying to act like they haven't noticed when, in fact, they can't seem to look away."

"Tricia always tells me I should be more discreet."

"She might be right, but I don't mind."

Their eyes held in the growing darkness and once again Elliot felt a confusing attraction. He wanted to blame it on the intimate atmosphere but sensed there was something else happening. A connection he hadn't felt in a long time.

He pulled in a breath to say something to her when suddenly the door swung open, and a flashlight bounced its light around the room.

Elliot startled then saw Kane standing in the opening.

"There you are," he said, his voice shaky, sounding very un-Kane like. "You kicked my heart into overdrive man. When I saw your truck in the ditch..." Kane dragged his hand over his face and, as he moved into the room, Zach pushed past him and rushed to Elliot.

Zach grabbed him, holding him close in a tight hug, whispering his name over and over. Elliot was surprised at the jolt of emotion Zach's arms around him created.

When he pulled back, Kane also pulled him close.

"I'm so glad you're not hurt," he murmured. Then he pulled back, his eyes wide. "How is Kinsley?"

Elliot nodded toward the couch where Kinsley sat with her foot still elevated.

"Hey. What happened?" he asked.

"I sprained my ankle," Kinsley said, shifting herself on the couch. "It'll be fine."

Elliot could see Kane's eyes flicking over Kinsley, as if to make sure everything else was okay with her. Then he frowned. "So why is your ankle wrapped in Elliot's shirt?"

"Didn't have a tensor bandage," Elliot said with a laugh. "I used what was at hand."

Kane shot him a wry smile. "Good thinking."

"When we saw that truck in the ditch…" Zack shook his head, his hand on Elliot's shoulder. "I thought the worst."

"How did you know where to look?" Elliot asked.

"When you didn't come home we tried your cell phones but nothing was going through."

"Mine's dead, and we have no idea where Kinsley's is," Elliot said.

"Anyway, we started combing the roads between here and town and found the truck. When we didn't see you inside I remembered that Tanner's place was close, and here you are." Kane shook his head, as if still trying to absorb it all.

"Well let's put that fire out, get you guys out of here and back home." Zach rubbed Elliot's arm, his smile warming Elliot's heart.

"Here, let me give you a hand," Kane was saying to Kinsley, holding his hand out to her as Zach and Kane took care of the fire.

She hesitated, shooting Elliot a panicked look, and he thought of the rip up the back of her skirt.

"It's still raining out there, you might want this." He grabbed his coat off the firewood stack and brought it to her. He gently helped her to her feet and caught a grateful look as he wrapped his coat around her waist, tying the arms in the front.

"Maybe be better if you put it over her shoulders," Kane said, sounding puzzled.

"No. That's fine. This works," Kinsley said.

Ignoring his brother's confused look, Elliot slipped his arm around her waist to support her.

"Let's get out of here," he said, slanting her another smile.

When she returned it his heart skipped, then raced.

So easily he had fallen into a place he had rigorously avoided.

He dragged his gaze away from hers, forced his wayward heart to settle down. He had too much riding on the line right now to be distracted by this attractive woman. A woman who was exactly the wrong one for him.

But as he helped her out of the house and through the still-driving rain, holding her close to protect her, he felt the pull she exerted on him.

Thank goodness they both had their exit plans in place.

$$\backsim\!\!\backprime\!\!()\!\!\backprime\!\!\sim$$

"Are you sure your leg isn't too sore?" Faith knelt by the bed, fussing with the tensor bandage she had put on Kinsley's ankle. "Tight enough? Too tight?"

"It's fine. Don't worry about it." Kinsley sat back, grabbed her laptop, and opened it up. "I hope you took some pictures of the dress." She needed to get back on track. The time she'd spent with Elliot had hit her harder than she wanted to acknowledge. It had been a moment of closeness and connection, and she knew she would have a hard time returning to the businesslike relationship that had kept him at arm's length. She couldn't afford to let someone as attractive, appealing, and transient as Elliot get anywhere near her heart.

"I didn't." Faith gave her an apologetic look. "I was so worried about you and Elliot. When I heard about the accident..." She pressed her hands against her chest in a dramatic gesture.

"When do you think the guys will be back?" Kinsley asked, keeping her tone businesslike.

After Kane, Zach, and Elliot dropped Kinsley off at the ranch, they went back into the rain to pull Elliot's truck out of the ditch.

"I'm not sure," Faith admitted. "It depends on how badly the truck was damaged and how easy it will be to pull out."

"I sure hope they can find my purse."

"You lost that too?"

"Yeah. Somehow it flew out of the truck. And the flowers..." Kinsley heaved out a heavy sigh. "That'll be a disaster. I can't imagine that they would've survived that crash or the storm." She bit her lip, thinking. "We might have to come up with another plan."

Maybe this was a blessing in disguise. Maybe now she could convince Faith to go with the traditional florist. Though she had to admit, as they were picking out the pots of plants, she was already imagining where she would put them. They were certainly a cheaper option than going completely with florist's bouquets and arrangements and, for the price, they got a lot of flowers.

Cheap. Tacky. Unconventional.

Drake's sarcastic voice slipped into her thoughts followed by a picture of his mother's disapproving face. She shook her head, as if to dislodge the memory. Why did she care what they might think? This was her plan, and she wanted to work with Faith, not force her own vision on her as Drake and his mother often did with hesitant brides.

"Well, let's wait and see how they look when the guys come back," Faith said with an encouraging smile. "You said Elliot tied a tarp over them, so maybe they didn't get too blasted by the rain."

Faith got up from the floor, walked around the bed, and sat down beside her. "I feel really bad about the accident. I feel like I could have prevented it somehow."

Kinsley chuckled. "What? You think you could have single-handedly kept that deer out of our path?"

"It's the butterfly effect. Maybe if I had come along with you guys, you might have left a little earlier or a little later and not had that deer jump in front of you and hit the ditch."

"Or," Kinsley said with a light laugh, "if you had come along maybe we would have actually hit that deer, and who knows what could have happened then?"

"I suppose," Faith agreed.

"Besides, if I hadn't been wearing those crazy high heels I wouldn't have twisted my ankle."

"I'm sure Elliot was merciless in his teasing. He used to bug me whenever I wore them too. I'm sure he figures the only thing a girl should wear that has heels are cowboy boots. He always did like the more earthy types."

Kinsley brushed away a niggle of unease. What did she care about Elliot's preferences in footwear for women? Or the type of women he liked?

"So where did someone like Carmen fit into his ideal? She certainly doesn't seem the cowboy-boot type."

"I think he just went out with Carmen because they'd been friends for so long. I don't think either of them were fully committed to the relationship. Besides, Elliot's dad didn't like her."

"Is that why they broke up?"

"Partly. But I think it mostly had to do with the fact that Elliot couldn't get rid of his need for his father's approval, and Carmen didn't want to compete with that."

Kinsley's thoughts flitted back to her conversation with Elliot in Tanner's house.

"Does Elliot ever see his father?"

"Not if he can help it. Though Dennis won't leave the poor guy alone."

"What do you mean by that?" Again she thought of some of the cryptic comments Elliot had dropped in the conversation.

"Dennis will phone him. Ream him out for something he did wrong on one of his rides. He was such a horrible dad, and yet, he always makes it sound like he's so concerned about Elliot's well-being. Always trying to give him tips on how to ride better. I think Dennis still thinks he's some kind of rodeo legend." Faith folded her arms across her stomach, shaking her head. "It's been years and years since Dennis won his title at the CFR. But he still acts like it was just yesterday and the fact that he's been there and Elliot hasn't is something he can't let go of. And for some reason, neither can Elliot."

Kinsley absorbed this information, her heart once again going out to Elliot. To have such a dysfunctional father, someone who was so unkind. So uncaring.

"Was his dad abusive?"

"I'm sure he was. Tricia told me that whenever he'd come back from staying at his dad's place, Elliot would have more bruises. One time he came back with a broken arm." Faith shot Kinsley a horrified look, placing her hands on Kinsley's arm. "You can't say anything to Elliot about that. He told her in private, and she told me, and now I'm telling you. Elliot's pretty closed-mouthed about how his dad treated him. It's like some secret he's ashamed of."

Kinsley thought of Elliot's comments to her about his father having a mean left hook. Why had he told her if he was keeping it from other people?

Why did you tell him about your accident?

She shook the questions off. Even as she tried to tell herself it was just a casual conversation, she knew the time they had spent in Tanner's house was something unique for both of them.

However, she didn't want to dwell on that. She couldn't be distracted by a good-looking cowboy with a messy past and a questionable future.

"You seem interested in Elliot. What happened in Tanner Bond's house? Did he kiss you?"

"What? No. Why would you say something like that?" But even as Kinsley pushed back at Faith's questions, her cheeks warmed.

Because, whether she liked it or not, there had been a second she thought he might. A second she wished he had.

"I don't know. It's like there's something different between you two. You don't seem as prickly around each other."

"You noticed that in the few minutes that the guys were back here to drop me off?"

Faith nodded, giving her friend a shrewd look. "Yeah. I know how appealing Elliot is. But Elliot never wanted the girls that he could get easily. He always wanted a challenge. You're a challenge to him because you're so different from any of the other girls he's ever dated or hung around with."

Kinsley didn't want her cheeks to warm the way they did. Didn't want to see Elliot as anything more than a reluctant assistant.

"I see how he looks at you. And, my friend, whether you like it or not, I saw how you looked at him just a while ago too."

"He helped me out when I twisted my ankle."

He did more than that and you know it.

Kinsley dismissed the insidious voice even as she remembered him carrying her on his back as if she was no heavier than a child.

He was strong and confident.

And far too appealing.

"So, let's talk about flowers," she said, forcing her attention to the real reason she was here. This wedding and its success. "When they return, if the plants aren't salvageable, we should make alternate plans." She was determined to keep Faith on topic. "I also hope they found my cell phone. All my contacts are on there." She would need to get in touch with Jill soon.

Faith was quiet, and Kinsley chanced a look her way.

"Elliot is a good guy, you know," Faith said. "He comes across all cocky and confident, but he has a good heart."

"I'm sure he does. But that doesn't matter. I'm not interested." She opened up a new document, sucking in a slow breath.

"I guess it's just as well," Faith agreed, settling beside Kinsley on the bed. "Elliot has had one thing on his mind for the past five years, and that's winning at the Canadian Finals Rodeo. And if he gets that, then he's got his sights set on the National Finals Rodeo in Las Vegas next year." Faith frowned as if she didn't understand her future brother-in-law. "He's been working toward that ever since I came to Rockyview. Apparently he got hurt so many times when he started, Zach wanted him to quit. But he wouldn't. So Zach hired an ex-saddle bronc rider to help him out. He's been chasing that CFR championship ever since. And, like I said, the NFR after that. Though I don't know what he'll do if, by some stroke of good fortune and amazing riding, he gets them both. His life will have lost its purpose."

Kinsley knew she should shut this conversation down but curiosity made her ask, "Why do you say that?"

"He'll never admit it, but his whole life Elliot has been trying to prove to Dennis that he's worth something. That he's important. He thinks he can do that by winning what his dad did. But it won't satisfy him, because even if he does, Dennis won't recognize it. Won't give Elliot the approval he's been looking for. Elliot could win every competition he enters, score the highest, do the best, but I don't think Dennis would ever acknowledge it." Faith heaved out a sigh.

"It sounds like he had a difficult relationship with his father," Kinsley said. She already knew that, of course, but for some irrational reason she wanted to hear Faith's take on it. Wanted to find out more about the man who was edging more and more into her thoughts.

"If you want to call it a relationship. Elliot says he can't stand the guy, but somehow Dennis has this hold on Elliot he doesn't want to recognize. That man has caused Elliot so much pain in so many ways." Faith's expression grew somber as she fiddled with her engagement ring, and Kinsley felt a tremor of pity for Elliot she knew he wouldn't appreciate.

"Do you think he would quit the rodeo if he doesn't make it to either of the finals?"

Faith paused a moment. "I don't know. It's such a thing with him. It's defined his life. It's become his entire focus, trying to please a parent that won't be pleased."

Just like Drake, constantly trying to curry favor with his own mother, that critical old bat.

Elliot was the same.

The cold thought planted itself, stuck, as her practical mind called out, *Danger, danger.*

Caring for a man like him would take too much out of her, and she couldn't do that again.

CHAPTER 8

*K*insley limped down the stairs, annoyed at herself for sleeping so long. If she'd had her phone she could have set an alarm. Instead she slept most of the morning away. She blamed it on the painkillers she'd taken. She had hoped to get an early start.

And to see if Elliot was still around?

Nope. Not at all. And that certainly wasn't the reason she was wearing pants today. And a more casual shirt. The pants were more comfortable. That was all.

Last night she and Faith had eaten cereal for dinner while they watched television, waiting for the guys to come back. But by the time nine o'clock rolled around, Faith gave up, helped Kinsley up the stairs to her room, and then left for her place in town.

Kinsley had gone to bed as well and hadn't heard if the men had even made it home. But she thought Elliot might still be around this morning.

"Good morning," Zach said, looking up from his paper as she entered the kitchen. "Looks like the ankle is still sore."

"It is, but I'm sure it'll be okay." She was surprised Zach was still here. Usually he left with Kane first thing in the morning. Guess they all made it back. "How is Elliot's truck?"

"It's fine. Was a real struggle to get it out of the ditch. He never could have, like he figured. We pulled it into the shop last night, looked it over. It needs a new tie rod and a new rim and windows replaced but once we get that done it will be drivable."

She wanted to ask where Elliot was but kept that question to herself. Last night, after Faith left, she had told herself to pull it together. To not let one afternoon alone with a very appealing man distract her.

"Did you want breakfast? Elliot made eggs and he told me to save some for you."

It was small kindnesses like that that allowed thoughts of him to tiptoe back into her mind again.

"Thanks, but I think I'll check out the flowers," she said, granting him a smile. "If they've been loaded off the truck yet." And maybe Elliot was outside. Maybe she'd see him.

"Oh, yeah. Elliot was out early this morning unloading them before he left."

"Left? For where?"

"He's off to another rodeo."

Of course he was. Another rodeo and a reminder to her of his focus and the things he was chasing.

However, she still couldn't help a lingering disappointment.

"And how are you doing?" Zach asked, his eyes kind, holding hers.

"Just a little achy. But it will pass." She wasn't sure if he was asking after her physical or mental health but chose to play it safe. "I better get outside and look at those flowers."

"Oh, and Elliot told me to tell you they found your purse. Your phone got wet so he put in a bowl of rice. It's on the counter there. Don't know what good that would do."

It was a small thing, but Elliot's consideration only kept him in her mind.

"The rice helps draw the moisture out of the phone," Kinsley told him. "I'll leave it there until tonight then take it out."

"I guess you two know what you're doing."

You two. The simple words created a connection and an unwelcome jolt. As if Zach sensed as well that things had shifted between Kinsley and Elliot.

Zach propelled himself to his feet. "I need to get going too," he said. "I thought I would stick around until you got up."

"Sorry about the eggs."

"That's okay. I wish we had a dog to feed them to though." He gave Kinsley a quick smile then walked over to the kitchen counter.

Kinsley watched him, surprised at how much smoother his movements were. "You seem to be moving about better," she couldn't help remark.

Zach shot her a look over his shoulder. "Yeah. I took Elliot's advice and started seeing a massage therapist the last couple of weeks, and that's helped a lot." He turned to face her. "Maybe you should do the same?"

She bit back a retort, knowing he was just being kind. Her mother often accused her of being too touchy when people gave her helpful hints and bits of advice that, overall, were useless.

"Thanks. I'll take that into consideration."

Zach smiled as if he sensed her evasion. "Sorry. I know I shouldn't be giving you advice. I'm sure you've heard all kinds of it before. I know I have. It's just that it worked for me."

"I'm glad it did. I might have to try it again." She returned his warm smile, held his gentle gaze. "Did Elliot tell you where he left my purse?"

"It's over there. On one of the chairs. He cleaned it off for you too."

She found it and picked it up. The leather was water-stained but, as Zach said, clean. Another small considerate act that glided too easily into the lonely part of her soul.

"Tell him thanks," she said as she unzipped it, checking for her wallet, pens, notebooks, and all the other detritus of her life she collected in her purse. Everything was there. The only reason her phone hadn't been was that she'd been holding it when they got into the accident.

"You can tell him yourself when he comes back on Sunday."

That's right. He was coming back to continue helping with the wedding.

The thought warmed and frightened her at the same time.

"I'll make sure to do that," she said. "Is it okay if I leave my purse here?"

"I can put it in my office," he said. "Tricia will come back today with the kids, and I don't want them getting into it."

"Okay. Thanks."

"The guys put the flowers in the shop, so you'll probably find Faith there."

"Shop?"

"The large building by the corrals and the barn. Where we do all manner of fixing and stuff." Another grin.

"Ahh. A garage."

"Nah. Out in the country we call them shops."

"Duly noted." She gave him another smile, then left.

She wore more sensible shoes this morning, figuring it was best not to tempt fate with a wrenched ankle and high heels. She took her time, favoring her ankle as she headed over to the so-called shop, reveling in the bright sunny morning. The earth smelled fresh, cleaned, washed by the rain last night. She had to navigate a few puddles, and the grass was soggy. Tendrils of fog wisped the hills and the mountains beyond. It was a beautiful day, she thought, feeling a touch of envy for Faith that this wondrous setting would be her home.

And a stunning backdrop for a wedding.

Kinsley held the words close, lifted her chin, and took a

deep, calming breath. The wedding would be perfect. She just knew it.

Faith was, as Zach had told her, in the "shop." The large overhead door was open, letting the sunshine in, and Faith was fussing with the pots all laid out on the concrete floor.

"Hey you," Kinsley called out as she came nearer.

Faith frowned as she looked up. "You didn't need to come out. I thought you would be resting."

"I've got things to do," Kinsley said, reaching into her pocket for her phone to capture a picture of the future bride surrounded by pots and buckets of color.

Then remembered that her phone was drying out.

"They're all safe and sound." Faith stood as Kinsley joined her. "A few broken stalks, and we lost a few leaves and blooms, but mostly they look fresh and oh so purty."

Kinsley let her eyes rove over the plants, her gaze critical, but, as Faith assured her, they did indeed still look fresh.

"I'll forgive you the 'purty' comment because I'm so thankful they survived. We cleaned Adelle at Growing Things out, so if they weren't—"

"Didn't happen so we're not going there." Faith dropped her hands on her hips, smiling as she looked over the flowers. "So flowers are done. What's next?"

"Bouquets, boutonnieres, centerpieces for the tables and wedding dress?"

"Wedding dress is under control."

Kinsley held back her comment about wanting to see the dress.

"And yes, I will go to Carmen's with you today and then to Mia's flower shop," Faith said, forestalling Kinsley's next question.

"Excellent. We can go anytime you're ready."

Faith nodded, still looking over the brightly colored pots of flowers. She released a gentle sigh. "I just love how this looks. I'm excited to see how you arrange them all."

Kinsley had to smile at her friend's pleasure. Her happiness was Kinsley's. Then she looked past Faith and saw the buggy in the dark recesses of the shop. Unease slithered through her stomach.

"So you're still stuck on coming in on that buggy?" She tried to sound positive. Encouraging.

Faith shot her a puzzled look, and Kinsley knew she hadn't hit the note she was aiming for.

"Yeah. And you still don't seem too thrilled about it all."

"The buggy will need a lot of work." Kinsley decided to go with her objections. "And we're only a couple of weeks away from the date." She had to remind herself that things were coming together. That it would all work out. As long as she stayed on task and Faith didn't come up with any last-minute additions.

"Zach and Kane are done haying. Mason and Tricia will be back soon. Elliot will be back on Sunday. There'll be enough manpower to get it done."

"And the horses?"

"Mason and Tricia assured me they have the perfect pair. Evenly matched, so the pictures will turn out good."

Kinsley fought down a flicker of panic, recognizing the same emotion from the many other weddings she had worked on. She had to remind herself that Drake's perfectionism and his mother's constant criticism inflicted much of the panic.

This wasn't his wedding, or his mother's. She was doing this one on her own and she was more than capable of taking care of it.

"Well, we'll deal with that later."

Faith shot her a knowing look then shrugged. "Fine. Let's go to Carmen's."

"I need to get my phone first."

"You don't have it on you?"

"Elliot put it in a bowl of rice last night. He said it got wet."

Faith gave her a coy smile. "Now wasn't that sweet of him."

"Yeah. Really sweet." Kinsley turned away before Faith could see the flush that warmed her cheeks at Faith's comment. Seriously. She had to get things under control.

Partnership. Think of your partnership with Jill. How you won't let anything stand in the way of this opportunity.

With that she squared her shoulders and walked to the house to get her purse, phone, and laptop.

The visit to Carmen was uneventful. They were to meet her at her home but when Kinsley phoned to double-check, Carmen told them to come to the coffeehouse. One of her workers had called in sick.

With Carmen's help and suggestions the menu came together quite nicely. Carmen assured her that everything would work out well, and Kinsley was feeling more positive by the minute.

Mia Verbeek, the florist had some fantastic and original ideas for the bouquets and, again, Faith was willing to go with them. At least she wasn't a diva bride.

On the way back from town, Kinsley called the company who would put up the tent and finalized the date and time for setup. They were also supplying the tables and chairs and linens. Then another quick call—thank goodness for Bluetooth —to verify that the DJ who would do the music would also supply the sound system for the speeches and program.

"Wow, you are efficient," Faith said in admiration as she ended the last call.

"That's why I get paid the big bucks," Kinsley said.

"Okay, now I feel bad you're doing this gratis."

"No. Please, no. I offered, don't forget that. And believe me, the bucks aren't that big. At least they weren't with Drake's company. Mind you, I never got to see the balance sheet."

"Why not?"

"I was never a full partner like his mother and him."

"I'm glad you dumped him. The more you talk about him the less I like him. He sounds like a screwball Momma's boy."

"Well, Momma's boy might be an exaggeration. He and his mother could fight pretty good if push came to shove." And, sad to say, sometimes it did.

"Wow. Well then, you're better off without him."

"That's for sure. And I'm not letting some guy's dream or vision overwhelm mine. Ever again."

Faith was quiet for a moment. "That sounds definite."

"It is. Drake represents so much time wasted while he went after his dreams and kept me hanging, so to speak. I waited too long to discover that."

"I can understand that. Your heart was broken."

Kinsley let those words settle. "I don't know if it was broken so much as worn down. A steady drip, drip of inattention. Of being relegated to second place in his life. It grew tedious." She gave Faith a quick smile to soften the somber mood that had penetrated the car. "But thankfully, Kane and you have found each other again, and you've made a commitment to each other."

"And it's because of Drake that you don't want to have anything to do with Elliot?"

"Elliot has his own stuff, but probably, yes. I don't need complications. For the first time in years I'm on track to do what I need to do. Take care of me."

Another moment of silence fell as Kinsley drove down the winding road to the ranch. Her words sounded defensive and challenging and when Faith spoke up, Kinsley knew she had heard the same thing.

"So Elliot did kiss you yesterday?" Faith sounded curious and, if truth be told, a bit hopeful.

"Again. No. Why do you keep asking that?"

"Just because it seems like things have shifted between you guys. Just a sense I have."

"Well you better keep your senses to yourself. It didn't happen." Kinsley bit down another retort, realizing she was protesting maybe too hard. She breathed a sigh of relief when her cell phone ringtone sounded through the car speakers. She glanced at her console, not recognizing the number, but answered it anyhow.

"So, are you out and about?"

Elliot's deep voice sounded even darker coming into her car and, quite frankly, just a bit intimate.

"Yeah. And I'm here with her," Faith sang out.

Pause, then, "Okay. I see. Well, I was just calling to see how you're doing, Kinsley. That's all."

"I'm fine." His "that's all" created a surprising and unwelcome disappointment.

"Your ankle is okay?"

"It's sore…" She let her sentence trail off, far too aware of Faith sitting beside her, listening intently to the conversation. Such as it was.

"Fine. Good to hear. Like I said, I just wanted to check in. Drive safe."

And with that the phone call was over.

The moment of silence that followed was broken by a light chuckle from Faith. "Well, well, well," she said, drawing the words out. "Elliot is calling you."

"Just being polite." Kinsley tried to keep her tone noncommittal, casual even as her renegade heart upped its beat.

Faith blew out her breath in a sound of disbelief. "Elliot has never just 'checked up' on someone that I know of." She made quotes with her fingers. "He's the kind of guy who sails through life with no attachments."

"I wouldn't call his past sailing through life," Kinsley said.

"You're right." Faith was quiet, and once again Kinsley hoped she would let it go. "Anyway, nice to know my future brother-in-law can be considerate."

Kinsley didn't want to be talking about Elliot. Again.

So she switched the topic back to the wedding. Faith, thankfully, played along. The conversation the rest of the ride was much easier to navigate.

The next couple of days were busy with setting up seating arrangements and deciding on table settings. On Sunday Faith, Kane, and Zach went to church. Kinsley stayed home. While she would have liked to attend with them, she was uncomfortable going to a new church where she didn't know anybody. Uncomfortable with the stares she knew she would have to face.

So she sat on the deck, on the porch swing, reading her Bible, letting the peace of the ranch enfold her.

And trying not to listen for a truck returning from a weekend of rodeo.

🙒🕇🙖

"So you guys are really serious about restoring this buggy?"

Elliot looked up from the bolt he was loosening and had to do a double-take. Was this Kinsley of the tailored suits and businesslike attitude?

Today she wore blue jeans and a T-shirt. Her hair was still pulled up, but at least it was just in a ponytail that hung down her back.

She seemed friendly, accessible, and approachable. He released a gentle smile. He hadn't seen her since Friday, but the entire weekend she was on his mind. The distraction she created had cost him a couple points on his rides. Thankfully he won, but he still had to put up with the critical phone call from his father as he was driving back last night. He knew he shouldn't have taken the call, but it was like an itch he couldn't

115

scratch enough. As if he hoped that someday it would be different.

But it was Monday. A new day and a new week, and he didn't have his phone with him.

"You're looking good," he said, pushing those thoughts aside.

"I didn't feel like wearing a skirt and a tensor bandage. Can't wear high heels with that, and running shoes would ruin the look with the suit."

Elliot grinned at her as he sat on the old buggy seat. "And how is your ankle?"

"I have to be careful, but it doesn't hurt as much as before. Got some good first aid."

Elliot rested his elbows on his knees, toying with the wrench he was holding, the day suddenly offering more promise. "And the phone is still working?"

This netted him a coy smile. "You know it is. You called me the other day. But thanks for putting it in the rice."

"Good to hear."

"But back to my original question. You're still fixing this buggy up?"

"It's what Faith wants, and Kane told me what Faith wants, Faith gets."

Kinsley made a face, and it wasn't hard to read the concern in her expression. "If you're worried about the horses…"

She waved his comment off, but Elliot knew she was worried. He thought of what they'd talked about in Tanner's house. No wonder it scared her.

"Look, we need to do something about this. You can't be on a ranch and be afraid of horses." He set the wrench down and vaulted off the buggy. He walked over to her and took her arm to support her. "I want to introduce you to one of the horses we're using."

She pulled back and almost fell. He caught her, but as soon

as she regained her balance she yanked her arm free from his hand. "No. It's fine. I don't need to see them."

Elliot dropped his hands on his hips, tilting his head to one side, catching his lower lip between his teeth. He could see the dread etched on her face.

"I think you do. You'll be around them, after all." Elliot took a step closer, holding her gaze. "I'm not asking you to ride them. Just come and see them. I'll be careful."

She closed her eyes, and he could see her fighting her own fears.

He took a chance and laid his hand on her shoulder, giving it a gentle squeeze. "I'll make sure nothing happens. I promise you. Just trust me."

Kinsley paused, pulling in a deep breath. Then she looked up at him, her eyes latching on to his. "You're absolutely sure it'll be okay."

More of a statement than a question, but he nodded, adding what he hoped was an encouraging smile.

She still looked concerned. He tucked a stray strand of hair behind her ear, his fingers lingering on the soft skin of her neck. "Absolutely sure. You'll be fine. You're tougher than you think."

She released a harsh laugh, but then to his surprise she walked toward the corrals. Her limp was a reminder of what she had gone through and a reminder of how careful he had to be with the trust she had just placed in him.

"I'm guessing this is where the horses are?" she asked.

"So far so good," Elliot said catching up to her, keeping pace with her. "Mason and Tricia are working with one of the teams right now, so you get to see them up close."

Though Faith had commissioned him to do the training, once Mason and Tricia found out, they volunteered. A job Elliot gladly conceded to them. Especially now that he had to restore the wagon to make it wedding-worthy.

They walked together through the farmyard, neither saying

anything. But somehow Elliot was comfortable with the silence. So many of the girls he had spent time with loved to fill the empty spaces with chitchat. Naturally gregarious by nature, he still enjoyed moments of quiet even when he was with someone.

A few minutes later they came around the barns and headed toward the round pen. Elliot could see Mason and Tricia in the circle, working with one of the horses that was to pull the wagon. He was pleased to see that they had managed to get the collar on him and the traces clipped on the collar. Seamus was standing quietly while they worked the rest of the harness.

He could hear Mason's low murmur as Tricia adjusted the saddle portion of the harness.

Seamus looked up as they approached, whickering lightly.

Tricia looked over her shoulder and smiled her welcome.

"I'll be with you in a minute," she said, turning her attention back to the harness she and Mason were working with.

Then, when she was done, she walked backwards from the horse then climbed up the fence and jumped down, hurrying over to them. "Hey, brother," she called out, launching herself at Elliot, throwing her arms around him. "I'm so glad to see you again." She squealed and hugged him. Hard.

Nothing like a happy homecoming, he thought, stepping away from Tricia.

"It's only been a few weeks since I was here," he reminded her.

"Doesn't matter. We haven't seen each other much the past while. I celebrate any time you're around."

"Well I'm glad to be home to help with the wedding."

"Are you? That's not what Faith said," Tricia said with a chuckle.

"I imagine you met Kinsley already," he said, shrugging Tricia's comment off as he caught Kinsley's wry glance.

"We said hello last night, but it was a gong show. Kids were tired and cranky from the long drive and Mason was bushed from all the driving. I tell you, we're not heading down to Sweet Creek again anytime soon." Tricia flashed Kinsley a smile. "Hope the kids weren't too noisy for you."

"It was fine," Kinsley said. "I hardly heard them."

"Where are they now?" Elliot asked.

"Dad's watching them. Just for a few minutes, then I got to get back until it's time for them to have their afternoon nap." She sighed, glancing at Mason, who was adjusting the harness. "This horse training business is taking more time than I figured on. I might need to look at getting a nanny for the kids."

"Don't look at me," Elliot said, raising his hands in a defensive gesture.

"As if I could count on you to stick around," Tricia snorted. She turned back to Kinsley. "And I hear the wedding plans are coming around? I saw the flowerpots. That's a genius idea."

"Thanks, but it wasn't mine. That was Faith's vision."

"I was wondering. Doesn't seem like the usual wedding planner concept I see on my Pinterest boards."

"Ah. Pinterest. The bane of many a wedding planner," Kinsley said with an unexpected touch of wry humor.

"I bet. I'm sure there are more Mason jar ideas than you know what to do with."

"They have taken over the wedding boards for the past few years. I think they're a little overdone, but it could work with Faith's overall rustic theme. And I found some unique ideas we could use. I've seen some spray-painted or frosted—"

"I'm here to see the horses," Elliot said, breaking into the scintillating conversation. "Mason jars are just things to put peaches and plums in. Can we go now?" He took a step away from the girls, hoping he wouldn't get roped into painting said Mason jars. "I thought I should introduce Kinsley to the horses. Just so she knows what to expect." He gave Kinsley an encouraging smile. "So. Should we go?"

"I guess." Kinsley pressed her hand to her midsection then took a deep breath.

"You make it seem like an ordeal," Tricia joked.

"Speaking of ordeals, you might want to go help Mason with that crupper," Elliot said before Tricia could get started on another topic.

"Right. Of course. We'll talk later," she said to Kinsley, then jogged off to join her fiancé.

Elliot resisted the urge to take Kinsley's arm to help her along. Though part of the reason for the hitch in her step, he was sure, was her sore ankle, he also suspected the other was her previous injury. And he knew she wouldn't thank him if he tried to help her.

"I thought there were two horses," Kinsley said as they walked to the gate.

"There will be. I think the other one is still in the corrals. They're both part of a team that Zach talked about training to use in chuck wagon races at one time."

"He never competed?"

"They were still young when he bought them," Elliot said as they came closer to the pen. "Training horses for the chucks requires a lot of commitment, and by the time we all came around I think he shelved that dream. It also costs a lot of money, and I don't think us kids were cheap to have around." He added a smile just to make sure she knew he was teasing.

"I can imagine the grocery bill was fairly enormous."

"Hence the canning of the peaches," Elliot added. "So if you're looking for Mason jars, I'm sure there's dozens and dozens of them downstairs in the cold storage room."

"Well, we'll see how that all comes together." Kinsley bit her lip and rested her hands on the top railing of the fence panel between the large posts of the round pen.

"This one's Seamus. He's probably about eighteen years old. Tricia used to compete with him once Zach gave up on said chuck wagon racing, so he's been around the block a few times. His teammate, Sancho, is a little younger, but they're from the same stud and mare. So brothers, if you will."

Elliot tried to look at the horses through her eyes. Tried to see what could possibly terrify her and understand her point of view. To him they were just horses. Calm, quiet. Bombproof.

Her hands were clenching the top of the fence, and he easily saw the hurried rise and fall of her chest.

"So just look at them for now," Elliot said. "Just get used to being around them."

"I'm hardly around them if I'm on this side of the fence," Kinsley said with a shaky voice.

"Every journey starts with one small step," Elliot replied.

She shot him another wry look. "I didn't know you were so profound."

"I have depths yet to be plumbed. I'm a man of hidden thoughts and complex ponderings."

"I'm intrigued," Kinsley said.

Elliot grinned. It was worth spouting off just to see the twinkle in her eye, the curve of a smile on her lips.

The longer they stood there the looser she clung to the fence. It helped that despite Mason and Tricia struggling with the harnesses, Seamus stood patiently, flicking his ears at a few stray flies, but otherwise unfazed at the incompetence that Mason and Tricia were displaying.

"I'd offer to help, but I know even less about that business than you do," Elliot called out.

"Not really a spectator sport," Mason returned, sounding annoyed.

Elliot rested his arms on the top rail of the fence, grinning. "I should get some popcorn."

But Mason just ignored him, still working on the breeching, getting it under the horse's tail. "I sure hope Faith appreciates all the work we're doing for this," Mason said as he walked around the horse, adjusting and pulling on the belly band. "Not exactly what I signed up for when I agreed to help Tricia train her horses."

"You're gonna be part of this family," Elliot said. "May as well get used to getting roped in to help with things you know nothing about."

"Good thing I'm a fast learner," Mason said.

"I take it you've never harnessed a team of horses before?" Kinsley asked him.

"It's been a few years," Mason admitted, looking at her over the top of Seamus. "Thank goodness I've got a patient team to work with."

"You can come in the pen if you want," Tricia offered. "Seamus is so calm. He won't mind the extra people."

Elliot wanted to take Tricia up on the offer, however, he also knew that it had to be up to Kinsley.

But Kinsley was already shaking her head no.

"Are you sure?" he asked. "I'll come in with you."

To his surprise his offer made her hesitate.

"I don't know."

Should he push? Hold back?

Her reluctance bothered him. He sensed if she would just make one small move, he could build on that.

"Or we could just step inside the pen," he said. "You don't have to do anything more than that."

"One small step for Kinsley, one giant leap for overcoming my fears," she said, rubbing her hands against her legs again.

Her answer surprised him but also generated a spark of hope.

"Okay, follow me," he said.

He walked toward the opening, watching her the entire time. When he unlatched the gate to get into the round pen, he saw her hesitate, but then she lifted her chin and walked slowly past him.

He was right behind her, vigilant, making sure she wasn't going to either fall or freak out.

He heard her long, slow intake of breath and had to curl his hands into fists to stop from touching her. Supporting her.

A pause in her step, a faltering movement, her limp suddenly more pronounced.

Seamus nickered softly, as if inviting her to come forward.

"Just wait a minute," Mason said to Kinsley. "I'll take the harness off. He'll feel more relaxed then."

This made Kinsley stop but, thankfully, she didn't step away.

It took Tricia and Mason less time to remove the harness and the collar than it did to put it all on, and then Seamus was free.

"Just take a couple of steps toward him," Elliot said, keeping his voice quiet more to keep from spooking Kinsley than Seamus. "Then stop and wait."

"What will happen?"

A tiny reed of fear threaded her voice, but Elliot was so proud of her for not leaving. For at least trying.

"He'll come to you and then stop to see what you want to do."

"But he'll stop."

"He will." Elliot kept his focus on Kinsley but was also keeping part of his attention on Seamus, making sure he didn't come too close.

Kinsley clenched her fists but stayed where she was. Sure enough, Seamus was curious enough about their presence that he took a few ambling steps forward and, as Elliot promised, stopped. He snorted but stayed where he was.

"And now you can move a bit closer," Elliot said, his voice persuasive.

Kinsley hesitated a moment but then took a few halting steps toward Seamus who, thankfully, stayed where he was, watching.

"Lift your hand slowly and just touch his head." Elliot was right beside her, hovering but trying to look like he wasn't hovering.

Again Kinsley wavered, but, to Elliot's surprise, she did exactly what he told her to do. While she moved, Elliot sent up a silent prayer that Seamus would behave. Not make any sudden movements. But Seamus lived up to Elliot's expectations and even lowered his head as Kinsley's shaking hand reached out.

She touched the blaze on his face, withdrew, but then reached out again with more confidence.

"You better behave yourself," she said to him as she stroked his head.

Seamus blinked slowly, looking the picture of relaxation.

"Do you want to come in closer?" Elliot asked, pleased at her progress. "Stroke his neck."

"Um, I think I'm okay for now," Kinsley said, but she continued stroking Seamus's nose, looking far more relaxed than she had when she stepped into the pen.

He wanted to encourage her, tell her she was doing great, but realized how patronizing that would sound. She'd been around horses before. She knew, roughly, what to expect. She just needed to find her way around them again.

Seamus nudged her hand, as if he too was pushing her to do more than stroke his forehead. She chuckled lightly then took another uncertain step closer.

Then she was standing beside the horse, rubbing her hand over his neck, her mouth wreathed in a smile that made Elliot jealous of Seamus.

"You're a good boy," she murmured as she rubbed his neck, patting him lightly. Then she looked up at Elliot. "You were right. He's very calm."

Their eyes met, held, and he couldn't look away. It was as if everything else faded and it was just the two of them, their gazes locked.

His breathing shifted and, before he even realized what he was doing, his hand was resting on her shoulder, his forefinger gently caressing her neck.

Her lips were parted and her breath came quicker. Elliot shifted just a little closer. Nearer.

Then she seemed to come to herself, blinked, and broke the connection by looking away.

What was he thinking?

Elliot dropped his hand, suddenly flustered. Suddenly aware of Tricia and Mason watching him.

"So, I better get back to working on that wagon," he said, shifting his stance. Moving away from Kinsley.

"Of course," she said, her smile suddenly forced and wooden. "I should go too." She sounded breathless, and he wondered if she'd been as affected by their brief connection as he had.

He knew he should leave it be, but he wasn't ready to let her go. He wanted to talk to her. Alone.

And what? Ask her if she would let you kiss her? Because that wouldn't be stupid at all.

Yet he felt as if he was on the cusp of something different. As if maybe, possibly, things were shifting between them, and he wanted to see where it was going.

He gave Mason and Tricia a half-hearted wave, ignoring their knowing looks. He opened the gate for Kinsley, not trusting himself to look at her as she walked through.

He latched the gate and slowed his pace to match hers, his thoughts racing. She had affected him in a way that was surprising and not unwelcome. He wanted to spend more time with her. And not working on the wedding.

"Hey, I was wondering if...well..." his words drifted off as he found himself, for the first time in years, unsure of what to say around a woman.

"If what?" she asked, looking at him, a faint smile curving her lips.

He hesitated, not sure how to ask.

"So this is where you all are hanging out?"

The horses in the corral beside them whinnied as the familiar voice sounded across the yard. Elliot turned to see Denise, astride a horse, coming at a trot toward them.

Elliot stifled a stab of annoyance at her sudden and inconvenient appearance.

And then he heard Kinsley's swift intake of breath. He shot her a concerned glance and saw, again, the same look on her face that he'd seen when he almost ran her over the first time they met.

"Slow down, Denise," he called out, taking a step between Kinsley and the oncoming horse. "Pull up right there."

"Sure. Of course," she said, sounding puzzled as she stopped her horse. "Everything okay?"

"Kinsley is...uncomfortable around your horse." He didn't know if Kinsley would appreciate the comment, but he didn't know what else to say.

"Pinto is fine. You know that." Denise sounded put out and puzzled at the same time.

His old girlfriend had been riding since before she could walk. Elliot knew she couldn't imagine why anyone would possibly feel uncomfortable around a horse.

"I do, but please, just keep your distance."

"Sure." Still puzzled, Denise vaulted off her horse in one easy movement. She slipped the reins over Pinto's head and then hesitated, unsure what to do next.

Elliot saw Kinsley's hands curl into fists, could almost feel the tension radiating off her. She had been so comfortable with Seamus, he was surprised she was this upset with Pinto. The horse was just standing there, as quiet as Seamus had been.

"Come and say hi to Pinto?" Denise was asking Kinsley. "He's extremely well behaved."

Kinsley licked her lips, then lifted her chin in a defiant

gesture. Elliot thought she would say no. He was surprised when she moved past him. She was walking stiffly, as if trying to hide her uneven gait, but she had a determined look on her face.

Pinto turned toward her, lowering his head as she came close.

"He loves getting scratched between his eyes," Denise said, her tone encouraging.

Kinsley hesitated for a fraction of a second, then, moved closer and rubbed Pinto's head.

Elliot grinned at the sight. She was more confident this time than she had been with Seamus.

"Hey, Pinto," she murmured as she scratched his head. You're a pretty horse."

"He's the best," Denise said. "Do you want to take him for a ride?"

Kinsley took a quick step back at that, giving Denise a quick, decisive shake of her head. "Thanks. That's generous, but I should get back to...back to work."

"Right. You're planning the wedding. Sure hope the weather holds for it."

"Me too." Another bright smile, a hesitant look back at him, and then she was leaving them. Elliot could tell she was trying hard not to limp, but her step was still uneven. His heart broke for her.

He wanted to rush after her, to tell her how proud he was of her, but guessed it would A, look patronizing, and B, sound patronizing.

Neither of which she would appreciate.

Denise walked her horse over to the corral where Mason and Tricia were putting the harness back on Seamus. Guess they wanted the practice. While Denise had ridden up they had gotten the collar on and wrestled the harness on the horse more quickly this time.

"She scared of horses?" Denise asked once Kinsley was out of earshot. He hoped.

Elliot didn't want to talk about Kinsley without her there. Nor did he want to expound on why. Kinsley had confided in him and he didn't want to betray her trust.

"So what brings you here?" he asked, shifting the topic.

"Just wanted to say hello. Not often we're both in town at the same time."

"That's true. How's the job?" He would have preferred to catch up to Kinsley, talk to her, explore the changing emotions between them. But Denise had ridden all the way over here, he had to at least be polite.

Denise chattered on about her new job working as a consultant for a feed company. How much she loved it and how she got to travel.

Elliot wasn't the least bit interested, but he played along, determined to be polite.

He and Denise had dated a few years ago. He had broken it off because he knew it wouldn't work out between them. She was heartbroken and he'd felt like a heel, but he knew what a good relationship should look like. He'd seen it in Zach and Grace's marriage. Their closeness and connection was what he wanted for any future relationship. Denise was a great girl, just not the right girl.

"Anyhow, just thought I'd stop by. I guess..." She hesitated, and he cringed inwardly, preparing himself for what she was going to say. "I guess I was hoping we could go out riding."

That wasn't as bad as he thought it would be, but still, not a good idea.

"I doubt I'll have time, Denise. With this wedding and the rodeos I have to hit yet..." He let the sentence trail off, hoping she would get the hint.

She gave him a forced smile, which showed him she caught it just fine.

"Okay. Well, good luck. Looks like you're on your way to the championship."

"One ride and one rodeo at a time," he said.

Denise nodded, got on her horse, pulled her hat more snug on her head, turned, and rode off.

Elliot refused to turn around to catch Tricia's reaction. Tricia had never cared for Denise. So he walked toward the barn, ducked around it, and hurried back to the shop where the wagon waited for him.

As he picked up the wrench he had been using to take the seat off the buggy he thought back to Kinsley's appearance a few moments ago.

And he wondered why she had come to the shop. Maybe he'd have to find a reason to go the house and then, oh-so-casually, ask her.

CHAPTER 9

*T*hat came close to being a very dumb mistake. She had simply gone out to the shop to check on the progress of the wagon. That was all.

Was it really?

Kinsley clenched and unclenched her fists as she walked away, overly conscious of the hitch in her step. Overly conscious of how she looked in blue jeans compared to that stunning woman who had shown up on horseback. Of course this happened shortly after she had done that cute little thing with the horse. Petting it so sweetly. Even though deep inside she was terrified, she had overcome that. She had been proud of herself. And, she had to admit, thankful to Elliot for giving her that little push. For a moment, as she stood close to Seamus, she felt like maybe she could overcome this fear. A small step in the right direction.

And then the blonde bombshell showed up, moving easily on her horse, as if born there. Had she imagined how Elliot's eyes had lit up when he saw her? Didn't matter.

Give yourself a shake, she told herself. *This is just God reminding you of why you shouldn't have anything to do with that guy.*

But it still hurt. She had spent most of her teen years and adult life trying to prove that physical appearance wasn't the true measure of a person. She shouldn't judge another woman the way she hoped not to be judged.

As she stepped inside the house, she heard the kids crying. They'd been quiet when she left, playing in the family room. But now it sounded like things weren't going well.

She followed the sound down the hallway to the bedrooms, and sure enough, Zach was sitting on the bed holding Cash on his lap, while Hope was sobbing her little heart out.

"I don't want to sleep," she cried. "Want Mommy."

"Mommy is busy," Zach said. "You lay down and have a nap, and as soon as you wake up you can go see her."

"I want to see Mommy too," Cash said.

"Later," Zach said. Kinsley could hear the desperation in his voice. He sounded like he was at his wits' end. Then he looked up and saw Kinsley hovering in the doorway. "Are you busy?"

Kinsley hesitated, feeling like she should back away from the situation. She had been working on the wedding program, downloading graphics. It still needed to be put together, and later this afternoon she had to call the woman Faith was hoping would play for the wedding service. Someone named Marianne who played with Faith on the worship team at church.

But when she saw the lines bracketing Zach's mouth, she knew she couldn't just walk away.

"What you need me to do?"

"The kids just need to settle down. They don't want to sleep. And they're both exhausted. Can you try?" He looked so bereft that Kinsley couldn't find it in her heart to leave.

"Why don't you go, and I'll see what I can do?"

That was all the invitation Zach needed. He stood, still

holding Cash, and handed him to Kinsley as she came around the end of the bed.

Kinsley planted her feet to get her balance, then took the little boy from him. She wavered a moment, but then sat on the bed.

"Oh, I'm so sorry," Zach said, holding his hand out toward her. "I forgot about... I never thought..."

Kinsley could see he was struggling. She also knew that Zach was just trying to be considerate.

"He's just heavier than I thought. It kind of threw me off."

"He is a chunk," Zach agreed, giving her a careful smile. "Are you sure you'll be okay?"

Hope had stopped crying, obviously curious about this new development. She scooted closer to Kinsley, slipping her arm through hers.

"I think I'll manage," Kinsley said. "I'll read them some stories. I imagine I just need to keep them occupied."

"A nap would be great," Zach said. "But we'll take what we can get."

"You can go now. I've got this under control."

Kinsley sounded more confident than she felt. But after being confronted with Denise and her obvious proficiency with a horse, she needed a win. If there was one thing she was good at, it was entertaining little kids.

At least that's what her sisters always told her when she flew to Ontario to visit them.

Zach closed the door behind him, and Kinsley was alone with the children.

"You my friend?" Hope asked.

"Absolutely," Kinsley assured her. "Are you sure you don't want to have a nap?"

Hope shook her head, keeping her eyes fixed on Kinsley's face. "Read a story?"

Kinsley chuckled, then nodded. If she could get them snuggled in bed to read to them, they might settle into sleep.

"I get the book," Cash called out, wiggling off Kinsley's lap.

"No I do," Hope retorted, scooting off the bed, toddling right behind him.

"Why don't you each get two books," Kinsley said. "And I'll read them to you."

A few minutes later, as Kinsley had hoped, they were curled up in the bed, one on each side of her. She was leaning against the headboard, holding the books as she read.

The kids had their arms tucked into hers, their heads leaning against her arm. It felt so domestic, so cozy.

Kinsley swallowed as she turned the page, unable to stop the feelings of melancholy that drifted over her.

When she and Drake got engaged, she had imagined scenes like this many times in her head. Sure, she had wanted to be a part of the wedding business that Drake and his mother ran. It was work she knew how to do. And work she was good at. It was a lucrative career in which she could use her business degree.

And yet, a part of her yearned for this as well. A home. Children. It was what her sisters had, and though she tried hard not to envy them, it was difficult not to feel a measure of bitterness against her old fiancé for taking away all those years of her life. For holding up her dreams while he chased his own. While he put her needs aside for his.

By the third book, the children's heads grew heavy against her arms. She finished the story, letting her voice go quieter and quieter. And then she waited a few more minutes just to make sure. They were breathing deeply by now, and when she was sure they wouldn't wake, she extricated herself from them, moving awkwardly across the bed.

She tucked them in, watching them for another moment,

smiling at how innocent they looked. Rosy, chubby cheeks, waiting to be kissed. Dimpled hands curled up by their heads.

She walked slowly out of the room, gently closing the door behind her.

Zach was in his recliner, snoring quietly.

Chuckling, Kinsley walked up the stairs to her bedroom where she usually worked. But wanting to keep close tabs on the children, she gathered up her laptop and her notes and brought them downstairs.

She spread everything out on the kitchen table and began working. A couple times she looked up, listening to make sure the children still slept. It felt very domestic, sitting here at the gallery table in a home that held sleeping children. A home that exuded warmth and welcome. However, even as she sat there enjoying the ambience, her thoughts drifted to Elliot. Had he and Denise gone riding?

And why did she care?

She cared, because for a moment as Elliot was encouraging her with Seamus she felt a spark between them. A connection she easily recognized as building attraction. Growing awareness. Yes he was good-looking, she would be a fool not to admit that. There was something else to him though. A vulnerability.

She shook her head. She was indulging in foolish thoughts. She clicked on the space bar, waking her laptop up.

And she got back to work, keeping her focus on what was in front of her.

Real and tangible plans. Not foolish dreams.

ᕱ

"So you didn't go riding with Denise?" Tricia teased Elliot as she scooped up the mashed potatoes at suppertime.

"I had work to do," Elliot grumbled. He didn't want to talk

about Denise. Not with Kinsley sitting right across the table from him.

"She sure seemed like she wanted to go," Tricia continued. "Maybe she was hoping to light the old spark."

"Elliot has enough of those old sparks still smoldering around the country," Kane said. "I don't think he needs to go relighting any of them."

Though Kane's grin showed Elliot he was joking, he also sensed an undercurrent of disapproval.

"I've got other things on my mind," Elliot returned.

"How's it coming with the wagon?" Faith asked. "You think you'll have it done on time?"

"I'm sure I will. I'm no carpenter, but I'm handy with a sand blaster and a paintbrush."

The talk eased into the usual supper conversation. The wedding and how things were progressing.

"Have you heard from the photographer yet?" Kinsley asked.

"He told me he'd call me back tomorrow," Faith said.

"It would be nice to nail him down," Kinsley said. "I'd like to talk to him about how he wants to go about this."

"He shows up, he takes pictures," Faith said with a chuckle. "How hard can it be?"

"Well, there's a little more to it than that," Kinsley said. "Do you want family pictures, or do you want pictures of just you and Kane. Do you want casual pictures, or do you want formal pictures."

"Sounds like you know what you're talking about when it comes to wedding photography," Elliot said.

The entire suppertime, Kinsley had been avoiding his gaze. Though he tried to make eye contact with her, she never connected with him. He had to wonder if Denise had something to do with it. Things had been going just fine until she showed up.

"I know a few things," Kinsley said.

"A few things? Like I said, I've seen your pictures," Faith said. "You always do such an amazing job."

"Then why don't you get Kinsley to take pictures?" Elliot asked. He was determined to catch her attention. And as her frightened gaze swung to his, he clearly had.

"I'm not taking the pictures," Kinsley protested. "I'm not a professional photographer."

"We don't have to worry about that just yet," Faith said. "Are you able to come with me to look at the wedding dress tomorrow morning?"

"Of course," Kinsley said. "I'd love to."

"Take your camera along," Faith added. "You may be no professional photographer, but I would love some pre-wedding pictures of the dress."

Kinsley smiled, and Elliot could see that despite her protests, she was looking forward to the idea.

Hope was banging her fork against the plate, as if looking for attention.

Kinsley gently took the utensil away from her, smiling as she did so. "Do you want more to eat?" she asked.

"Not hungry," Hope said. "Read another story?"

"Is that what you were doing when I left you with the kids?" Zach asked Kinsley.

"You left the kids with Kinsley?" Tricia asked her father. "You were supposed to watch them."

"I was tired," Zach grumbled. "Besides, Kinsley offered."

"I'm so sorry about that." Tricia looked stricken. "Dad was supposed to be taking care of the kids. Not you."

"She did a good job of that," Elliot put in. "She's a natural." As soon as he spoke, he realized his mistake. Kinsley was frowning at him, and so were Tricia and Faith.

"How would you know?" Faith asked.

Elliot just shrugged, hoping he looked more relaxed than he felt, as he scrambled for something to say.

After Denise left, he waited an appropriate amount of time then went to the house to get a drink of water, his excuse to talk to Kinsley. He wanted to make sure she was okay, and, even though he didn't really want to admit it to himself, he hoped somehow to assure her that Denise meant nothing to him.

"I came to the house for a drink of water. I saw Zach sleeping in the recliner and I heard Kinsley reading to the kids." *Not bad*, he thought. A decent reason, and one that wouldn't require any more explanations.

He had seen how Mason and Tricia were watching him with Kinsley in the corral. The last thing he needed was them teasing him in front of her. But when he glanced over at her again, she was finally looking back at him. He took a chance and gave her a careful smile.

"I have to confess," he continued, "I wanted to stick around to hear how the story ended."

"The bear made it home," Kinsley said. "The kitten made friends with her enemy, and the dragon found the book he was looking for."

"I'm so glad. I was hoping the dragon would get his happily ever after."

Kinsley's mouth quirked up as she returned his smile, and Elliot felt as if he had cracked the most hilarious joke.

"Sometimes that happens in stories."

The despondent tone in her voice made him wonder how many unhappy endings she had experienced. "Sometimes it happens in real life too," he added.

Her only response was a half-hearted shrug, which could mean anything.

"I don't think there's such a thing as a happily ever after," Faith said putting emphasis on her final word, "but I do believe in happy-for-now."

"I sure hope so," Kane put in. "After all, we are getting married soon. I'd like that to be a happy occasion."

Faith gave him a smile then stroked his stubbled cheek. "And I'm so glad we are and it will be."

They exchanged a look so full of love that Elliot felt a pang of gentle jealousy. Yes, he was happy for Faith and Kane, happy for Tricia and Mason.

Yes, he had a plan for his own future.

But for the first time in a long while he realized it was a short-term future. And that a part of him wanted what his brother and sister had.

CHAPTER 10

Kinsley struggled to stifle her gasp of dismay as Faith came out of the bedroom the seamstress, Nelly Boyko, used as a dressing room.

The wedding dress Faith had been so excited about was a disaster. And Faith's disappointed expression told Kinsley her friend felt the same.

"I think we need to do something about this neckline," Faith said, plucking at the material draped from shoulder to shoulder.

Kinsley guessed the seamstress was going for a Grecian look, but the linen she used did not lend itself to draping.

"I can see what you're talking about," Nelly said. "You said you wanted a natural fabric," she said, her tone defensive.

"I know," Faith said. "I guess I was counting on you to help me out."

Nelly pursed her lips as if unhappy with Faith's comment.

"I'll see what I can do," she said. "But I will charge you a little more for the alterations."

"I would think alterations would be part of the package," Kinsley said, not happy with Nelly's response. "Faith needs to be happy with the result."

"Of course she does, however, it's extra work I didn't count on." But Kinsley could see that Nelly was still annoyed. Well, if she was going to be annoyed anyway, Kinsley figured she may as well go all out with the honesty.

"And while you're altering, that waistline is too high," she said, walking around Faith, tugging and lifting the material. "And the draping in the back is all wrong."

"Well, like I said, I'll see what I can do," Nelly repeated, looking completely put out.

"I'll go take this off now," Faith said, giving Kinsley a wan smile.

When she left, Kinsley turned back to Nelly.

"If you charge for the alterations, what amount would Faith be looking at?" she asked. So far they were well within budget, and she wanted to keep it that way.

"She hasn't given me any clear direction as to what she wants the neckline to look like," Nelly said. "But the way I designed it, I might have to change the entire bodice."

"Where the waistline is sitting is not Faith's fault," Kinsley said, determined to press her point.

"I suppose you're right," Nelly conceded. "I should have measured her better."

"Another thing I need to know is what timeline we're looking at for the changes," Kinsley said. She had to stifle her nervousness, as the wedding was coming up quickly.

"I can get it done by the end of the week," Nelly said.

"Can you do it any sooner?" Kinsley asked. If the changes were unsatisfactory, that was cutting it too close.

Kinsley didn't want to think about that. She had to trust that the alterations would work out. It would be almost impossible to find a suitable dress off the rack a week before the wedding day.

Faith returned, carrying the dress. She gave it to Nelly, biting her lip as she did so. "The zipper up the back is a little uncomfortable," she said. "Maybe you could look at that as well?"

Faith sounded tentative, and it annoyed Kinsley.

"Of course she can. Just add that to the list." Kinsley shot Nelly a stern look as if daring her to challenge her.

But Nelly shrugged and took the dress, then laid it down on the table behind her.

"I'll let you know when it's ready," she said sullenly.

Kinsley was quiet as they walked out of the house toward the car.

"You didn't like the dress, did you?" Faith asked once they were in the car and on their way to town.

Kinsley wasn't sure what to say, but Faith had read her reaction well. Anything she said to the contrary would be a fib.

"How much will the dress cost?"

When Faith told her, Kinsley had to stifle a groan.

"It costs that much because it's custom-made," Faith said, her tone defensive.

Experience had told Kinsley to wait and let the future bride assess the situation herself. Hopefully Faith would arrive at the same conclusion as Kinsley.

"She came highly recommended," Faith continued.

"Are you happy with the dress?"

From the way Faith was chewing her lip, Kinsley got her answer.

"We have no other options, do we?" Faith asked. "I don't have time to run into the city and try on dresses and wait for alterations."

"You're right, that would take too long." Kinsley's thoughts flipped around, trying to think of what do to.

A thought snuck in, hovering on the edges of her mind. *You could let her use your dress.* It still hung in the garment bag pushed into the back of a closet in her apartment in Calgary. The dress she spent months looking for. Months, and a lot of money.

She should have sold it or donated it, and moved on. But she couldn't seem to part with it.

And now?

For some reason her thoughts slipped to Elliot. But no sooner had his smiling face appeared in her mind than she dismissed it. Yes, he was attractive, yes, it seemed like there was a connection between them, but there was no way she was making that huge jump. Not with a guy too much like Drake.

"Where are you?" Faith asked, obviously noticing Kinsley's momentary distraction.

Kinsley glanced at Faith, mentally sizing her up. "What size do you wear?"

"Eight," Faith said. "Why?"

"Do you think we're the same height?" Kinsley asked.

"I know we're exactly the same height," Faith said. "I borrowed your clothes when we were in school together. Why?"

Kinsley hesitated. So many dreams and plans for her own life had been woven into that dress. Could she let go?

And what are you keeping it for? Do you need the reminder of Drake's casual treatment of you?

"If you're interested, I still have my wedding dress," she said, throwing the words out before she changed her mind. "And I'm sure it would fit you."

"Really? Your wedding dress?"

"I think, at one time, I sent you pictures of it, and you said you loved it."

Faith frowned, as if trying to draw out the memory.

"Lace on the top with a halter neckline. Gauzy skirt. Beaded waistband."

Faith's expression grew dreamy. "I remember now. It was gorgeous." Faith laid her hand on Kinsley's arm. "But you can't give that dress away. Someday you'll get married. I know it."

"Maybe. Not for a while though. I have plans I want to see happen first."

"The wedding planner business?"

"Yes. That's why I'm doing your wedding, remember."

Faith made a face then shrugged. "I know, but..."

"But what? You don't think I'm good enough?"

"Of course you're good enough." Faith waved dismissively. "You're fantastic. Organized, on task, and you know how to see the big picture."

She stopped and Kinsley waited, hearing the objection in her silence.

Then Faith sighed and fiddled with her engagement ring. "Like I said, you're really good at this. That's why I asked you to do my wedding. However, I feel like this job is not really you."

A tiny shiver of apprehension snaked down Kinsley's spine. "What do you mean?"

Another sigh, another twist of her ring. "I mean that when I see you taking pictures, that's when I see you come alive. That's when I see you smile. You're superb at this wedding stuff, there's no doubt, but I just feel like you could be doing something else. Something you want to do in your heart."

"Like you with your music?" As soon as Kinsley spoke the words, she regretted them. She knew Faith had "followed her dreams" when she broke up with Kane and left with a band to play her guitar.

"Sometimes you need to fail to know how to succeed." Faith chewed at her lip as if remembering those failures. "I think by being a music teacher, I've found a good blend between my dreams and being practical."

"It is a perfect balance," Kinsley agreed. "So what do you think would be the balance for me?"

She threw the question out with a laugh, but at the same time Faith's doubt in her career choice resonated in a way she hardly dared acknowledge. Questioning her choices at this stage was disconcerting and disorienting. Jill had offered her a potential partnership. It was a fantastic opportunity. She was a single woman and had to make her own way in the world. This was a way to do that. She couldn't depend on fickle men to plan her future.

"I think you have a good eye for what will work. I think you have good instincts. And you take amazing pictures."

"So you've been saying," Kinsley returned dryly.

"And I'll keep saying it."

"I'm not taking the wedding pictures," Kinsley said knowing exactly where Faith was going with this. "I won't have time."

Faith sighed and pulled her phone out of her pocket. "Guess I'll try calling Jeff Wylie again."

Kinsley kept her eye on the road while Faith made the call. Even though she'd been adamant about not taking the pictures, she couldn't stop herself from imagining how she would go about it if she did. What kind of shots she would take. How she would set them up.

She shook her head to dislodge the thoughts. She had enough going on right now.

Like a wedding dress that couldn't be salvaged and that needed to be replaced.

"Yeah, Jeff, just want to double-check with you about my wedding. I haven't heard from you. Please, please call me back."

The anxiety in Faith's voice created a flicker of confusion. Kinsley's thoughts raced through her mind, chasing each other, trying to find a solution.

If they didn't get this guy…

Did she know anyone else they could get on such short notice…

There might be someone she could call, but would they be any good?

You could take the pictures.

Kinsley sucked in a steadying breath as panic beat at her chest, a flurry of fear. She needed this wedding to go well. How could she manage and control all that, and horses too, if she had to be the photographer as well? And if Jill showed up, what would she think of Kinsley's juggling act?

Faith put her phone back in her purse and, thankfully, didn't look over at Kinsley.

"I heard back from the people with the tent," Kinsley said, moving to a safer topic. "They'll be coming a day earlier than we expected because it worked out better for them. Which is great. They'll set out the chairs and tables then as well as the dance floor."

"That's nice to know," Faith said, but Kinsley could hear the forced enthusiasm in her voice.

"And I have to run to Calgary to pick up the tablecloths and napkins as well as some items for the tables Jill said we could rent. If you want, I could pick up my dress and bring it back here for you to try on."

Faith didn't respond, which made Kinsley think she had overstepped.

"I'm sorry, Faith. If you really like the dress that Nelly made for you—"

"I don't. It's hideous. And now I can't get a photographer." Faith's voice broke into a sob. "I don't know what to do. Things are falling apart."

"Oh sweetie…" Kinsley reached out to squeeze Faith's shoulder. "We'll figure something out."

Faith sniffed then dug in her purse, pulling out some tissues. She wiped her eyes and blew her nose. "Are you sure about your wedding dress?"

"I'm sure. It's time to move on." Put the past behind her and look ahead. "Like I said, I'll pick it up when I go to Calgary."

Faith drew in a wavering breath. "Other than the dress and photographer, who is kind of important, everything else seems to be on target, right?"

"You said that Tricia has her bridesmaid dress already?"

Faith nodded.

"Kane and Elliot are going to town to pick out their clothes?"

"Yes. Kane will be done hauling the hay home by then."

"And Elliot is working on the wagon. Tricia and Mason are confident about the horses." She wasn't, but she didn't want to voice that opinion. "The flowers look healthy and beautiful. We just need to double-check with Mia about your and Tricia's bouquets. We can nail that down in the next couple of days to give her time to order them and put the bouquets and bouton- nieres together."

"And Marianne Den Engelson is able to do my wedding music?"

"Also committed." Another panicky win for Kinsley. She had spent most of yesterday afternoon chasing Marianne down between writing up the wedding program and getting that sent off to the printer.

"Then I guess things are coming together." Faith drew in a deep breath. "I'm really disappointed with the dress. Are you sure you don't mind lending me yours?"

"I told you. It's just hanging there. It needs to be used. It needs to find a new purpose."

"I feel bad about taking it, but it's a gorgeous dress. Such a dream."

"Please don't feel bad. I need to get rid of it."

And as she uttered the words she realized how true they were.

⌒◯⌒

"How's the wagon coming along?" Kane asked as he strode into the shop late that afternoon.

Elliot looked up from the bolt he was tightening on the frame of the wagon and gave his brother a tentative smile. "I've just about got the seats done. They need another coat of varnish and then I can bolt them on." He jerked his chin toward the

146

wooden benches he had been working on all morning. Kane walked over and stood in front of them, his hands on his hips.

"They look great."

The approval in his voice warmed Elliot's heart. There was a time when he wouldn't have cared what Kane thought, but since coming back to the ranch, his brother's opinion mattered more and more.

"I'm no carpenter, but I think they turned out well."

"Better than well. It looks professional."

More praise.

"Thanks." It was all he could say.

A moment of silence followed his reply, and Elliot took the wrench to the other bolt holding the frame for the seat.

"Will it be finished on time?"

"I'll have it back together by the end of the week. Then I should take it out with the horses a few times to make sure they're okay with it and that the wheels don't fall off."

"I'm not worried about Sancho and Seamus," Kane said, walking back to the wagon, running his hands over the sideboards. "But a few trial runs would be a good idea. Especially since I get the idea Kinsley is not too crazy about the horses."

"Not at all. But she has good reasons." As soon as the words left his mouth, he felt like smacking his forehead. Kinsley had told him what she had in confidence. He had no right to go blabbing about it.

"What reasons are those?" Kane asked.

"Not mine to say," Elliot returned.

Kane was quiet a moment, but Elliot knew his brother well enough to guess he was gearing up to say something important.

"She's an attractive woman," Kane said.

"She is that," Elliot agreed. "And I'm sensing you'll say something about that."

Kane sighed. "I saw how you two look at each other, and I'm guessing there's some attraction going on."

"Is this where you lecture me about not breaking her heart? About being careful?" Elliot couldn't keep the snap out of his tone or the edge out of his voice.

"Faith told me how Kinsley's marriage was called off and how her heart was broken. So yeah, I'm telling you to be careful with her."

Elliot was quiet, letting Kane's words settle, giving them some weight.

Then he spoke up. "Kinsley is an adult, and so am I." And he left it at that. He wasn't going to talk about something he wasn't sure of himself. He didn't want to bring his changing feelings for Kinsley out into the open to be examined in the cold light of day.

He was attracted to her. And unless he was being obnoxious, he sensed that she was interested in him as well.

"Well, just be careful," Kane said. "I know you have your plans, but she has hers. And I don't see them meshing."

Elliot chose not to reply to that.

"At any rate, I'm glad the wagon will be finished," Kane said. But he didn't leave. Which made Elliot wonder if there was something else on his mind.

He worked in silence a little longer as Kane walked around the wagon, inspecting it some more.

"You okay with this idea?" Elliot asked, preferring to talk about something ordinary. "Faith arriving in this wagon?"

"It's what she wants to do."

"But what do you want?" Elliot's mind slipped back to a comment he had made previously to Kinsley. What Faith wants, Faith gets.

"It's Faith's wedding, and I want everything to be perfect for her."

"I think that's admirable, but it's your wedding too," Elliot said.

"To be honest, I would have preferred to elope."

"Like Tricia and Drew did?"

"With a happier ending, of course." Kane glanced over at Elliot. "That little adventure didn't turn out real well for you either."

Kane knew he was referring to the broken arm and bruised ribs Elliot suffered in the accident that killed Tricia's husband. Elliot had been best man for that wedding too.

"True enough. It was a hard time for everyone." Another moment of silence. "It was hard being put out of the running for the CFR."

"And it gave you a lot of free time."

Elliot sat back on his heels, still holding the wrench as he looked at his brother. He thought of what he and Kinsley had talked about that afternoon in Tanner's house. How she had encouraged him to talk to his brother. Make things right between them. "I know we've never talked about what happened that summer, not in-depth at any rate," he said, his voice quiet, serious.

"Doesn't matter. It's history."

Kane's terse reply made him want to stop there. Take it and let it go. But every time they were together there was an under-lying current of tension he wanted out of the way.

"Maybe to you, but it's one of the main reasons I'm here. To make peace. To find a way past this. You asked me to be your best man, but I'm sure you would have preferred if Lucas could do the job. I'm glad to do it because I need to figure out how to make things up to you. I'm sorry if you thought something was going on between me and Faith—"

"I know there wasn't. Faith and I talked about that."

"Well, I'm glad you're getting married. I'm glad you guys worked your way past all that other stuff."

Kane held his earnest gaze, frowning. The silence between them seemed heavy. Weighted with guilt and regret.

"We have," Kane said softly, leaning his elbows on the wagon. "But there've been consequences to her following her dreams."

"But she quit the band," Elliot said, puzzled at how grave Kane sounded. "That turned out good in the end, didn't it? She's got a good job now, and you two will have a good life together." He threw the words out with a glimmer of hope even as Kane's words about consequences sent a chill into the atmosphere.

Kane said nothing, his expression still serious. Elliot wondered if there was something he'd missed. Something he didn't know.

"So what are some of these consequences you're talking about?" he prodded, coming off the wagon to stand beside his brother.

Another beat of silence greeted his question, then Kane turned to him, his eyes dark. "Faith had a relationship with one of the band members. She got pregnant." He stopped there, pressing his lips together, as if he didn't want to release the next words. "But she lost the baby."

Elliot stared at him, shock coursing through him at Kane's blunt admission. "Pregnant?"

Kane clung to the side of the wagon, his knuckles growing white. Elliot could see how difficult this was for him, but wasn't sure what to say. Did Kane blame him?

"She's asked my forgiveness," he continued, "and though it seemed patronizing to have to give it, seeing as how we were broken up at the time, we found our way to each other. Like I said, we've worked through it." Kane closed his eyes, lowering his head.

"I'm sorry to hear that." Elliot was stunned, trying to absorb this all. "I'm sure that's been difficult to process."

"It wouldn't have happened if she hadn't gone touring with that band."

A chill feathered Elliot's spine at Kane's words and the anger that laced them.

"So you are saying that's my fault after all?" Elliot asked.

Another moment of silence, then Kane pushed himself straight. "If you hadn't encouraged her to go traveling with them, a lot of bad things in her life wouldn't have happened."

Elliot took a step back, the restrained annoyance in Kane's voice washing over him. It hurt more than he wanted to admit.

"I can see why it's easy to make me the target," Elliot said. "Probably easier to blame me than to think maybe Faith made a bad choice. But she wasn't a puppet. She had her own reasons for doing what she did." He kept himself from saying that one of those reasons was the pressure Kane and her grandfather put on her to go to law school. Become a lawyer in her grandfather's firm. A respectable job. One that Kane and her grandfather thought would be perfect, but a job she didn't want at all.

He waited for Kane's answer, but his brother was slowly shaking his head, still looking away from him. As if still trying to deal with this ghost in Faith's past.

"I hope you can find a way to get past this," Elliot said. "I hope for your and Faith's sake that this doesn't come between you."

"We've talked about it," Kane said. "I thought I was done with it, and then you returned..."

"And it all came back." Elliot finished the sentence for him. What surprised him the most was how much this hurt. He knew Kane wouldn't exactly welcome him with open arms, but he didn't think the past would be such a shadow on the present.

"I can leave if you want me to." As Elliot forced the words out he realized how difficult they were to say. "I'm sure you can find someone else for your best man."

But even as he spoke, he realized he didn't want to leave. Things had changed for him in the past few weeks, and the dream he had been chasing grew less important. The restless and wandering life he had been living grew wearying.

Being on the ranch made him return to one of the best times in his life.

And there's Kinsley.

"Of course I don't want you to go. This is your home as much as it is mine," Kane said. "You're as much Zach's son as I am."

"Except I didn't get adopted." Elliot was hoping to make the comment sound like he was kidding, but the sudden anger on Kane's face made him realize the joke had landed with a thud.

Kane shook his head and then, to Elliot's shock and surprise, Kane grabbed him and pulled him close in a rough man-hug.

Elliot held himself stiff for a moment, unsure of what to think. He felt a sliver of discomfort, but when Kane wouldn't let him go, he relaxed into his brother's embrace. Then, even worse, felt a shiver of sorrow envelope him. He couldn't cry. He never had even when Dennis was whaling on him with his belt, his fists or whatever came to hand.

He couldn't start, because he didn't know if he would ever stop. And cowboys don't cry. They man up.

Yet it felt so good to be hugged by his brother. To have that physical connection.

Then Kane thumped him on the back and drew back, still holding him by the shoulders as he looked into his eyes. "You're my brother. I know Mom and Dad would have adopted you in a heartbeat if it wasn't for—"

"If it wasn't for Dennis," Elliot finished.

"But adopted or not, you're my brother. And I wanted *you* to be my best man, not Lucas. You were always my first choice."

"Despite what happened?" Elliot couldn't stop the surge of blame at the thought that he had taken part in the difficulties Faith had dealt with.

"Not despite what happened," Kane said. "What you said just now makes sense. Faith made her own choices. She wasn't a child. I guess, yeah, it was always easier to blame you than think she wasn't perfect."

"None of us are," Elliot said.

"No. But thank goodness God loves us still, despite our messy lives."

Elliot felt another shiver of sorrow at the easy way Kane spoke God's name. God the Father. He still struggled with that idea. But he brushed it aside. For now, God would have to wait. For now he and his brother had breached the chasm that had divided them.

And for that he was grateful.

"And now that we've got that out of the way, I need to ask a favor of you," Kane continued.

"What favor?"

"We need to go to town and pick out what we'll wear for this wedding."

"Really? Shopping?"

"Hey, if I can do it, you can," Kane said, shooting him a warning glance.

"Ugh, I hate buying clothes."

"Cowboy up, mister. Besides, it won't be hard. Faith said keep it simple, so a nice shirt and new blue jeans is all we need." He glanced down at Elliot's scuffed and worn cowboy boots. "And maybe some new footwear."

"What? These are my lucky boots." Elliot held one foot up, inspecting it. "I wear them everywhere."

"Which is exactly why, given that we live on a ranch with animals, and that they've been in countless rodeo arenas, you will need some new boots."

Elliot chuckled, Kane grinned, and then together they walked out of the garage.

Brothers in arms, Elliot thought as a weight he'd been carrying for years slipped off his shoulders.

CHAPTER 11

*K*insley pulled up to the ranch, her head buzzing. It had been a long busy day, and she was tired.

She turned her car off, thankful for the quiet that washed over her after the busy traffic and endless roads of the city. She'd only been away from Calgary a week and a half, but it hadn't taken her long to get used to the peace and quiet of the ranch and the country roads.

Rolling her head eased the kink in her neck, but her hip ached with all the sitting. As she got out of the car she faltered, then took a moment to stretch it out.

"Are you okay?"

Kinsley spun around just as Elliot came sauntering toward her, the sun catching glints in his perpetually tousled hair.

"Of course. I'm fine." She couldn't help the defensive tone that entered her voice. The past few days she had been growing more and more self-conscious around him, and she hated it.

"So you got everything you needed in Calgary?"

"I sure did," she said, wondering why he was here. Had he been waiting for her?

"You were gone a long time. Did you take some time to catch up with old friends?"

And why was she even the smallest bit pleased that he had noticed her absence?

"No, I spent a lot of time in my car driving."

"That sucks. I hate traffic."

"Especially considering that for you, a traffic jam means waiting ten seconds to make a left turn in Rockyview."

Elliot laughed, which gave her a small thrill of pleasure.

"You got me pegged," he said as he took a few steps closer. "So did you miss me when you were gone?"

"I haven't been gone long enough for that."

"I actually kinda missed you," Elliot said, giving her his most charming smile.

"I'll bet you did." Kinsley tried to sound like she was joking, but was surprised at the little thrill of pleasure his words gave her.

A strand of hair, lifted by an errant breeze, caught on her lipstick. She lifted her hand to remove it but Elliot was already there, his fingers teasing it away.

His fingers lingered on her face for a heartbeat, sending shivers dancing down her spine.

"I know you don't like to look messy," he teased, his eyes flicking down, then up again.

"I had business to do today." And why did she feel like she had to justify what she was wearing? Suddenly she was self-conscious of clothing she had chosen with such care this morning because she wanted to look professional when she stopped at Jills's shop.

Jill had offered to let her use one of her backdrops for the head table as well as candleholders and a variety of other decor items that would add to the table centerpieces. Thankfully it all fit in her car.

"You look very professional. And uncomfortable." His eyes teased her as he loosened the single button of her blazer.

She swallowed, her heart racing.

It was a simple gesture. But the way he looked at her created an intimacy that, she was sure, he was doing on purpose.

"What are you doing?" she asked, feeling a need to call him out on his actions.

He didn't answer her question and took a step back, his expression shifting. Instead of answering he looked into the back of her car. "Faith told me you were picking up stuff in Calgary and that I needed to help you bring it to wherever it needs to go."

His practical question brought her back to reality and settled her on solid ground.

She just wished she wasn't so disappointed about his matter-of-fact statement. Wished he didn't create this vulnerability she wasn't sure what to do with.

"That would be great," she managed, turning away from him. She opened the back hatch and was about to take the boxes out when he stepped past her and took over.

"Where do you want these?" he asked.

"I think just put them in the garage for now," Kinsley said. "It's all stuff for the wedding."

"I kinda guessed that."

She picked up a box, ignoring Elliot's frown.

"I can take care of all this," he said.

"Maybe I don't trust you," she returned, trying for some levity.

"Maybe you shouldn't."

She tried not to read more into his comment than simple banter. So she simply handed him the boxes and he walked away, whistling.

Four trips later, they had the backdrop, the boxes of napkins, candleholders, cutlery, and wineglasses stacked inside the garage.

"It's a good thing the guest list isn't huge," Elliot said. "You'd have a lot more stuff stashed in here if it was, and I imagine it would be a lot more work."

"You're right about that," Kinsley agreed.

"I'm guessing things are going good with the preparations?" Elliot asked.

"All the boxes are getting ticked," Kinsley said as she walked back toward the car. She was tired and still stiff, and she was trying hard to keep her stride even. Though she had felt self-conscious around Elliot from the beginning, the last little while had seemed to be even worse. Especially after seeing Denise with her perfect body, perfect hair, perfect teeth, and perfect everything.

And she could ride a horse.

"So what did you do today?" Kinsley asked, needing to shift her silly thoughts away from self-pity toward practicality.

"Kane and I bought our shirts and pants for the wedding," he said. "And, you'll be pleased to know, I bought some new boots."

Kinsley glanced down at his worn and scuffed cowboy boots. "Those look like they've had a few miles put on them, that's for sure."

"A few miles and a lot of rides. But I figured I would cut loose for my brother's wedding."

Kinsley nodded as she opened passenger door of the car.

"And what is that?" Elliot asked as she pulled out the garment bag.

"Is Kane anywhere around?"

"He's working with the horses. Tricia and Mason went to town to get wedding clothes for the kids and I went back to the shop to finish up my work on the wagon. Faith told me to keep an eye out for you." He glanced at the bag she held. "So, satisfy my male curiosity. What's in the bag? Another suit for you?"

"You don't like my suits?"

"I think you look better in blue jeans." His eyebrow twitched upward and he added a grin.

He was flirting with her and, she had to admit, it made her feel good.

"So. The bag?" he repeated.

"It might be Faith's wedding dress. That's why I was asking if Kane was around."

"You got her dress in Calgary? I thought Nelly Boyko was making it."

"She was. Is. We looked at what she had done yesterday and...well...I thought we could give Faith another option."

"Looks like you got it at a fancy place."

"You can tell that from looking at the garment bag?" Kinsley teased as they walked toward the house together.

"For one thing, the name of the shop is written in gold swirly letters and for another, the address isn't exactly in a strip mall."

"You know where the high-end stores are in Calgary?"

"Sort of. Denise loved shopping and a couple of times she dragged me to a store close to that one," he said, waving his hand at the bag. "Let's just say I didn't blend. It was one of those memories seared on my subconscious and rises up now and again to haunt me."

Denise again. A good reminder that the way he was talking to her was how he talked to any woman. And yet...

"Well, you're right. This came from an exclusive wedding dress shop." One that Drake and his mother had a discount with because of the business they sent their way.

"I can't believe Faith would buy her dress at a boutique shop. She keeps saying how she wants this wedding simple and not spendy."

"This dress won't cost her a thing. It was..." She hesitated, fighting down the sting of humiliation of not only still having her wedding dress, but giving it away.

"It was…" he encouraged.

"Doesn't matter. I'd like her to try it on."

But as he opened the French doors for her, she caught his curious glance and the questions lying behind his gaze.

Kinsley was thankful the house was empty. She was tired and her hip ached, and all she wanted to do was soak in a hot tub and—

"Do you want a cup of coffee?" Elliot asked, walking over to the kitchen counter.

"Um. Yeah, but I can make it myself."

"I don't mind. I know a guy should never say this to a girl because it could be read wrong, but you seem tired."

"As in haggard and drawn?" she said, chuckling at his honesty as she draped the garment bag on the back of a kitchen chair.

"As if you could look that way," he protested as he filled up the coffeepot with water. "No. You're just walking slow. Does your hip hurt?"

"There's no beating around the bush with you is there?"

"Why? I know you injured your hip, and I can tell when you've been pushing yourself too hard physically. It's no secret."

To her surprise Kinsley felt a whisper of thankful relief. Elliot truly was easy to be around. No nonsense, and straightforward. She appreciated that.

"That's true and yes, I am tired. I did a lot of walking."

Which made Elliot glance down at her shoes. "Seriously, girl, you've got to lose those high heels. They're bad for your back no matter how hale and hearty you are."

Kinsley eased them off her throbbing feet. "Losing them now."

"I mean as in forever," Elliot said. He put a new filter in the basket and filled it with coffee grounds, his movements quick and efficient. He knew his way around this kitchen. "You can look professional without sacrificing your physical health."

"Says the man who has heels on his cowboy boots."

Elliot laughed at that. "Those heels keep my feet from slipping through the stirrups when I'm riding. There is a practical purpose for them. What's the purpose of yours?"

"If you don't buy my professional argument, then I'm tapped."

Elliot chuckled at that. And as the coffeepot burbled he put out mugs, pulled cream out of the refrigerator, and set everything down on the table in front of her.

"No sugar, right?"

"I'm surprised you remember."

"I keep my eye on you," he said, tapping his temple.

"That sounds creepy."

He gave her an exaggerated leer. "Maybe I'm a creepy guy."

"I don't think so."

He grinned and shrugged then waved his hand at her wedding dress. "Do you want me to take that upstairs to your room? Just in case Kane comes into the house."

"It's okay. I can do it." She pushed her chair back, struggling to get to her feet.

But Elliot was already standing, his hand gently pushing her back down.

"You're tired. I can do it for you."

She was about to protest again, but the thought of getting up and trudging up the stairs was too much for her right now. So she nodded.

"I'll be right back," Elliot said with a grin. "And I promise I won't read your diary."

She laughed at that, and before she could say anything else, he grabbed the garment bag and was gone.

Elliot's attention made her smile. Despite his casual attitude, she felt cherished, taken care of.

Drake, who always prided himself on his gentility, had done nothing like that for her.

Nor had he ever stood up for her.

She braced herself for the usual twist in her stomach, the embarrassment and humiliation that accompanied thoughts of him. Especially with Elliot handling the wedding dress she was supposed to be wearing as she married Drake.

But to her surprise, thinking about him merely brought a glimmer of annoyance and a surprising sense of freedom. She was making her own way now, she wasn't piggybacking on his success or his mother's. As Drake had often jokingly intimated. Though the words were spoken with a smile, she still struggled with the idea that they only employed her on sufferance. Only a part of the company because she was marrying him.

"Okay, I didn't snoop, but my goodness, you are a tidy person," Elliot remarked as he bounded into the kitchen.

"As Benjamin Franklin said, for every minute spent organizing, an hour is earned."

"Were you scrambling through potential quotes to toss at me because you guessed I would make some comment?"

"I have a few more up my sleeve, but that one seemed to be the most appropriate. I'm glad I could finally use it." She smiled up at him and he stepped closer, and for a moment she wondered if he would touch her again. Her heartbeat ticked upward, and her breath caught in her throat.

Then he turned away and poured a cup of coffee for them both.

"Here you go," Elliot said as he set the mug down in front of her and then sat down right beside her. "Nice and hot, just the way you like it."

"You seem to know an awful lot about me," Kinsley said.

"I'm an observer. I pay attention," Elliot said. "It's what's kept me alive at times."

"Really? How?"

"I need to know how to read a horse, see how he's reacting, and what he might do as he jumps out of the chute."

"Do you have another rodeo this weekend?"

He nodded, looking down at his mug, his finger running up and down the side.

"You don't seem too enthusiastic about it," Kinsley said.

"You're not the only one that's tired," Elliot said, looking up at her, his hazel eyes holding hers again. "It's a long season, and with every rodeo I don't get injured, I get a little more nervous."

"I thought you'd get more confident."

"It's all about odds. Sooner or later the horse will turn the wrong way and I won't be ready. I'll get bucked off or I'll get kicked. Anything can happen."

"Yet you keep going."

"I keep going," he repeated. He gave her a vague smile and took a sip of his coffee. "So, do you want to tell me about the wedding dress? The way you hesitated I'm guessing there's something else behind the story."

"You really come straight to the point, don't you?" Kinsley said, guessing he didn't want to talk about the rodeo and his pursuit of greatness.

"Life's too short for prevarication," he said. "And don't tease me about prevarication. Just because I'm a cowboy doesn't mean I don't know how to use fancy words."

"It's a good word," she said. "As for the wedding dress, it is, well, was, mine."

Thankfully his face didn't change expression at all. "So the obvious conclusion would be that you didn't use it?"

"That's an adequate conclusion."

"So because I'm a straight shooter, I'm coming right out and asking what the heck was wrong with the guy that you have a 'used-to-be-mine' wedding dress?"

Once again Kinsley smiled at his directness.

"He had a problem with commitment. He had his own plans,

and his own dreams, and I thought at one time I fit in with them but then I realized I didn't."

"It all sounds kind of vague. How did you know you didn't fit in with them?"

Kinsley bit her lip, the old bruise on her soul still tender. She looked away from Elliot because she didn't want to see the pity on his face, and yet, she had an overwhelming urge to tell him. "I overheard a conversation. The kind people have when they think you're not there. Which is seldom the good kind. Drake's mother was telling him that she didn't think I was the best partner. Either in the business or in his life. After all, how would it look to future brides, if the person planning their perfect wedding looked like me. Walked like me. And then, when I thought he would stand up for me, I heard nothing. No defense. No support. And I realized that if he couldn't stand up for me now, it would only get worse. So I broke up with him."

Silence followed her explanation. Then Elliot reached over and cupped her chin in his hand, turning her face toward his. "No offense," he said, "but what were you doing with such an idiot? You're a woman of discerning taste, and you were engaged to that loser?"

In spite of the shame spiraling through her, Kinsley couldn't help but giggle. "When you put it that way..."

"I know the usual comment is to say you're better off without him, but it couldn't have been easy to face such a shallow guy. To listen to, pardon my words, such incredibly lame excuses."

She chuckled again. "It wasn't easy. Thankfully I ended the relationship first, so at least I could walk away...actually make that limp away...with my pride intact. That was a year and a half ago. I've found my own way through life since then. Trouble was, I was connected to the business he and his mother ran. I had commitments to a few weddings I had to finish up, so

I had to deal with them both for another eight months. Once the commitments were fulfilled, I could leave."

"Awkward."

"In the extreme," she admitted.

"So, are you over him?"

Kinsley tested that question, teasing out old feelings, then nodded. "Yeah. I am. Hard not to feel some shame—"

"He was the idiot. He's the one who should feel ashamed."

Kinsley was quiet a moment, absorbing his words. The shift in her emotions. The pleasure she felt when he stood up for her. Like Drake never did.

"You're a good guy, you know?" she said. "A really good guy."

Elliot's smile shifted and grew melancholy. He leaned one elbow on the table. "Thanks for that. I've not heard anyone say that in a long time."

Kinsley thought of Dennis and the comments Faith had made about how anything Elliot did was never good enough. And she gave in to an impulse she knew she would later regret but couldn't stifle.

She leaned closer and gently brushed a kiss over his stubbled cheek.

His swift intake of breath and his tight clasp on her hand showed her that maybe she should have thought this through.

His eyes darkened, and when he didn't let go of her hand, when he moved closer, his face blurring, she knew she had done something that changed everything.

But as his lips claimed hers, as his hand snaked around her neck, holding her in place, she didn't care.

Not one bit. Not for now anyway.

Elliot drew back, reluctantly pulling his lips from her soft, warm ones, his heart racing like he had just gone ten seconds on a bucking bronc.

Why had he kissed her?

She started it.

He swallowed, lowering his hand but unable to look away from her. Kane's words reverberated through his mind.

Be careful.

And now, hearing her story, he understood exactly why.

And yet...

She was smiling at him. She wasn't angry with him. But then Kinsley lowered her gaze, her hand trembling as she placed it on her chest, which was moving up and down. Rapidly.

That small gesture gave him hope. It seemed the simple kiss had affected her as much as it had him.

So he took another chance and stroked her cheek with his forefinger.

Just then they heard voices, the door of the porch burst open, and Elliot quickly lowered his hand.

Tricia, Mason, and the kids were back.

"Ah, you made coffee," Tricia said, sniffing as she came into the kitchen, her hands full of crinkling bags. Then she stopped, glancing over at Kinsley. "Hey. You're back from the big city."

Kinsley nodded and, to his surprise, her cheeks flushed. He hoped Tricia didn't notice.

"That's perfect. I wanted to show you what we picked out for the kids to wear for the wedding." She set the bags on the table just as Mason entered, carrying a squealing child under each arm.

While Tricia opened the bags to show her, Kane and Zach entered the kitchen followed by Faith, who was talking on her cell phone.

And that was the end of the quiet.

Elliot wanted to chase everyone out. Send them all away. Relive the moment he and Kinsley had shared.

Kiss her again.

But the growing chaos whisked away the emotions of the moment.

Tricia and Faith got busy getting supper ready. Kinsley was approving the shirts he and Kane had bought and the clothes for the twins.

When Zach, Mason, and Kane retired to the living room with the kids to keep them busy while supper was being made, Elliot felt at a loss, not sure where he wanted to be. In the kitchen with the chattering women, unable to talk to Kinsley, or in the other room where the kids were already shrieking and laughing as Mason and Kane got them riled up.

For a moment, he felt like he belonged in neither place.

So he walked out the door and sat down in one of the chairs sitting under the pergola.

At least it was quiet here. The setting sun sent long shadows across the yard, bringing a faint chill.

A door opened behind him and, stifling a twist of annoyance, he turned to see who wanted what from him.

But it was Kinsley.

"Hey," was all she said, her voice breathy, bringing peace with her presence. "It's pretty noisy in there, and no one seems to need my help. I haven't even had a chance to tell Faith about the dress."

"I know how you feel," he said, pulling a chair for her around with his booted foot. "As for Faith, she'll remember once everything has settled down. In the meantime, have a seat. We can both sit out here and wait for the chaos to settle down."

To his surprise she wasn't wearing her high heels, but she was still walking unevenly, favoring her hip.

He wanted to jump up, help her to her chair, but knew she wouldn't appreciate it. So he stayed where he was, watching as she carefully lowered herself into the chair then lifted her bare feet onto another chair in front of her.

She just sat there, quiet, and he was happy to share the peace with her. A few stray leaves rustled across the patio, teased by the wind. But other than that only blessed quiet and peace.

They sat that way for at least five minutes in comfortable companionship.

"How is the wagon coming along?" she asked, finally breaking the silence.

"Almost done." He glanced back, still able to hear the clang of pans, the chatter of the children, and the murmur of conversation. He guessed it would be awhile before dinner was done. "Do you want to come and see?"

"I guess I could, though I don't have shoes on."

"I could piggyback you again."

She looked down at her narrow skirt then got up. "Wait here. I'll be right back."

"Just don't get roped into helping with supper," he said, reluctant to have her leave in case Faith decided she needed to talk about the wedding or anything else that might come to mind.

"I won't."

"If you're coming out again, meet me at the front door. That way you don't have to come back through the kitchen."

With another smile, she left. He got up, walking around the house before anyone came out to see where he was.

A few minutes later the front door opened and Kinsley stepped out.

She wore a simple shirt, blue jeans, and sensible shoes. Her hair hung loose from her usual tight ponytail, flowing over her shoulders.

"Much better," he said approvingly.

"I can be taught." She gave him a smile.

They walked in silence again, to the garage. Elliot pulled the large sliding door open, watching her to catch her reaction.

She stopped, staring, then a slow smile flowed over her soft lips. "Wow. Cinderella's pumpkin has nothing on this carriage. It looks amazing."

Her approval was a gift he took and held close.

"I built the benches myself. Cut a section out of the sides of the wagon so that Faith can get in and out easier."

"Did you make these as well?" Kinsley walked closer, bending over to touch the wrought-iron steps that now gleamed black from the lacquer paint he had layered on. It had taken four coats to get the shine.

"I've done some welding from time to time. Zach taught me."

He had sanded the wood of the sides and painted them also. The benches were shining in the low light, a satin finish to them.

"Do you want to try it out?" he asked.

"Now?"

"Why not?"

"I don't know... Tricia and Faith will expect us for supper, and I'm sure you won't get the horses rigged up that quickly." She straightened, running her hands along the edges he'd spent so much time sanding smooth. He guessed her hesitation had more to do with being behind a team of horses than the girls' expectations.

"You're right. After supper then?"

"I want to show Faith the dress, and I have a few emails to answer."

"Tomorrow?"

"Maybe..."

Elliot walked over to her side, took her hand, and squeezed it gently. "I know you're scared, but you won't be riding the horses. And I'll be careful."

"Will the horses know that?" she asked with a nervous laugh.

"You saw Seamus. He's completely bombproof. Sancho is even quieter."

Still she hesitated.

Elliot waited, willing her to say yes.

"Why do you keep doing this?" she asked. "Getting me to be around horses?"

Because he wanted to create one more connection between them?

Because he hoped to help her?

Because he thought he might have a chance to kiss her again?

All of the above?

"I'd like to help you get past this," he said. "I guess because I'm so used to horses, I can't imagine what it would be like to be afraid of them."

"I wasn't always," she said, her voice quiet.

"Well then, let's work on that," Elliot said. "We can start with your history and build on it."

She seemed to consider his remarks, then, to his surprise, nodded. "Okay. Let's go after supper so I won't have time to change my mind." She turned to him, and though she had agreed, he could still see the hesitation in her eyes.

"You can trust me," Elliot said.

"I hope so."

Elliot heard Tricia calling them, and he gave her a wry smile. "I guess supper got done quicker than we thought. We should go before they wonder where we are."

As they walked together to the house, Elliot was surprised at the anticipation he felt at taking her out in the wagon, going for a ride on the ranch, spending time together.

He just hoped no one else wanted to come.

CHAPTER 12

"So I finally got a call from the photographer," Faith said as she handed Kane the bowl of potatoes.

Kinsley looked up from the piece of chicken she was cutting, not encouraged by the dejected tone in Faith's voice.

"And what did he tell you?" she asked, even though she guessed exactly what Faith would say.

"He apologized profusely, but said he couldn't make it." Faith pressed her lips together as if holding back other emotions.

"Oh, honey, I'm so sorry." Kane stroked her back in commiseration. "Maybe we can just ask people to bring their cameras and take pictures. I'm sure we'll get some decent ones."

And right then Faith's gaze swiveled to Kinsley, a pleading look on her face.

"I won't be able to do a decent job," Kinsley protested, knowing precisely where Faith was going with those puppy dog eyes. "I'll be organizing people, making sure the twins come down the aisle properly…"

But even as she expressed her reasons, they sounded hollow to her.

"There's enough other people to watch the kids," Tricia said, not helping Kinsley one bit. "Besides, it doesn't matter if everything doesn't turn out perfect. What matters is that Kane and Faith get married. And that they have nice pictures."

That was easy for Tricia to say, Kinsley thought. She had nothing riding on this wedding. No future partner watching to make sure that everything happened on time and moved smoothly.

"You know how stuck I am," Faith pleaded. "You know how hard it will be to find someone else. Someone half decent."

Still Kinsley hesitated, though if she were honest with herself, a part of her wanted to try. She had seen enough photographers working other weddings. And there were many times afterward, when she looked over the photos, that she caught herself criticizing them. Thinking she would have done something differently.

"Please," Faith pleaded, her voice breaking just enough to erase the last of Kinsley's misgivings.

She hesitated just long enough to let Faith know she was doing this on sufferance.

"Okay," she said. "I'll do it. But you can't expect me to do the full range of pictures your photographer would do. I'll have things I'll need to coordinate for the wedding and will have limited time."

"I understand," Faith said, her voice light with relief. "I don't need a thousand pictures. Just a few really nice ones."

"It would actually work out better if Kinsley takes the pictures anyway," Elliot put in. "I could take her to scout out potential locations. And, even better, we can get some early morning pictures with you guys in the wagon because she's right here."

Kinsley shot him a warning glance, wondering what he was up to.

But the smile he gave her was full of innocence.

"That's a great idea," Faith said. "I had only thought of

coming in on the wagon. We could take some awesome pictures of all of us beforehand, which wouldn't have worked with the timeline before. Jeff said he couldn't come until an hour before the ceremony." She clapped her hands, as thrilled as a little kid. "This could all work out perfectly."

"I can take Kinsley out with the wagon after supper to scout out some potential locations," Elliot suggested.

"Oh, things are working out even better than I had hoped," Faith said, smiling at Kane.

"I'm glad for you," Kane said with an indulgent smile. "And I'm even gladder for me. Happy wife, happy life."

The rest of the meal went by far too quickly for Kinsley. Though she had already agreed to the ride with Elliot, now she felt an added pressure.

As soon as the meal was done, Zach, Elliot, Kane, and Mason left to harness the horses. Kinsley helped clear the table with Faith while Tricia cleaned up the kids and gave them a bath.

"I know you're hesitant about taking pictures, but you'll do a great job," Faith said as she scraped the leftover potatoes into a glass container and snapped a lid on.

"You know I'm no professional," Kinsley said.

"You keep saying that, but I think the only difference between you and Jeff is experience. And the fact that you've never been paid for your work. But, once I pay you, that will change." Faith shot her an encouraging smile as she closed the refrigerator.

Kinsley rinsed the dishes, struggling with a mixture of emotions. So many things had come at her the last few weeks, she wasn't sure how to sort them all out. In a few minutes she was going out with Elliot and, she was sure, he would try to kiss her again.

And she would let him.

And where is that going?

"Look, I know you're worried about this, and I don't know

how to reassure you other than to say I have faith in you. And not just 'cause my name is Faith," she said with a chuckle at her own joke.

"Thanks for the confidence. You know it's more than just the taking pictures. I need this wedding to go well."

Faith leaned against the counter beside the sink, her arms folded. "I know you do." She hesitated a moment, biting her lip, and Kinsley knew something else was on her friend's mind.

"But what?" Kinsley asked, helping her friend along.

"Is that really what you want to do? Organize weddings the rest of your life? I mean, you're fantastic at it, don't get me wrong. I wouldn't have asked you to do it if I didn't think you could do a fantastic job. But I remember a letter you sent me a while back. You didn't sound happy, and I don't think it was just because of Drake."

"I had a few things going on," Kinsley admitted, not sure she wanted to delve into that uncertain time of her life. Yes, she was dealing with Drake's lack of commitment. Yes, she had some issues with his mother, but Faith was right. There had been an underlying dissatisfaction with planning wedding after wedding and with all the drama that surrounded each event. The emotions. The handholding necessary to get this event to the conclusion. At times it was all too much.

She shook her head and suddenly realized she hadn't told Faith she had the dress.

You were occupied with other things.

"I can't believe I didn't say anything sooner," Kinsley said. "But I brought the dress back from the city."

Faith pushed herself away from the counter. "I want to go see it. Right now."

Kinsley was only too happy to put off thinking about the wagon ride coming up, so she rinsed and dried her hands and led Faith up to her bedroom.

She pulled the garment bag out and laid it on the bed. "Do you want to open it?"

"No. You do it," Faith said, standing at the foot of the bed. Though Kinsley knew Faith had seen pictures of the dress, she still had some misgivings. If Faith didn't like it, they were back to square one. Negative square one, she thought.

She unzipped it, surprised to catch the lingering scent of the perfume she used to wear. The perfume Drake liked so much. She had flushed it all down the toilet after she broke up with him. Seemed fitting.

But she was even more surprised that the scent didn't create even the smallest tinge of sadness. Instead, all she felt was relief that the stress of waiting and wondering had been cut out of her life when she ended her relationship with Drake. As she pulled the dress out Faith's gasp told her everything she needed to know, and the look of amazed awe underscored it all.

"Ohh…" was all she could say as she came near Kinsley. She carefully lifted the gauzy skirt of the dress, holding it out. The sun streaming in through the window beside her caught the delicate sparkles scattered through the filmy material. Just enough to create whimsy, but not too much to make it look overdone.

"It is so beautiful," Faith breathed, touching the ruching on the shoulders, the beaded waistband. "Exquisite. But then, I should have known you would have picked out a stunning dress."

"You should try it on," Kinsley said.

Faith needed no more encouragement. Without a lick of self-consciousness she unbuttoned her shirt and stripped off her blue jeans.

Kinsley couldn't help a flicker of envy at Faith's perfect body, her long slim legs, her unmarked skin.

She handed her friend the dress, helping her zip it up at the back. Faith turned, smoothing her hands down the skirt, her face suffused with wonder, looking like every bride Kinsley had worked with who had just found the perfect dress.

"It fits like it was made for me," Faith said. Then her lips trembled, and she covered her face with her hands, a tiny sob slipping out.

"What's the matter, sweetie?" Kinsley slipped her arm across Faith's shoulders, giving her a gentle one-armed hug.

"It's so beautiful," she sniffed. "When I saw that dress that Nelly made I was so worried. I thought the whole wedding was going to flop. And now..." She swallowed and drew in a quavering breath, giving Kinsley a tremulous smile. "And now I've got such a beautiful dress, and it's all because of you."

Her gratitude created a weightless thanks. And, to Kinsley's surprise and pleasure, not the tiniest bit of regret.

"I'm so glad you like it. It is a beautiful dress. I fell in love with it the first time I saw it."

Then Faith's eyes grew wide as she pressed her fingers to her lips. "I'm so sorry. You had dreams for this dress and now—"

"Stop right there," Kinsley said, twitching the shoulder into place, fussing with the skirt, fluffing it out. "I'm glad you can use it, and I'm even happier that you love it so much."

"Are you sure—"

"I wouldn't have offered it if I wasn't." Kinsley gave Faith a broad smile. "Frankly, it's a relief to have it out of the house and put to use. I kept thinking I should get rid of it but knew it wouldn't be appreciated because it was so-called secondhand."

She had dealt with more than one bride who turned up her nose at the idea of a pre-owned dress. Granted, if they could afford a wedding planner, they could afford to buy the dress they wanted and not settle. But still...

"It's like a fairy tale." Faith sighed, lifting the filmy skirt and turning to look in the dresser mirror again. "It's so much lovelier than the one I thought was my dream dress. I can't thank you enough."

"Then don't start," Kinsley said.

Faith was about to say something more when a voice from below called Kinsley's name.

"You better go," Faith said, shooing her along. "Before the guys get into trouble with Tricia. I'm sure she's trying to get the kids in bed."

"And we don't want Kane to see the dress before I take the pictures," Kinsley agreed.

She gave Faith a final smile, stepping back to take another look at her old wedding dress on her dear friend.

Then, with a feeling of unexpected lightness and relief, she grabbed her camera bag, closed the door behind her, and made her way down the stairs.

⌒⟨⟩⌒

"You sure you don't want me to come along?" Mason asked, holding Sancho's harness, stroking his nose.

Elliot gave him a warning look but only received a grin in answer.

"I don't know if you should trust this guy," Kane said as Kinsley approached the wagon, her camera bag slung over her shoulder.

"Not helping, brother," Elliot said, frowning at him.

What was with these guys? It was as if they knew exactly what was happening between him and Kinsley. It was, Elliot had to admit, kind of transparent. The photo tour was simply an excuse to get her away from the ranch. Everyone seemed to know it.

Sancho shook his head, making the harness jangle.

Seamus pawed the ground, anxious to get going.

"Ready?" Elliot asked, giving her a reassuring smile.

"I hope so," Kinsley said, but Elliot could see the concern etched on her face.

"I'll help you up into the wagon, and we'll just take a few rounds through the yard before we head out."

"Don't worry, you'll be fine," Kane assured Kinsley, taking her camera bag from her.

Elliot was sure she would've preferred not to have an audience as she got aboard, but right now he needed Mason and Kane to help with the horses, so they had to stick around.

He climbed up behind her, helping her settle in on the front seat. She looked flushed, and her eyes were bright. He wasn't sure if it was fear or anticipation or maybe a combination of both.

"You'll be fine," he said, giving her hand a gentle squeeze.

Kane handed up her camera bag and Elliot tucked it behind the buckboard of the wagon. He unhooked the reins from the handbrake and threaded them through his fingers.

"Okay, wagons ho," Elliot said. He clucked to the horses, released the brake, and with the creak and sway of the wagon, they were moving. As promised, he drove the horses around the yard, feeling more confident with each turn they made, each quick response the horses gave him. Kinsley initially sat still as a statue beside him, clinging to the side rail of the seat. But with each uneventful roll of the wagon wheels, she seemed to relax.

"Drive safe," Kane called out as Elliot turned the horses away from the ranch yard, heading down an old wagon trail to the hills beyond.

Elliot would have much preferred to do this trail on horseback, where he had more control, but the old road was even, and they moved along at a nice steady pace.

It was early evening yet, and the sun was still high in the west.

"You should have good light for taking pictures," he remarked.

He glanced sidelong at Kinsley, who now had her hands on her lap as she looked around.

"You doing okay?" he asked as the horses plodded along.

"I think I'm enjoying myself," she said with a saucy little grin.

"Well, that makes my job easier," Elliot returned.

"Where are we headed?"

"We'll be going up a gentle hill, to a lookout point where I'm sure Faith will want to have pictures taken. After that we'll stay along the edge of the hill, work our way down, toward an old wooden bridge over a creek that would also be a great place for pictures."

Kinsley picked up her camera bag, unzipped it, and pulled out her camera and another lens, which she quickly swapped out. She snapped a few pictures then checked the back of the camera, made a few adjustments, and took a few more.

"What are you checking for?"

"Adjusting for the light. Setting the shutter speed, aperture, that kind of stuff."

"Ah yes, the old aperture-setting trick," he said.

"You don't fool me, you don't have a clue what I'm talking about."

"Hey, I just use my phone for pictures. Works for me."

"I took a course that said the best camera is the one you always have with you. Phones can take awesome pictures these days."

"But not as good as that beast you have there," he said, nodding at her camera.

"Not such a beast, though I would love to try a mirrorless camera. They're smaller, but I'm just not sold on them yet."

"I'd ask you what the difference is, but judging from the size of that camera bag, the extra camera, and all the gear you have stashed in there, I'm thinking you'd yak my ear off."

"No, I wouldn't. I'm not that knowledgeable."

"Well you must know a few things, otherwise Faith wouldn't have been campaigning so hard for you to take the pictures. She always said that was her first priority. Pictures."

"Over getting married?"

"Well, that's a given."

He flipped the reins, urging the horses on. They had noticed his distraction and slowed their pace. "Gee," he called out, tugging on the reins to get them turning. "You feeling okay?" he asked, glancing at her.

"I am," she said, flashing him a grin. "I'm glad you thought of this. A much gentler introduction to being with horses than riding."

She steadied herself against the gentle rocking of the wagon. Her camera whirred a few times, and she looked at the display. Then took a few more.

"What made you get into photography?" he asked.

"I dabbled in it during high school."

"Let me guess, yearbook and school paper?"

"You are so perceptive and yes, I'm a walking cliché. Actually, a limping one. I had my challenges trying to take pictures of the sports teams."

"Please don't do that," he said, frowning at her.

She returned his look, puzzled. "Doing what?"

"Put yourself down like that."

The only sound in the ensuing quiet was the muffled plod of the horses, the jangle of the harness, and the creak of the wagon. Had he pushed too far? Said too much?

Kinsley snapped a few more pictures as they headed up the incline to the grove of trees ahead, then lowered her camera to her lap. "It's an old habit."

"From school?"

"From life." She gave him a melancholy smile. "I guess it was...is a way of beating people to the comments. Making a joke before they can. That way I feel like I'm in charge."

Elliot said nothing to that, weighing her comments, giving them the space they deserved.

"I get that," he replied after a moment. "But you shouldn't

assume that everyone will say something negative, or even think it."

"Maybe not, but I've heard enough in my life."

"Right now I think there's nothing I'd like more than to punch your old fiancé in the nose," he said, assuming that was who she was talking about. "Actually, I'd like to do it twice."

"Elliot, that's not a good idea," she said, but he could hear the underlying chuckle in her voice.

He pursed his lips. "You're right. Three is the magic number."

Kinsley laughed at that. "Then I hope you never meet him. Drake is fond of his nose."

"I hope so too. Because he might not be as fond once I'm done."

"I don't think you would really do that," she said, leaning to one side and, to his dismay taking a picture of him. "You're too kind for that behavior."

"Oh, you don't know my dark side." He shot her a teasing glance. "I am my father's son, after all."

She lowered her camera, her expression serious as she studied him a moment. "Zach isn't like that," she said, seeming to deliberately misunderstand him.

"No. He's not. But Dennis is. Like I said, mean left hook."

"Not everything is determined by our DNA," she said, turning away from him to snap a few more pictures. "We can make choices. God has given us that ability and power."

Elliot held that thought a moment, saying nothing.

"And, whether you believe it or not," she continued. "I think God placed you in the Tye family to show you other choices. Other ways of living."

"Well, Zach and Grace were the best examples I've ever had of faith in action," Elliot agreed. "And you're right. They showed me another way of living. Another way of thinking. I'll be forever grateful for that."

"So I believe that you can choose to put aside the behavior

Dennis has meted out to you and choose the way Zach raised you. Choose what Zach has told you, not what your biological father has."

Elliot held her words close, treasuring them. But, a small part of him, the part that had been repeatedly lambasted by Dennis, struggled.

You'll never be good enough. They're just taking care of you for the money.

"While we're on the topic of fathers, I'm intrigued why Kane calls Zach Dad, but you always call Zach by his first name."

Kinsley kept taking pictures as if his reply didn't matter to her one way or the other.

But it dug into his soul, turning over the insecurities he had buried deep.

"Just habit, I guess," he said, though that wasn't an entirely correct answer. If he were to examine his motives more closely, he would have to acknowledge that it was more than a habit.

"I was just curious." She gave him a careful smile. "I'm not trying to say anything by it."

"I know. It's just..." He hesitated. "I think I never felt like I had the right."

"To call Zach Dad?"

"Yeah. I was jimmied back and forth so much, it was easier to call them by their first names. Plus, Dennis would have a fit if I'd called Zach Dad." As soon as those last words slipped out, he regretted them. What was it about this woman that made him say so much? Next thing he knew he would be spewing his passwords.

"From what you told me, he seems possessive."

"Yeah, he was. He was even jealous of my girlfriends."

"Is that why you're not married?"

"You're getting personal now," he said, nudging her as if joking.

"Like I said, you know my sad history. Let's keep things even."

"I'm not married, because I've never had the big romance," he said, thankful for the shift from his father to his love life. Much easier topic. "Not even Carmen or Denise, regardless of what Faith and Tricia will tell you. I've been too busy focused on Rodeo."

"I don't want to denigrate your choices, but sounds like you've given up a lot for that dream."

"I have…" He let the sentence trail off, his mind slipping back over the past few years.

"You look grumpy," Kinsley said. "I hope the horses are behaving."

"They are." He pulled in a deep breath, a sudden loneliness coursing through him. The same loneliness he tamped down each time he was on the road. Each time he came back to his motel room—or tent if the weather was nice—and realized how alone he was. Sure, he had friends and rodeo buddies, but a lot of them had either a girlfriend tagging along or a wife.

Was it that same loneliness that drew him to Kinsley?

He shot her another sidelong glance in time to catch her looking at him. Once again that attraction sparked between them. Once again he wanted to touch her. Kiss her.

He got to their first destination and pulled the horses to a halt, tied up the reins, and turned to her, letting his feelings roam.

She smiled back at him, taking his hand in hers as she set her camera down.

The touch of her hand, the way her eyes held his, the emotions that sparked between them, overcame his thoughts.

He gave into impulse and drew her close.

She responded almost immediately, tangling her hands in his hair as their lips met. Moving, seeking, soft and warm.

It felt right and, after a while, as he drew back, looking into her eyes, he felt a sense of coming home. Here, on the ranch, up in the hills he rode as a young boy, making good memories with the Tye family. Now making others...

Just memories?

"And now what?" she asked, her hand trailing down his cheek, resting on his neck. Warm, soft, tender.

"What do you mean, now what?"

"I'm not sure what to do with this. Where are we going?"

He thought of her wedding dress. Of the broken promises in her past. Thought of his own plans and the question mark that would follow once he got to where he was going.

"I'm not sure either," he said quietly. "But we could give it a chance. See where it goes."

"And you're heading out again this weekend?"

"Yeah. And right after the wedding again."

"So, once you win the Canadian Finals, you're looking to Vegas? The National Finals?"

"I'd like to win it, for sure."

"Did your dad—Dennis—make it to the NFR?"

He frowned at her. "Why did you have to bring Dennis into this?"

She was quiet a moment and then, to his dismay, drew back at the muted anger in his voice.

"I'm sorry," he said, catching her hands, squeezing them lightly. "I don't want to talk about Dennis."

"But he's so entwined in your life right now."

"He's not. He's not a part of my life."

"He's the reason you're chasing the rodeo, isn't it?"

He pulled in a breath. He didn't like the way this conversation was going. He had brought her up here to show her potential settings for pictures, to explore the relationship he knew was building between them. To look ahead, not back. Looking back never did him any good. "What if I want to prove to myself that I'm better than him?"

"Is that a good reason? You've had better examples of how to live your life. Don't you think you might be making wrong choices for the wrong reasons?"

He blew out a sigh, dragging his hand over his face, wishing she would stop. Yet, some perverse part of him knew she was right. But if she was, then what was the point of what he was doing?

"Look, right now, this is all I've got. Rodeo. It's who I am. I'm not a part of this ranch, so rodeo is all I've got." He tossed the words out, then jumped off the wagon. He strode away but then caught himself. He couldn't leave her there up on the wagon with the horses.

So he turned around to help her, but she was already making her way down the steps.

"I didn't want to be on the wagon, in case the horses took off," she said, her voice matter-of-fact.

"I'm so sorry," he said, walking toward her to help her take that last, larger step. "I shouldn't have done that."

"No, you shouldn't have," she said, giving him a wry smile. "And I'm sorry for prying. I'd like to say it's none of my business, but part of me wants it to be."

"I'm glad you care." He paused, sucking in a deep breath. "I don't like talking about Dennis—my father—with you. I feel like...like it's a stain on something that, I think, is special."

Her mouth tipped upward in a half-smile. "I think this is special too."

He slipped his arm around her waist, turning her to the opening in the trees. "I stopped here not only to kiss you, but to show you this." He waved his hand at the valley below them and the mountains across, standing sentinel, their granite peaks dusted with snow. "Faith was hoping to take pictures here with that as the backdrop."

"I should have my camera," she said.

"Just look at it for now," he said. "Just enjoy it."

She leaned against him, wrapping her arms around his waist, the two of them now blended together.

He drew in a breath as he laid his head on hers once again. It was as if the world was turning in slow circles with them at the center.

They stayed that way a moment, then, a few moments later, she drew away.

"Sorry. I want to catch this before the light shifts."

He ran back and got her cameras and handed them to her. "I didn't know which one you wanted."

"Both of them. Thanks so much."

He stood back, smiling at her infectious enthusiasm. And as he watched her snap photo after photo, as he saw the passion on her face, he wondered, again, why she hadn't made this her career choice.

"We've got another place to look at," he said. "Climb aboard."

She took a few more photos then reluctantly backed away.

"The next place is just as nice," he promised her.

"I'll have to trust you."

"I think you should anyhow."

She gave him a curious look as he helped her aboard. "You know what? I do."

He felt as if she had given him the best gift ever.

CHAPTER 13

"This is perfect," Kinsley said, taking a few more pictures of the bridge.

"Why are you taking so many?" Elliot asked, still sitting in the wagon, keeping the horses in line.

"I want to see exactly how the light will fall this time of the day. Make sure I'll get the right angle."

"Only if it doesn't rain."

"Don't even say that word." Kinsley shot him a warning glance. "I've been praying steady for good weather."

"That's good. I'll add mine, for what they're worth."

"What do you mean?" The cynical tone in his voice caught her attention.

"I haven't spent as much time with God as I should," he returned, lifting one booted foot to rest on the buckboard. With his hat tipped back on his head, his faded jeans, worn boots, and plaid shirt, he was the epitome of a cowboy. And every kiss he gave her, every crooked smile, lifted her heart. "I can't imagine my prayers will have any influence, but I'll add them too."

"You don't think God is waiting for you? He never leaves, you know. We're the one who moved if God feels distant." As soon as she spoke the words she wished she hadn't. It was as if this entire time together she'd been prying. Digging.

Protecting yourself?

Maybe. Her past relationship had taught her hard lessons on the importance of looking out for herself. Of not jumping into any relationship, or drifting into any relationship, without knowing what she was in for.

He slanted her another signature grin. "For someone who has had her own share of junk to deal with, you're surprisingly optimistic about God."

"His love surrounds me and has held me up through that junk." She shrugged, wishing she could find the right words to encapsulate a relationship that permeated her being. That was as much a part of her as her hair and eye color. "Haven't you felt it as well? How could you not, living here?"

He twisted his mouth to one side as if considering her question. "I did when I was with my mom, Grace. She would tell me she was praying for me. I think it was her prayers that eventually brought me back to the Tye ranch for good."

"Given what you told me about Dennis, I would say that was an answer to prayer."

Elliot smiled. "You're probably right. But I hate to cut things short." He glanced at his watch. "We should get back before Kane starts fussing and sending out the scouting crew."

"He is very much the big brother, isn't he?" Kinsley asked, walking back to the wagon but giving the horses a wide enough berth. She felt a little better around them, but they still gave her the willies.

"He is that, but in a good way."

"Sounds like you've found some measure of peace, the two of you."

"Yeah. And thanks to your advice, we cleared a lot of things up." He bounded down from the wagon and helped her up and into the seat. "Good to go?" he asked as she slipped her cameras back in her bag and zipped it closed. She pushed it against the buckboard and sat back.

"I am."

"Great." He held out the reins to her. "You're in charge."

She shot him a panicked glance, holding her hands up. "No. No way."

"C'mon, you know how quiet the horses are. It's been a real snooze driving them. What could go wrong?"

"That question rates right up there alongside 'hold my beer, watch this' when it comes to potential catastrophes."

"You don't need to see a catastrophe with every horse."

"Says the banged up saddle bronc rider."

"That's different."

"They're not. They're still horses."

But Elliot still held the reins out to her. "Don't you want to see what it's like to control a horse? To be in charge not only of one, but two horses?"

She swallowed, biting her lip as she considered his offer.

"The best way to deal with a fear is to face it head on," he said. "You're not the only one who can do psychoanalysis."

"Touché, Dr. Elliot." She rubbed her hands over her jeans, but as she did, a picture of Denise popped into her mind. In charge, confident. Just the kind of woman who was a better match for Elliot than she was.

So she held her hands out to take the reins, adding, "You're keeping one foot on the brake, right?"

"I'll be right here. If necessary, I can leap onto the backs of the horses and control them that way."

"You've done that before?" she asked, aghast at the idea.

"Nope. But I've watched enough old Westerns to know how it's done."

She chuckled at his laissez-faire attitude.

"So here's how you thread the reins through," he said, his

hands covering hers. "You've only got the two horses, so it's much easier."

Kinsley followed his lead, focusing on the leather reins, trying not to get distracted by his head close to hers, his hands touching hers.

"Okay, give a little slap on their backs and say 'Giddy up.' Cliché, I know. When you want them to turn, you say 'Gee' for right and 'Haw' for left. And give a tug on the appropriate horse. Easy."

"Sure." Kinsley took another steadying breath, battling an unwelcome flutter of nerves. But when Elliot slipped his arm around her shoulders, she felt her nerves settle.

She slapped the reins just as Elliot told her, called out "Giddy up," and with a sudden jerk, the horses leaned into the harness and started walking.

"We need to make a left turn up ahead," Elliot said, pointing to where they would rejoin the trail.

Another breath and a nod of recognition, and Kinsley hunched her shoulders, pressed her feet against the buckboard.

"You'll need to relax a bit," Elliot said. "Your tension flows down the reins to the horse. Like electricity."

"Really?"

"Sort of. Just relax and trust me. I wouldn't let you do this if I didn't think you could handle these horses."

She nodded and lowered her shoulders, hoping that would help.

Seamus and Sancho lumbered along and when she tugged on the one and called out "Gee," just as Elliot predicted, the one horse, she couldn't remember which one, obediently turned, taking his partner with him. The wagon creaked and the horses plodded, and with each calm step she felt herself relax.

"See, you're a natural. Now, make the horses stop."

"Why? We're moving along so nicely." She was more than content to sit and let the horses have their head.

"Because I want you to see that you have control."

She tugged on the reins. Nothing happened.

"A little harder, honey. They don't have bits in their mouths, so aren't as sensitive to pressure. They'll feel it through the collars on their neck."

So she pulled a little harder and, to her surprise, the horses stopped. They stomped their feet and shook their heads, as if wondering what was going on, but they didn't move one inch forward.

"Now, get them going again," Elliot said.

Another slap of the reins, another "Giddy up" and they did exactly what she wanted.

"Told you, you can do this." Elliot leaned back and tipped his hat over his eyes, as if he was about to have a nap.

"What are you doing?" she asked, elbowing him in the side.

"Resting. It's been a busy few days." He lifted his hat and looked at her, grinning. "And just messing with you."

"I've got two 1200-pound animals pulling a wagon that I'm sitting on," she said through gritted teeth, trying to keep her voice low so as not to frighten the horses. "This is not the time to be 'messing' with me."

"Sorry. I couldn't resist. I love how you jump to the bait, though."

"Okay, you've had your fun." She took another breath as they broke through a copse of trees and onto the pasture. They had another hill to climb and then, if she were correct, the ranch would be in sight. The horses, sensing they were getting close to home, picked up the pace.

"Hold them back," Elliot said, sitting up. "Remember, you're in charge."

So she pulled on the reins again and, sure enough, the horses slowed.

"Turn them right, just 'cause you can," he instructed.

"Why? The ranch is just over that hill ahead."

"Just try."

So she did. Then she turned them left. Then in a circle. She thought for sure she would have to fight the horses but, true to Elliot's word, they obeyed.

"So, doesn't that feel good?" he asked as she made them turn once more.

She shot him a grin, surprised at how much fun she was having. "It does feel good," she admitted.

"Horses want to please. They just need to know what you want them to do. I'll pass on a good piece of advice I got from my dad."

"Which one?" Kinsley couldn't help asking.

"Zach. He told me that a dog is looking for friendship, but a horse is looking for leadership. So you have to provide that leadership. They are more comfortable if they know exactly what you're asking from them."

"Good to know."

"And one of these days, I'll see you on the back of a horse again, providing that leadership."

She wanted to refute his words, but instead she latched onto the idea that there would be a future time. Together.

What would that look like?

She didn't want to delve too deeply into that. Not yet.

For now, she was riding beside this amazing man, driving a team of horses.

In charge and in control.

"Stop here," he said. "At the top of the hill."

"Why?"

"Because you look so adorable right now. I want to kiss you again."

She couldn't resist that invitation, so she pulled the horses to a stop. Elliot put the brake on, tied the reins around it, pulled her close, and kissed her again. She slipped into his arms, responding to him in a way she never had with Drake. Then, with a satisfied smile, she leaned against him, absorbing the warmth of his body, the strength of his arms, content, for now, to put off going back to the ranch. To just sit here on this hilltop and enjoy the amazing view spread out below them and the man she shared it with.

⌣◯⌐

"This is so beautiful," Kinsley breathed, resting against him. "I can't imagine why anyone would want to leave this."

He didn't know if she had said what she did on purpose, but it created a tumble of unwelcome thoughts.

Why was he leaving all the time? Why was he always running as she said?

Do you have to keep doing this?

He didn't like the questions she created in him. He resented the uncertainty she brought into his life, and yet, he knew she was only unearthing the indecision that had been dogging him the past few years.

He didn't respond to her comment. Instead he turned her toward him, drew her close, and kissed her again. And again. Easier to do that than face the questions she brought up in him.

But she drew back, her eyes troubled.

"What's wrong?" he asked.

"We keep kissing each other. I know what it means to me. I guess I'd like to know what it means to you."

He knew he had to answer quickly, but at the same time didn't want to throw out some pat response. She deserved more than that.

Trouble was, he wasn't sure. Just as he was about to say that he wanted to see how things would go, his phone rang.

He wanted to ignore it, talk about where this was going, if it was going anywhere.

But he was waiting to hear back from a rodeo buddy about a ride this weekend.

With his eyes on Kinsley, he pulled his phone out of his pocket and swiped to answer it, not registering who was calling.

"Hey, Son."

The growly voice in his ear was like a hand tightening around his gut.

"Hey, Dennis," he said, hoping he sounded more casual than he felt.

Hang up. End this conversation.

But years of habit kept him on the line. Years of hoping maybe this time things would be different.

He turned away from Kinsley as if he didn't want her to witness this.

"Hey my boy, how you doing?" Dennis's words were slurred, and Elliot guessed he'd been drinking. Or was still drinking. His father never knew when to stop.

"What do you want?" Elliot asked, his voice clipped.

"Well, of course I phoned to congratulate you on your last rodeo win," his dad said, laughing. "Isn't that what a father's supposed to do?"

What a father was supposed to do was feed his son, take care of him, and encourage him. Not beat him or neglect him or berate him.

"Well thanks for that," Elliot said.

"Yeah, I wouldn't get too cocky." This was interrupted by a fit of coughing. "You'll never beat my ranking. And I know you'll never win. The only Meacher name on that CFR trophy will be mine."

In the background Elliot heard the clink of glasses and the strains of country music. Big surprise. His dad was sitting in a bar.

"You're right. The Meacher name won't be there when I win. I'm competing under my current last name. Tye."

Heavy silence followed this comment. Elliot knew the reminder would get under his father's skin. Dennis always grumbled that Elliot never competed under his proper name. The Meacher name.

"What have they ever done for you? You're *my* son. I took care of you when you were a kid and your useless mother took off. 'Course, I don't know why I bothered with a mouthy, arrogant kid like you. Faithless kid like you. You may think you're some great saddle bronc rider, but you'll never be what I was. Never." His voice grew louder and angrier with each word, and when he was done, he coughed again.

Kinsley wasn't looking at him, but Elliot could tell from the set of her mouth that she heard every one of his father's jeers.

"I'm saying goodbye now," Elliot said.

"Well then do it, do it and hang up," his dad taunted him. "But I know you can't. I know you miss me, and I know you need me. I taught you everything you know about saddle bronc riding. I made you who you are."

Elliot clenched his jaw, closing his eyes as his father's words resonated through his mind. "Yeah, you did, Dad, you made me exactly what I am."

And then he finally did hang up on his father.

He shoved the phone back in his pocket, sucking in a few deep breaths to still his pounding heart. How could his father do this to him every single time? He thought he had gotten past all this. Gotten past the anger that his father created, gotten past the insecurity Dennis created every time he spoke to him.

One more breath, then he turned to face Kinsley. She was looking at him, her head angled to one side, a delicate frown puckering her forehead.

"I'm guessing that was Dennis?"

He gave her a curt nod then was surprised to see her face harden.

"Why is he calling you?"

"The usual. To remind me I'll never be him."

"Why did you talk to him?"

Her question hung between them.

"Because I'm a sucker for punishment." As usual he was angry with himself for letting his father get to him.

"I have to confess I heard some of what he was saying. How you'll never get your name on the trophy." She paused there, frowning as she looked down at her hands. "Is that the reason you compete? To prove him wrong?"

Her answer triggered an immediate defense mechanism. "Of course not. I don't care what he thinks."

"Maybe not, but you let him talk you down. You didn't hang up on him."

"I did eventually," Elliot said.

"Eventually," Kinsley repeated.

A confusing mixture of emotions rose up in him. Annoyance, anger, frustration, all vying for attention.

"How many years have you been chasing this?" she asked.

"Probably about six. But I made it this year."

"So what happens when you win the CFR?"

"Then hopefully I go to the NFR."

"And after that?"

Elliot rubbed the back of his neck, frustrated at her line of questioning. "Why do you care?"

Thankfully this seemed to stop the third degree. She shifted away from him, looking to the mountains, pulling in a long, slow breath.

"This is an amazing place," she said. "I can understand exactly why Faith wants to have her wedding here. There's a rich heritage here. Don't you want to be a part of it?"

A weight attached itself to his heart, pulling him down. His mind ticked back over all the things he had done, the opportunities he had missed.

"It's not that easy," he said. "I've made mistakes."

"And you have a biological father you're trying to please and a foster father who cares."

Elliot held her steady gaze, not sure what to say. He struggled for an explanation, then to his dismay found he had none.

"Did you ever stop to think you might be trying to appease the wrong father?" she pressed.

As he held her gaze he realized what she was trying to say.

"You have an earthly father and a heavenly Father who only want what's best for you. Why don't you think of them more?"

"I do, but my reality is that Dennis is a part of my biological heritage. And I've worried enough years I might be like him." The admission burst out of him, the words echoing in the silence.

Kinsley was quiet a moment, as if taking that in, nodding her head.

"I'm not talking about this anymore," he ground out, her questions beating at the protective layers surrounding his heart.

He turned away from her, unwrapped the reins, took off the brake, and headed back to the ranch.

He knew he might be letting the horses go a little faster than they should. If he had his way they would be trotting, but despite his frustration with Kinsley, he couldn't do that to her.

They came into the yard and, as if she sensed the drastic change in his mood, she grabbed her camera bag and fumbled her way off the wagon as soon as he came to a halt, not waiting for him to help her.

He watched her go, knowing he should apologize.

But he didn't know what to say. So better to say nothing. Leave things as they were. Probably for the best.

He unhitched the wagon from the team, reminding himself to move slowly. Be deliberate and not let the horses sense his anger.

By the time he got the horses squared away he had settled

down somewhat, but he wasn't ready to go back to Kinsley and her questions.

His phone rang again but this time he looked at who was calling.

Trent Siler.

"Hey, buddy, I heard you need a ride to the rodeo in Williams Lake," Trent said. "I've got time off and thought we could make a road trip. Go a day early. I could be there in half an hour."

He knew he should talk to Kinsley. Apologize to her.

But his conversation with Dennis was still echoing in his mind. Her probing questions brought up things he preferred to keep buried.

"Yeah. Sounds good to me. I need to get out of here."

CHAPTER 14

"This is so exciting," Faith exclaimed, clapping her hands like a child as she watched the crew set up the tables inside the tent. "This makes it way more real."

Her excitement was infectious, and Kinsley had to smile. She'd had little to smile about the last few days. Last week Wednesday, after she and Elliot had finished their wagon ride, he'd brought her back to the ranch, packed up his bags, said a quick goodbye, and left.

She wondered if it was because of their conversation up on the hill. She knew she had pushed too hard, but she couldn't seem to let it go. She felt as if she had an investment in his life.

But it was now a week later, and all she had heard from him was a few random texts, telling her to save a dance for him at the wedding. As if nothing had happened between them.

The last week had created an unwelcome and unasked for restlessness that had wound around her heart. She knew much of it had to do with her changing feelings for Elliot combined with the fact they were both on different trajectories.

"Well, I hope it's real," Kinsley said. "Tomorrow you're getting married." She lifted the camera that hung around her neck all day and snapped a one-handed picture of Faith, standing in front of the tent, looking bemused.

"It still seems so surreal," Faith said. "I've been making plans for months now, and it's finally coming together."

And it was coming together well. The wedding party all had their clothes, the bouquets and the centerpieces for the table were being delivered tomorrow. Mason and Kane were getting the flowerpots to set out. The arch was finished and in place, and it looked stunning.

The chairs were out, ready for the ceremony.

Everything was on track, on budget, and on target. Kinsley knew she should be happy, yet that same restlessness she had been grappling with since Elliot left hadn't settled down. A new uncertainty had entered her life since that moment up on the hill.

And if she were honest with herself, it wasn't just Elliot. It was how much she enjoyed taking the wedding pictures. How much she enjoyed editing them on her laptop, when she was supposed to be putting the finishing touches on her friend's wedding.

"Where do you want us to put these?" Mason's voice behind her gave her a start, and she turned to give him directions about the plants.

Just in time to see Elliot sauntering across the yard toward her, hands in his pockets, cowboy hat pushed back on his head, smiling at her as if all was well in his world. Looking as if he hadn't kissed her, bared his soul to her, and then took off without a word.

She should be angry, but as he came closer she saw a bruise on his cheekbone, and he seemed to favor one arm.

He'd gotten hurt despite his promise to Faith and Kane.

She fought down a bite of anger, lifted her chin, and turned away from both of the men. "We're arranging about nine of them at the front of the tent," she was saying, choosing to ignore him. "There's a fountain right inside the door, by the gift table. I'd like a few set up there as well. Seven will go by the arch, and the rest at the back of the grouping of chairs."

"Well that's great, but which ones do you want where?" Mason asked.

"I put flags inside each pot to let you know where they're supposed to go. And I also have a few risers that are marked where they're supposed to go and which pot will go on them." She had spent most of yesterday and last night doing the pre-organizing, so that when the time came she wouldn't have to make any last-minute decisions. Or change her mind.

"Aren't you glad we went with potted plants?" Elliot asked as he came nearer.

Kinsley clenched her fists as she tried to reach for composure. He had walked away as if the passionate kisses they shared up on the hill had meant nothing. As if their conversation about his father hadn't even happened.

"I'm just glad you showed up and in one piece, sort of," she said without looking at him, keeping her tone cool.

Collected.

She watched as Kane and Mason unloaded the flowerpots. Her cell phone rang, and she pulled it out of the pocket of her pants, glancing at the screen.

"Hello, Jill," Kinsley said, walking away from everybody to find a quiet spot, ignoring Elliot yet fully aware of him.

"How are things going?" Jill asked.

She forced herself not to look back to catch Elliot's response to her ignoring him. "The tent is here, the flowers are getting put up. The arch is up, and the chairs for the ceremony are ready. The weather forecast looks fantastic, so I think everything is good to go."

"That's excellent. Of course, I wouldn't expect anything different. You're a very organized person."

"Thank you for that," Kinsley said, her future partner's

compliment feeling like a small gift.

"Just thought I would check in and see what time would be best for me to arrive."

Kinsley sucked in a quick breath, trying to still the sudden pounding of her heart. She had always known Jill was coming, but hearing her voice say it made it a reality. "The wedding starts at five o'clock," was all she said.

Though she would be taking pictures of the ceremony, Kinsley didn't want Jill around any earlier than necessary. In her initial interview with Jill the woman had focused on one thing ad nauseam.

As a wedding planner, all your attention had to be on the day. On how things were going. You had to be one step ahead of everything. Your finger on the pulse, your eye on the end game.

Mixed metaphors aside, she knew Jill wouldn't be impressed with Kinsley taking pictures as well.

"I'm looking forward to seeing how my future partner works under pressure," Jill said with a chuckle.

Kinsley pressed a hand to her stomach, stilling the frantic butterflies within. Her camera now felt like an anchor around her neck.

It will be fine. Everything will be fine.

"Can you remind me of the schedule again?" Jill asked.

"The service starts at five o'clock, and the dinner and reception are following right after that."

"Excellent. I'm assuming pictures are taken before that?"

"Absolutely."

"Glad to hear it. So many brides romanticize the whole walk down the aisle, but pictures are best taken before the ceremony when makeup and flowers are fresh. I imagine the photographer is doing a First-Look between the bride and groom at least?"

"Yes, I am," Kinsley said. Too late she realized how that sounded. But she hoped Jill wouldn't catch the slip. Or assume that Kinsley was in charge of setting this all up.

"Perfect. Well then, I'll see you tomorrow at four-thirty," Jill said. "I'm looking forward to seeing what you've pulled together."

She hung up, and Kinsley held her phone in a death grip. She closed her eyes, sending up a prayer for patience.

Dear Lord, please let this all work out.

"Everything okay?"

Really? Elliot? Now?

She spun to face him, thankful no one else was around. "So you decided to join us." She kept her expression neutral, hoping she wouldn't falter as she held his hazel eyes.

"Well, yeah, I'm the best man. I better show up." He angled his head to one side, his smile slipping. "You look upset."

She chewed at her lip, trying to find the right words. Trying not to let him see how his absence had annoyed her. Did she have the right to expect anything from him?

He kissed you. You kissed him. He's not just a guy you're working with anymore.

But the part of her that had been worn down by her ex-fiancé took over and self-preservation kicked in.

She pointed to his cheek, deciding to go with his injuries. "I assume you got that in the rodeo, as well as that sore arm you're favoring? Going to look great in the pictures."

"Well, you assume wrong," he said. "And Tricia assured me I could cover this up with some concealer."

Which meant he had stopped at the house.

"And my arm is just sore, that's all," he continued."That's all? You're lucky you didn't get hurt worse."

He gave her another lazy smile. "You were worried about me. That's kind of sweet."

His patronizing air, his idea that he could act so casual, as if she hadn't challenged him, hadn't had a soul-baring conversation, made her even angrier, but she had her pride. She wasn't letting him know that.

"I just finished talking to Jill, my future partner." That wasn't at all the reason, but it was easier to blame her frustration on that than try to deal with the emotions he created in her. "She wants to see how everything will go."

"We don't need to be nervous about her. You're amazing at this." He took a step closer, as if he would kiss her again.

Nope. Not happening.

She slanted him a look, tired of the whole charade. "What are you doing? So you're gone for like eight days, and you come meandering back, handing out compliments. And I'm supposed to smile and say, 'Oh aren't you sweet.'" The snap in her voice surprised her as much as it seemed to surprise Elliot.

"You're angry with me," he said.

"And the award for the most perceptive man goes to Elliot Tye." She clutched her clipboard, tapping it against the camera still hanging around her neck. "You drag me up to the hills, you kiss me, we talk about your father, and then you just leave. You send me some random texts from who knows where, and I'm supposed to just smile and simper when you decide to show up favoring your arm, with a bruise on your face, and be oh so happy to see you. As if you can just pick up where you left off."

Now his smile faded away. He rested his hands on his hips, looking down at the ground as he seemed to gather his thoughts. "You know it's complicated."

"That's a Facebook status, not an explanation."

"You're right. I'm sorry." He sucked in another long breath, then looked up at her. "I know I needed to apologize to you after taking off. I was confused, I wasn't sure what to think." He looked around, then back at her. "Can we go talk somewhere quiet?"

She should say no. She had several things to check up on, but the part of her that connected with him, the part that yearned for him while he was gone, overrode her objections.

"Okay. But only for a minute."

He gently took her arm and walked her past the tent, toward the shop where the wagon stood ready for tomorrow. He slid the door closed and turned to her.

She held her hand up, stopping him. "Don't you dare kiss me."

"Much as I'd like to, I need to tell you what happened."

"I would hope so."

He dropped on a nearby straw bale, leaning forward, legs spread, his hands clasped between. "I went to the rodeo and didn't do so great." He glanced up at her, releasing a light laugh. "My concentration was skewed, thanks to you. Then, out of the blue, Dennis shows up. Drunk and yelling at me. It was a mess."

"I'm sorry to hear that," she said, feeling her anger soften a bit.

"Yeah. I was too," Elliot said. He blew out his breath, his hands almost white-knuckled. "Later that night he got into a fight and got busted up pretty bad. His buddy called me. I went to reason with him, and that's when I got this." He pointed to the bruise on his face. "It's also when I wrenched the arm I injured in the car accident several years ago. I thought we were done when another guy came charging out of the bar and clubbed him with a baseball bat. Coldcocked him. I couldn't just leave Dennis there, so I took him to the hospital. I stuck around for a few days to make sure he was okay." He rubbed his hands over his face. "Needless to say, I didn't want to tell you all that in a text."

"But you're telling me now."

"Because you need to know." He got to his feet. "You need to know that I wasn't just ditching you. I was ashamed. But as soon as I saw you, I knew you needed to know everything."

"That makes things easier." And it did. Hearing that he had to deal with his father knocked all the objections right out of her.

"I was hoping it would."

"And I'm sorry you didn't score better."

"It was because of you, you know." His voice grew quiet, and he moved closer to her. She kept her eyes lowered, studying his shirt. It was wrinkled, as if he had shoved it into his bag, unconcerned about how it would look when it came out. "What you said, your challenge to me..." His voice faltered.

"I'm so sorry for what you had and have to deal with."

Elliot blew out a sigh. "Me too. I sure didn't need my hassle with Dennis after doing so poorly. I was so sure I would win. I drew a good horse. Thought I had a good ride."

"And what happens if you don't get enough points?"

He shook his head. "I can't think about that. This is too important to me to get distracted by maybes."

"Are you trying to convince me, or are you trying to convince yourself?" Kinsley asked.

Elliot looked her in the eyes. "You know, you threw a lot of questions at me up there on the hill, and maybe you were right, but I've had time to think about me. About you. And I don't think I'm the only one who might not have a complete handle on the future."

"What do you mean?" Kinsley asked, his words both thrilling and frightening her.

"I saw your face when you took those pictures. I saw how happy you were, I saw how much you enjoyed it." Elliot brushed a strand of hair back from her face, his lips curved in a smile as he did so. "And when I show up, you've got your clipboard in your hand, but your camera around your neck. You seem to think I'm chasing the wrong dream for the wrong reason, but I'm wondering if you're doing the same thing."

His words took her own misgivings, her own doubts, twisting them into a shape she didn't want to examine.

The past few days, taking pictures, working with them, editing them, had given her a joy she hadn't felt in a long time. At one time she had flirted with the idea of photography. In fact, her mother had even encouraged it.

"Jill, my potential future partner, is coming to the wedding," she said, forestalling and blocking those doubts from settling in her mind. Looking to the future she thought she had a handle on.

Until Elliot. Until he challenged her like she challenged him.

Elliot nodded, acknowledging her worries. Then he gave her his signature crooked smile. The one that had the potential to challenge her concentration. The one that made her feel unsteady.

"From the way Kane has been talking, you've planned this wedding so well that you could probably not even show up and everything will go smooth as silk. This Jill lady will be suitably impressed, if that's what you want."

"I want to do a good job for Faith," she returned, realizing how prim she sounded. But it was true. Yes, she wanted to impress Jill, but more than anything she wanted to help her friend have the wedding she dreamed of.

And that included taking pictures of the wedding, she realized.

"And I know you will." Elliot grew silent, looking at her, his expression drifting into seriousness. He held her gaze, then took her hand in his, looking down at their entwined fingers. "I'm sorry I didn't call you. Talk to you. Share with you. I'm not used to doing that when it comes to Dennis. I feel like…like all my life I've tried to keep the Meacher and the Tye family separate. It was so much easier that way. It's a habit I've carried into adulthood, unfortunately."

His admission opened a window into the life he'd been living. Into the struggle he'd been having.

"You've been trying to straddle two lives and two fathers," she said.

His smile told her she was dead-on in her assumption.

"Yes."

"But why even spend time on Dennis? Why even give him any control over you?"

She saw the flash in his eyes, how his mouth opened as if ready to protest. But he stopped himself, nodding as if considering this. "You might be right."

Kinsley thought of the wedding dress she had given to Faith. Seeing her friend wearing it felt as if she had cut a major tie with her past.

"I know it's hard to reconcile with the past and look to the future," she said. "But you can't let the past define you. Find your own way."

Elliot stroked her cheek, his eyes softening, his smile easy. His touch sent shivers down her spine. "You should add counselor to your résumé," he said.

Then he pulled her close and brushed his lips over hers. "I missed you," he murmured against her mouth, their breaths mingling.

Kinsley drifted into his embrace, wrapped her arms around his neck, and let herself leave her concerns behind.

❧❀❧

"I now pronounce you husband and wife." The minister smiled at Kane and Faith standing in the arch, their smiles so wide Elliot thought their faces would break. The sun was in the perfect spot, shining down on them with a benevolent light, creating the perfect setting for a perfect wedding.

The sun backlit Faith's veil, haloing her face, making her look angelic.

Kane's hair shone, his eyes glued to his wife, his shirt stretched across his broad shoulders.

They looked perfect together.

All had gone well. The horses had been on their best behavior as Elliot drove the wagon with Faith sitting in the backseat and her grandfather beside her. When they pulled up to the gathering, Elliot could hear a collective gasp of appreciation that made every splinter and blister he'd gotten working on the wagon worthwhile.

As beautiful as the wedding was, however, watching Kinsley working her cameras made him smile most of all.

While she took pictures up in the hills with the wagon and the horses, Kinsley kept her distance, but she seemed calm enough. Which made him thankful he had taken the time to acquaint her with the horses. She had even managed a quick smile as she arranged the wedding party around the wagon, frowned, then moved them around again. Despite her protestations, she seemed like she knew what she was doing and it was fun to watch her work.

But now, as she discreetly walked around the crowd, looking for just the right angle to catch the bride and groom, she was serious, concentrating on what she was doing, hidden behind her camera, snapping pictures of Faith and Kane as they embraced then shared a long kiss.

The crowd surged to their feet, clapping and whistling. Elliot joined in, truly happy for his brother.

Kane kissed Faith again, smiling down at her, his love so obvious it made Elliot's heart ache. The whole ceremony had been moving in so many ways. Faith had composed a song and sang it to Kane, guaranteeing that there wasn't a dry eye in the gathering.

Though he had seen Faith and Kane together since he'd come back, now, in this setting, it created a surprising discontent for the direction of his own life.

You don't want this. You have other plans.

But his eyes shifted to Kinsley even as he tried to convince himself of that.

She was moving back between the chairs, down the makeshift aisle, ready to capture the next few shots. As she walked, he caught her sidelong glance to the woman he had heard from Tricia, was Kinsley's potential partner, Jill.

Elliot decided he didn't like Jill. She looked like she had eaten four lemons, maybe five. Her clothes were even more austere than the ones Kinsley had worn when she first came to the ranch. Her harsh gray hair was short, cropped and the entire service Jill looked at Kinsley as if waiting for her to make a mistake. As if waiting for something to go wrong.

Faith waved her bouquet in the air, and Marianne, playing an electric piano, changed the music to an upbeat country tune. Faith hooked her arm in Kane's and together they almost ran down the grassy aisle.

"Should we keep up?" he murmured to Tricia as he took her arm.

"Let them have their moment. It will give Kinsley a chance to get some good shots before we come," Tricia said. "But they sure look happy, don't they?"

"They do. And you and Mason are up next," he said as they made their way down the grassy path. The twins had had their moment and were sitting with Zach.

Tricia grinned. "Yeah. I guess."

And again Elliot felt that unwelcome envy. His sister and his brother were finding their place in life and he felt as if he were still floundering.

The last few weeks it was as if his focus was shifting and changing. He didn't like how scattered his thoughts had become. And at the end of the aisle, crouching down, snapping pictures, was the reason for his confusion.

She had two cameras, large lenses protruding from both. He wanted to look over at her. Share a smile.

Share a moment.

But she had asked him, before the wedding, to please keep his distance and not distract her.

So he didn't wink at her when she set the wedding party up,

posed them, asked them to do this, that. Climb up on the wagon, come off the wagon. Stand by the wagon. Stand on the bridge. She was brisk and efficient and his admiration for her grew even more.

He respected her wishes, realizing that it was Kane's day, and his brother deserved his undivided attention.

Well, as undivided as he could make it.

But the wedding was now officially over. Kinsley had taken the posed and family pictures. Now it was time for dinner, short speeches, hopefully, and then a dance.

And Elliot intended on dancing as much as possible with Kinsley.

Thankfully Faith had refused to have a receiving line, and instead they all went directly to the tent where Carmen was laying out the myriad plates of appetizers she and Tricia had been working on all afternoon.

Kinsley was still taking pictures as they sat down at the head table. Elliot wasn't much of a flower person, but he could see how beautiful and tasteful the centerpieces on the tables looked. Festive, fun, and yet, stylish.

It had Kinsley's touch all over it. He hoped that Jill woman appreciated and acknowledged all the work Kinsley had put into this.

Everyone settled into their places, and Zach stood to give a blessing on the meal.

"I know I have a chance to make a speech later, but it's short, so I'll say what I need to say now." He turned to Faith and Kane, his expression growing serious. "I've had the privilege of watching you two work your way through your lives, make your decisions, and come to this place. Here as husband and wife. It hasn't been an easy journey for either of you, but I am so thankful that you two found each other again. I'm thankful for the grace of God in your life, how He has watched over you and how, as we just heard, He is here to bless your relationship and your life together. I know it will not be easy, there will be diffi-culties, but with God's help, and the support of your family and community, I know you'll make it. There is nothing more fulfilling than having someone you love beside you. Someone alongside who will share your experiences and memories in a way no one else can. A companion to do life with."

To do life with.

The same words the minister used when he spoke to Faith and Kane in his message.

He spoke of how wonderful it was to have someone beside you on the journey, someone invested in your happiness and well-being.

Elliot's eyes drifted to Kinsley, surprised to see her looking directly at him.

Was she thinking the same thing?

What had gone through her head as she watched her friend walk up the aisle in the dress that was supposed to be the one she wore to her wedding?

Then Kinsley's mouth shifted into a wisp of a smile. She lifted the camera and snapped his picture.

He shook his head in warning, and she just grinned.

Their connection held, and a warmth simmered below his breastbone, spreading, shifting his perceptions. Things were changing between them and that, in turn, was changing him.

This last rodeo had taken a lot out of him. He used to enjoy being gone, on the road, free. On his own. His life was one steady stream of movement, driving, challenging, pushing.

But now?

Now he felt drained. Rodeo wasn't giving him the satisfac-tion it once had. Chasing the CFR seemed less a dream and more an ordeal.

He turned his attention back to Zach who had paused a moment, grief shimmering across his face. "I wish your mother could be here to see this," he was saying to Faith and Kane. "I know how badly she wanted for her children to find their own place in life. To find peace and shelter from the storms life can throw at us, as, I believe, you two have found. The same thing we wish for all our children." Zach's eyes flicked to Tricia then to Elliot.

Tricia had already found her partner for the storms of life.

And him?

Elliot kept his gaze on his father, afraid what would happen if he looked once more at Kinsley. Afraid she would see the yearning for her that was minute by minute taking over his life.

Zach turned back to the bridal couple as he took a steadying breath.

"But know that if she were here she would give you the same blessing I am about to give you," he was saying. Then he lifted his hand toward them in a gesture of blessing. "May the Lord bless you and keep you. May the Lord make His face to shine upon you and be gracious to you. May the Lord lift His countenance upon you and give you peace." He paused a minute as if to let the blessing settle on them. "And now I want to pray over this amazing food we are about to eat." Another pause followed by rustling as the guests bowed their head, waiting. "Thank you, Lord, for Your love, Your guidance, and Your grace. Thank You for bringing Faith and Kane together so we could enjoy this celebration. Thank You for this delicious food that Carmen and Tricia have prepared for us. May we enjoy it, but as we do, may we be mindful of those who have so much less than we do. May we give as we have been given to. Bless our time together. In Your name, amen."

A murmured "amen" followed his words, then Zach ceded his place to Nathan Raphel, good friend of Kane's and Master of Ceremonies.

Elliot kept his head lowered a moment, Zach's words settling into his mind. Nourishing his soul. His father was always so sincere in his prayers. They weren't complicated or verbose.

Just words from a heart that Elliot knew served the Lord sincerely and completely.

A heart that had its own companion in his wife, Grace.

"Before we start supper, I have something special for the married couple," Nathan said as the DJ brought over a laptop, trailing cords connected to his soundboard. He and Nathan huddled over the keyboard, frowning, and then a burst of static and feedback screeched through the speakers.

"Can you see me?"

The voice that surged from the speakers sent Elliot's heart soaring. Lucas? Could it be? The last they'd heard from him was an email just after Faith and Kane got engaged.

"Yeah, we can see you," Nathan said, grinning over the computer screen at Faith and Kane. They both looked as shocked and excited as he felt.

And Tricia looked like she was about to leap out of her chair and grab the computer.

Nathan turned the laptop to face the head table and Elliot's own heart jumped at the sight of his foster-brother on the screen.

Which was immediately followed by a gasp of dismay from everyone at the table.

His face, his handsome, rugged face, was bandaged on one side. One eye was bloodshot, the other covered by bandages as well.

"Don't worry, this isn't as bad as it looks," he said, grinning. "I can see you all, can you see me?"

"We can," Kane said, his voice sounding strangled. "Good to see you, Lucas."

"I'm sorry I couldn't be there. I wanted to so badly. Nathan tracked me down, and we set this up as a surprise."

He shifted, his camera moved back a bit, and Elliot could see that Lucas was in a hospital bed.

"Are you okay?" Elliot couldn't help asking.

"I've been better, but the doc at the hospital here on the Kandahar base says I'm on the mend, so that's good. But I didn't call for sympathy or attention. I wanted to congratulate you, Kane and Faith, on your marriage. So happy for you guys. And I see that Tricia and Elliot are there too. So sorry I couldn't come in person." Lucas's deep voice trembled a moment, and Elliot sensed his disappointment at not being there with his family. "But I'm glad I could be here in spirit if not in body. Glad that the family could all be together. Dad, Elliot, Tricia, great to see you guys too." Lucas lifted a hand in greeting.

Elliot wanted to ask what happened. Wanted to know if he really was okay.

But this was not the time. He would sit down, tonight, and email his brother. Get more of the details, though given that he was in Afghanistan, Elliot was pretty sure he was injured in battle.

"So good to see you," Zach put in. "We pray for you every day."

This created a pause, and Elliot saw a variety of emotions flit over Lucas's face.

"Well, that's good," he said. "We could use all the prayers we can scrounge up over here. Anyway, like I said, this isn't about me. I'm so glad you two are married now. I'll be discharged in a few weeks, and then I'm coming back. We can connect then and I can…"

The picture wavered and the sound broke in and out. They caught only bits and pieces of what he said afterward. Finally, after a few more minutes of intermittent sound and frozen video they heard a muffled "goodbye."

The picture disappeared followed by a blip sound. The call had been disconnected.

Silence drifted up as the family realized what had happened to their brother.

Then Nathan closed the laptop and turned to the head table.

"So, that was greetings from Lucas. I'm sure he'll try to call again, though it took a lot of finagling with time and connections to get that done."

"Thanks for that," Kane said. "It was great to see him again."

Though Elliot agreed, the fact that Lucas was injured sat like a stone in his chest. And, from the look of dismay on Zach's face, Elliot suspected his father felt the same.

"It was hard to see him like that," Nathan said, "but he told us to reassure you all that he's okay. He really wanted to connect with you. He'll pull through this and hopes to come home soon."

"Well, that's good," Zach repeated.

"Okay. We only had a small window of time to catch Lucas," Nathan was saying, "so we had to put dinner off for a few minutes. But we'll start with the head table and I'll make my choices after that depending on how much you're willing to pay me." A murmur of polite laughter greeted his comment. "After dinner, we'll have a few speeches."

Elliot rubbed his damp palms against his pants, going over once more what he wanted to say to his brother. It would be fine, he told himself.

Then he stood and pulled the chair back for Tricia, again far too aware of Kinsley getting her camera ready to take his picture. It was as if every moment in her presence, with her carrying her camera, focusing in on him, created a growing intimacy.

An intimacy that was messing with his mind.

He blamed his changing feelings on the day. Watching your brother get married was a sentimental moment, and having a woman who was slowly becoming more important to him, who was making him more and more unsure of his choices, taking his picture, only added to the confusion.

A confusion he knew he couldn't indulge in.

Could he?

CHAPTER 15

"We are so thankful you all could be here to share this day with us," Kane was saying after all the other speeches were over, his arm around Faith, holding her close to his side. "And we are especially thankful to our heavenly Father for bringing us together. For the blessing of this relationship." Kane looked down at Faith, his eyes brimming with love. When he bent over to kiss her, Kinsley captured the moment.

Kane straightened and looked over the crowd, nodding to the DJ, who cued up the first song, a slow waltz.

The bridal couple walked onto the wooden dance floor. Kane turned to Faith, slipped his arms around her, and together they moved to the music.

Kinsley took a few pictures from her vantage point, then moved to catch another shot. She had gotten some great captures today, and now, as Elliot and Tricia joined them, she knew this part of her job, was coming to an end.

She crouched down, pleased to notice that her hip wasn't even that sore. She had been worried that it would hold her back, but that wasn't the case.

As she watched Faith and Kane dancing, she noted with

pleasure how the dress flowed around Faith's legs, how the bodice sparkled in the subdued light from the paper lanterns hanging in the tent. It was the perfect dress for her, and though, initially, it had been difficult to see her friend wear the dress that was supposed to be the beginning of her own happily ever after, now it didn't matter.

And as she took her last picture she saw, coming onto the floor, the man who had changed so much for her. Elliot took Tricia into his arms, but as he did, he looked over at Kinsley, giving her a smile so warm and intimate it made her heart shiver.

She swallowed and lifted her camera again, hiding behind it. However, as she took pictures of the bridal party, she zoomed in a few times on Elliot. He seemed to sense every time she did because he looked directly at her, pulling silly faces sometimes, other times blowing kisses. Despite his shenanigans she captured a few good, serious shots.

Then, as she straightened, the DJ changed the tempo of the music to upbeat country, inviting everyone onto the dance floor.

Kinsley snapped a few more pictures, then she walked toward the table where Jill sat so she could look them over. Faith had said she didn't want any formal pictures of the reception. She and Kane had put cards on each table asking people who took pictures with their phone to send them to a number printed on the card.

Kinsley was glad she was finished for the night. Her feet throbbed, and though her hip wasn't bothering her too much, she was tired mentally as well as physically.

"Things seem to have gone well," Jill said to her as Kinsley sat down. Jill had been sitting the entire time at the same table as Kinsley, scribbling notes in a small book. Every time she did, Kinsley's pulse picked up another notch. Was she writing good things? Bad things? Criticisms? Suggestions?

Kinsley struggled to keep her focus on the job she was doing at the moment, trying not to worry what Jill was writing down.

"I'm fairly pleased," Kinsley said. And she was. The wedding ceremony had gone smoothly, even with the distraction of taking pictures.

The dinner of appetizers had also gone well.

Carmen was a consummate professional. She had enlisted the help of some friends, her new boyfriend, Brent, being one of them, to help serve. They were all dressed in black pants and white shirts. People still drifted over to the tables to eat some more, but it looked like there had been more than enough.

"I was surprised you went with the transmission from Kane's brother," Jill said, closing her book and clipping the pen to it. "I don't know as I would have done it. It created a dissonance—"

"I thought it was an important thing to do," Kinsley cut in, quashing her fears of Jill's disapproval. "This is a close family, and even though it might not have been the most upbeat situation, I'm glad we did it. Lucas is a part of the family and he couldn't be here. I knew that was difficult for him and I knew it was also difficult for Elliot, Kane, and Tricia."

She sounded more defensive than she should. Jill's approval meant too much.

"I understand that," Jill said. "But I would discourage that in the future. Live transmissions like that don't always work and can interrupt the flow of the event."

"Kinsley has a real knack for knowing precisely what to do and how to make it happen."

Elliot's voice behind her made her jump. She turned, smiling at his defense. "I think it worked out really well," he continued.

"Elliot, this is Jill," she said as she introduced her future partner to Elliot. "Jill, this is Elliot. I'm sure you know he's the brother of the groom."

"I have to say I enjoyed your speech," Jill said, flashing a smile. Just like that, her prickly attitude was gone, and she was acting like every other woman did around Elliot. Grinning and borderline flirting with him.

"It came from the heart," Elliot said, placing his hand on his chest. He angled her a crooked smile, and Kinsley had to chuckle at how easily Jill fell under his spell.

"Well, it was a good speech, and I think this wedding has gone well." Jill's praise warmed her heart.

"It's been excellent. Kinsley has been fantastic. I'm also looking forward to seeing the pictures she took."

Jill folded her arms across her chest, her defensive body language eloquent as she turned to Kinsley again. "Are you sure that was such a good idea? Coordinating the wedding as well as taking pictures?"

"Faith was in a bind. Her photographer wasn't showing up." Again Kinsley tried not to sound defensive.

"Well, thankfully everything went smoothly." Jill gave her a tight smile, but Kinsley could tell she wasn't pleased with the whole setup. "But of course you won't be repeating this if you work for me."

"Of course not," Kinsley said. "This was a one-off."

"I would hope so," Jill said primly. "It's enough work, coordinating the wedding, without having to think of camera angles and shots."

"You just said this wedding went well," Elliot said. "I don't think you need to worry about what Kinsley can and can't do." Kinsley knew Elliot well enough by now to hear the faint edge of anger in his voice. While part of her was flattered with his defense of her, this was also her potential partner. And she didn't need anything to jeopardize that.

"Planning a wedding is a complex endeavor," Jill said, still smiling. "It requires being on top of everything at all times."

"Kinsley's pretty much in charge of everything," Elliot put in. "And the best part, she's able to roll with the flow."

Jill frowned at that. "Roll with the flow? What do you mean?"

Kinsley could see Elliot marshaling another argument, so she grabbed his arm, catching his attention and smiling up at him.

"I think we should have a dance," she said, realizing this probably also fell under the realm of "not something a wedding planner would do" but right now she knew she had to get Elliot away from Jill.

"I think that's a great idea," Elliot agreed, slipping his arm over her shoulders and walking away from the table.

"You need to know I'm not much of a dancer," Kinsley said, aware of the pickle she had created in her desire to get Elliot away from her future partner.

Now, as she watched other couples twirling around the dance floor, easily reading each other's movements, completely in sync, she wished she hadn't been so impulsive.

"Well if it's any consolation, I'm not much of one either," Elliot said. "So we can kind of fumble along together."

Coming from anyone else she would've felt offended, but combined with Elliot's grin and the way his arms held her close, it made her laugh instead.

"So, that Jill lady, are you sure you want to work with her?" Elliot asked, slipping his arms around her, moving slowly to the music, just as he had promised.

"She's one of the best in the business," Kinsley said. "It would be a huge win for me if I got the job."

"She doesn't seem like a lot of fun," Elliot said. "I didn't like how she was criticizing you."

"She wasn't criticizing me," Kinsley protested. "She was just—"

"Criticizing you," Elliot interrupted. He shot another glance to where Jill sat. "She's taking notes again. She's been doing that all evening. What is she writing in that little book of hers?"

"Maybe she's writing poetry," Kinsley joked, not sure she wanted to talk about Jill with Elliot.

Elliot said nothing for a moment as they moved over the dance floor, just taking small steps, swaying to the music. Kinsley hadn't danced in a long time, but surprisingly, with Elliot, she didn't even feel that self-conscious.

"So why her?" Elliot asked. "Why do you want to work for her?"

"I told you, she's the best in the field." She wished he would drop this.

"Better than Mr. Loser Drake?" Elliot asked.

"Way better."

"And wedding planning is the dream for you?"

Kinsley looked away from him, unwilling to hold his gaze. "You keep asking me these questions. Are you trying to make me unsure of what I should do with my future?"

Elliot was silent a moment, his arm tightening around her, his hand holding hers against his chest. "I just know that you seem a lot happier when you're taking pictures than when you're walking around with your clipboard, making notes, making plans," he said finally.

"That's because photography is a hobby, and making plans and writing on clipboards is my job."

"Well you just seem a lot happier doing your hobby than doing your job," Elliot put in. "And your job, this partnership with Jill, will mean you moving back to the city, right?"

Kinsley didn't know what to say to that. His question shifted their conversation to a different level. Was he concerned about her moving? Did that matter to him?

"But this isn't what I was hoping we would talk about as I was dancing with you," Elliot said. "I haven't had a chance to tell you how amazing you look."

Kinsley looked down at the slacks she wore. "I wanted something easy to move around in. And yet, something that still looked reasonably dressy."

The wide pants were made out of a pleated organza material that created the look of a dress, with the ease of movement of pants.

He fingered the hem of the gauzy blouse she had layered over top of it, and smiled. "Well, you pulled it off. Just like you pulled off this wedding. I know Faith is absolutely thrilled with how everything went even if Jilly over there doesn't seem to think you did things right."

"She was just offering her professional opinion."

"Which you'd probably have to follow if you worked for her."

And back they were to Jill.

"Can we not talk about her?" she asked, leaning back just enough to catch his gaze. She gave him a tentative smile. "I'd much sooner just be with you."

He returned her smile and then, to her surprise, pleasure, and dismay, in front of his family and all the gathered guests, he kissed her.

"Good plan. Let's get out of here."

"But my cameras-"

"No one will steal them."

"But it has all the pictures on it. From the wedding."

"Got it."

And before she could protest, he had her hand in his and was leading her off the dance floor. They stopped at a table where a couple sat.

"Dietrich, can you get Kinsley's camera and watch it for her? It's over there, on the table where the lady with the sour face is sitting."

The man named Dietrich just grinned at Elliot's description of Jill. "I'll guard it with my life," he said, getting up.

Elliot tugged on her hand but Kinsley waited until Dietrich picked up her cameras and brought them back.

"You can trust him. He runs the hardware store."

Then he led her out of the tent. The sun was just setting behind the mountains and the air was cool out here, but refreshing.

"Where are we going?"

"You don't trust me?" he asked, grinning at her.

"I do." And as she spoke the words aloud the truth of them settled into her. She did trust him.

They walked across the yard, headed, it looked like, to the shop, where he had been working on the buggy.

He let go of her hand, grabbed a large handle on the door, and slid it open.

"Come on in," he said to her, his voice holding a curious note.

She followed him, to a stack of straw bales with a blanket draped over them. "Sit down," he said to her, doing so himself and tugging on her hand.

As she did, his arm wrapped around her, pulling her back against the blanket-covered bales behind them.

"I've been wanting to get you alone all day," Elliot said, holding her close, resting his head on hers. She caught the faint whiff of the cologne he was wearing and nestled closer into his shoulder.

They were quiet for a moment, just enjoying being together.

"I have to ask you," Elliot said, his voice quiet. "How did it feel to watch Faith wearing your dress as she got married?"

"I was just thinking about that a few moments ago," Kinsley said. "And to tell you the truth, I was glad. I was glad I could help her out."

"That's good to know," Elliot said, tipping her chin up to look at him. His eyes traveled over her face, his fingers caressing her cheek and neck. "I thought it might bother you. I felt terrible for you."

"You don't need to feel bad for me. I'm over the heartbreak

that my very ex-fiancé caused me." She added a wide smile, knowing right down to the depths of her soul that she spoke the truth. "Besides, I have someone else occupying my mind."

"Really? Who might that be?"

"As if you don't know." Kinsley chuckled. She slipped her hand up the back of his head, tangling her fingers in his long thick hair, and drew him closer, their lips meeting in a warm, soft kiss. He pulled her even closer, and their bodies melted together. Kinsley's heart rate increased as their kiss deepened. Every part of her yearned for him, yearned for the closeness they were sharing, yearned for more.

Finally they pulled away, his forehead resting against hers, his face a soft blur.

"Oh, Kinsley," he breathed. "You are taking over my life."

She felt the same, but a small part of her held back. This was here, and now, but what about tomorrow? And the day after? Would they be able to be together?

She lowered her gaze, giving herself a little bit of physical distance. She wanted to ask him about the future, but fear held her back. She had made herself vulnerable to one man before, and despite what she said about Faith wearing her wedding dress, Kinsley knew she didn't dare give herself wholeheartedly to this man. There were complications in his life that she wasn't sure how to deal with. Wasn't sure what the repercussions for herself would be.

"I'm sorry if I spoke too soon," Elliot said, misunderstanding her silence. "I don't want to push you."

She shook her head, keeping her eyes focused on her hand resting now over his shirt pocket. Over his heart. "You're not pushing me to places I don't want to go."

She felt and heard his sigh of relief as his chest lifted below her hand.

"I know this sounds cliché, but I never felt like this about anybody before."

His words both exhilarated and concerned her. She wanted to express those concerns, but right now the way he was looking at her, the way he was holding her, made her feel attractive and wanted and loved. And right now, after watching her friend get married in her old wedding dress, right now all she wanted was to hold on to this moment. To cling to this connection.

And tomorrow?

She quashed her doubts, stifled her questions, and leaned into Elliot's arms, allowing herself this moment. Allowing herself to escape her concerns and just be with this man.

"You still working on the pictures?"

Kinsley looked up from her laptop, stifling a yawn as Elliot dropped onto the wicker chair beside her. She had woken up early this morning and started editing the pictures.

Then, when the truck arrived to take the tent down, she went outside to oversee the job.

But Mason, Nathan, Elliot, Tricia, and the company's employees were all helping. They shooed her away, so she took her laptop and sat on the patio. That way she was available if anyone needed her.

"How's the takedown coming?"

"We're done."

"Already? I was going to come and—"

"What? Supervise?" Elliot asked. Kinsley fought a stab of guilt. "Is that what Miss Jill would say you should do?"

"Probably."

"I had a chance to chat with her before she left last night."

Horror coursed through her. "Please tell me you were polite."

"I was the perfect gentleman," Elliot said with an impudent grin that made her question his sincerity.

"I hope so."

"She didn't seem any nicer than when I talked to her with you." Elliot leaned back, lacing his hands behind his head. "I still don't know why you want to partner with her."

Kinsley didn't know if she was being overly sensitive, but it seemed that there was a subtext to his question.

"Like I told you, she's the best. And she's offering me a full-time position, which is a whole lot better than the part-time one I had before working with Drake." She adjusted the black setting on the picture and sat back, looking at it more critically. No. She needed a different filter.

Elliot pursed his lips, seeming to ponder her reply. "So working for her would be quite a coup then?"

"Oh yeah. I can only imagine what Drake and his mother would think."

"Which is the point?"

Kinsley looked over her laptop at Elliot, wondering what he meant by that, but he was staring at the sky, looking as if he didn't have a care in the world.

But she did.

After they'd kissed in the barn, they'd walked outside and kissed under the stars. Talked and kissed some more. And with each kiss Kinsley knew things were moving to a place she couldn't back away from. With each kiss her plans grew less and less sure and her concerns increased.

But she couldn't change the course of her future. Not without knowing what Elliot was going to do.

"I don't know what you mean." Kinsley said.

"When I came out here, you were smiling," he said. "Working on those pictures."

"I was reliving the day. It was perfect."

"Yeah. And a lot of that was thanks to you, but you seem a lot more relaxed taking pictures, which, by the way, should be an incredibly stressful job."

"So you keep saying. Sorry I wasn't more twitchy."

Elliot closed her laptop and set it aside, leaned in and took her hands in his.

"I don't think you would be happy working for this Jill chick."

Kinsley pulled in a steadying breath, seeking the right way to say what lay on her mind. But he kept talking.

"I think one of the reasons you want to work for her is that this could be a way to show your ex-fiancé how valuable you really are."

Kinsley let his words sift into her mind, weighing them. And as they settled, they ignited a tiny spark of recognition. Of realization.

She tried to stifle it, but the harder she tried the more she realized how close he was to the truth. A truth that had been hovering at the edges of her mind but she didn't want to face.

"Why do you care?" she asked, sidestepping the doubts he was seeding in her mind and coming directly to a point she needed to discover. "Why does this matter to you?"

"I want to see you happy."

"What stake do you have in that?" The frustration his probing had created spilled out into her questions. And from the surprised look on his face, he heard it too.

He looked down at their joined hands, his thumbs running over the backs of hers.

"I care about you. I care about your happiness. A lot."

His simple words forced a sharp intake of her breath. And yet, his vagueness created another unease. "And why does my happiness matter to you?" she asked.

"Things are changing between us," Elliot returned. "You know that as well as I do." He looked up, his eyes drilling into hers. But she also saw the faint question in them.

"And what are they changing to? Where are they going?" She used her questions to deflect his words. She cared for him too, but the indecision that nipped at her heels was woven through those feelings. But who was going to move first?

"I'm not sure," he whispered.

Kinsley yanked her hands back from his. "Then I'm not either." There was no way she was making any kind of commitment or change of plans for someone who didn't know what he wanted.

"You're sitting there questioning me about my future. What about yours?" she pressed, taking another tack.

"What do you mean?"

"You're heading off to that rodeo next weekend, aren't you?" she asked. "And then after that another one. And after that I don't know how many more until you qualify for the CFR. And like I said before, then what?" She got to her feet, needing to put some distance between them. "You're questioning my motives for working for Jill. What about your motives for wanting to get to the CFR? I know you're doing it because of Dennis. But I don't know why you care what he thinks. You told me yourself that he abused you. Why does his opinion matter so much? He should be completely unimportant to you."

Elliot's hands clenched and unclenched, and she could see a nerve jumping in his forehead, a clear indication of how he was fighting for control.

"I have to do this," he ground out. "I have to prove that I'm better than him. Beat him at his own game. Win in his arena."

"You can play another game." She paused, praying for the right words. "Make a choice that doesn't involve him. You're a better man than he is. That's already been proven. Don't let him determine your future. Don't dance to his tune."

Elliot sat for a few more seconds, then he surged to his feet, the chair he was sitting in shooting away from him with a screech.

"I'm not dancing to his tune," he ground out. "I'm making my own choices."

"Are you? I saw what you looked like after your father phoned. After he criticized your last rodeo and your performance."

"And how was that?" His narrowed eyes and clenched jaw were a clear indication she was flirting with disaster, but they had edged back and forth on this topic enough. Last night she had come very close to making a declaration of love to him. Yet she'd held back, and now she knew why. As long as his father was such an influence in his life, she couldn't give him her heart. As long as Elliot's focus was some nebulous plan to best his father, she didn't dare hitch her wagon to his star. She had gone that route before and wasn't going to let a man's dreams take priority again.

And what about you? What are you doing? Are you willing to make that sacrifice?

She felt as if they were coming to an impasse. A game of emotional chicken with very, very high stakes.

"As he was talking to you, you looked like you'd been kicked in the gut."

Elliot just glared at her, dropping his hands on his hips. "I told you, he doesn't matter to me."

She forced herself to hold his eyes, to not give in. This was too important. "Then don't go to the next rodeo. Stay here."

"And what would that prove? I don't ride in that rodeo, I for sure don't make it to the CFR."

"And what would happen if you didn't make it there?"

He looked at her as if she had lost her mind. "It's all I've worked toward for the past few years."

"I know you have, but why? When you came back from that last rodeo you looked worn out. Weary. You won, but you didn't seem to have any joy in it. You say I'm happier when I'm taking pictures, but I think you're happier here. On the ranch."

He glared at her, that muscle working in his forehead. "Rodeo is tiring. And I need…" He stopped, shaking his head as he looked away from her. "So maybe you're right. Maybe I'm doing it for the wrong reasons. Maybe I care too much what Dennis thinks…" He let the sentence trail off as his eyes traveled over the mountains cradling the valley the ranch sat in. He drew in a long, slow breath, as if gathering himself. "I can't let him beat me at this. I can't."

Had he yelled this out, she would have been able to fight back. But the heavy resignation in his voice was something she couldn't argue with.

And once again she was faced with a man who tried too hard to please the wrong person.

"Then go. Do this, but I can't be with someone who's working so hard to gain his parent's approval. I can't live like that again."

"So you're saying I have to make a choice?" he asked. Now the anger had slipped into his voice. Now the veiled fury was evident. "It's either you or the dream I've been chasing?"

"Is it your dream? Is it what you really want?"

She spoke quietly and put extra emphasis on 'you.'

And as Elliot looked away, his eyes closed, his fingers massaging the back of his neck, she sensed he wasn't entirely convinced.

"I…I need to do this…" His hesitation, his wavering, made her feel guilty for pushing him, yet again. "If I don't, he wins."

His words echoed between them and a shiver feathered her spine.

"What do you mean, he wins?"

"I mean, he wins. He'll never let me forget."

Kinsley pushed her chair back from the table and stood, gathering her balance and her courage. "You asked me what I'm saying. I'm saying you don't have to make a choice. You have to make a decision. For yourself and your own life."

"No. That's not what you're saying," he said, slicing the air between them. "What you're saying is you want me to give up all my hard work and dreams so that you don't feel like I'm Drake all over again. If you think I'm walking away from this because of something you need to have happen, because of something that happened in your past, then you don't know me at all."

She looked up at him, his anger washing over her like a wave.

She fought down her own emotions, her own pain. "You're right. I don't know you."

Then without another word he spun on his heel and walked away.

Guess he'd made his decision.

Kinsley turned away, unable to watch him leaving. She stumbled across the patio to the French doors. She entered the house and closed them behind her. Her heart stuttered in her chest, creating an ache deep inside her. Her eyes prickled with unshed tears, her throat thick with grief. How could she have let this happen again? How could she have allowed him to slip so completely into her soul that his leaving was like a tearing away?

She made her way up to her bedroom, dropped onto the bed, and stared up at the ceiling, tears pooling in her eyes and coursing down her temples. Too many feelings. Too many emotions.

"Dear Lord, what do I do?" Her petition was a whisper, drifting up to heaven. She knew she cared for Elliot more than she had ever cared for anyone before. He had said the same to her, and yet, she felt confused, unsure of how to support him. *"What do I do?"*

She knew his relationship with his father, his pursuit of this goal, was unhealthy. She couldn't allow herself to get caught up with another man who had an all-consuming, single-minded purpose. She knew it would only end in heartbreak for her. Elliot could never please a man like his father, and Dennis would always be a shadow over their life.

But oh, how Elliot had captured her heart.

And oh, how it hurt.

Right then her phone rang. She didn't want to answer it, but the thought that it might be Jill made her jump up and stumble across the room to grab her purse.

She pulled her phone out and swiped the screen before even letting the number register.

"Hey sweetheart, how's it going?"

Kinsley sank onto the bed, clutching her phone. Was this God's answer to her prayer? A phone call from her mother?

"Not too bad," was all she could manage.

"You sound tired," her mom said.

"You always say that, Mom." Kinsley lifted her legs up and sank back onto the pillows, knowing this would not be a short conversation. Her mother didn't phone often, but when she did, their conversation ranged over a variety of topics. Faith, work, life.

"And how did the wedding go?" she asked. "Did you get that job with the wedding business?"

"I don't know," Kinsley said. "I haven't heard anything from Jill yet. So we'll see. I don't know how happy she was with my work."

"Why do you say that?"

"Faith's photographer bailed on her, and she asked me to take the wedding pictures. So I was juggling two jobs."

"Isn't that wonderful?" her mother said, excitement in her voice. "I know how much you love photography. Even though we told you it wasn't a practical career move, I always thought your heart was in that more than this whole wedding planning business."

Kinsley bit back an angry retort. This was the second time in thirty minutes she'd been challenged about her career choices. She didn't like it. Far easier to challenge Elliot.

That's different, she told herself. *That's an unhealthy relationship that's going to poison him. And I can't be around to see the fallout.*

And yet, even as her mother's words mingled with Elliot's, she felt that ember of doubt that had been glowing ever since she began working with Drake and his mother. An ember that had been fanned both by Elliot's questions and the reality of how much more she'd enjoyed taking pictures of the wedding than organizing it.

How much happier she was when she had a camera in her hand.

And what kind of future could she have with that?

"Even if that were true," Kinsley said, "right now I need a steady job, and working with Jill would be a great opportunity." Why did she sound like she was trying to convince herself more than her mother?

Her mind ticked back to Jill's note taking. She wondered if she even had a chance with this job.

"You know your father and I would be more than willing to help you out," her mother said.

Kinsley held that thought a moment, wondering what that would look like. Wondering what kind of help she dared ask for. But she dismissed the idea with a shake of her head. "I know that, and I appreciate it," she said. "But if I was going to do something like that, I'd have to do it on my own."

"You always were so fiercely independent," her mother said. She sighed. "I always thought it was because of your accident, but I think your accident only brought out the stubbornness that was already in you."

"Maybe," Kinsley said. "But if I start a business, I need to know it can hold its own."

"You could fall back on your degree while you build up your dream career," her mother said.

"That's a thought," Kinsley said. "I could get a job at a bank again."

"Last time we talked you mentioned a young fellow named Elliot."

"Yeah, Kane's foster brother."

"So, anything starting up with him?"

Her mother was an unabashed matchmaker who was never subtle about her intentions. After Kinsley broke up with Drake, her mom had given her twenty-four hours to grieve and then handed her a list of single men from the church and the community. Complete with phone numbers. It was no secret that her mother had never particularly cared for Drake. Which probably hadn't helped the relationship any.

She wondered, if her mother met Elliot, what she would make of him?

"No there's nothing starting up with him." Kinsley swallowed down a tremble.

"You sound upset," her mother said, as ever attuned to the tiniest shift in Kinsley's temperament or voice.

"It's just... It's been a busy week. Actually, a busy couple of weeks. Planning the wedding and taking pictures, and now I'm editing them."

Thankfully her mother allowed her space and was quiet a moment.

"You have to send me some. You always take such beautiful pictures. In fact, I was showing some of your work to a friend of mine at the library, and he was wondering if you do freelance work. That's why I was suggesting..."

Her mother paused, and Kinsley knew exactly where she was going.

"First of all, I really don't want to move back to Ontario," Kinsley said. "Besides, like I told you, I'm really hoping this opportunity with Jill comes through. And if it does, I won't have much time to take pictures."

"Always the wedding planner..." her mother said with a sigh. "You do realize you'll never meet any eligible young men this way."

"I don't know about that," Kinsley returned, striving for a light tone. "All those groomsmen and friends of the groom. Possibilities are endless." She paused a moment, then plowed on. "And how are the cats doing?" she asked, latching onto a completely different topic, one that would steer her mother away from this difficult conversation.

Thankfully her mother took the hint and started describing the latest litter of kittens. As her mother spoke, Kinsley closed her eyes, easily seeing the place she had grown up, the wide open spaces. Though she always said she would never go back, living in the city did make her miss her hometown from time to time.

If she started working with Jill, she would be smack dab in the middle of Calgary. High-rises and concrete and traffic.

"You make sure you get some rest," her mother said. "And don't forget to go for your regular walks. You know how important that is for your leg."

"Thanks for your concern, Mama" Kinsley said. "Thanks for calling."

"Kinsley, I... I..." Her mother's hesitation surprised her, and Kinsley wondered what else she had to say.

"I need to tell you that Drake just got engaged," she continued.

Kinsley smiled. "Well, I'm happy for him. I hope she doesn't mind working with his mother."

"Well, actually, Drake quit working for her. He and his girlfriend moved up to Ottawa."

"Thanks for telling me, Mama," Kinsley said. "But it doesn't bother me. Not at all."

"Well I just thought it might be good to hear it from me before you heard it from someone else," her mother said. "I hope you have a good day, and, sweetheart, please think about what I said. I just want you to be happy. Don't *you* get stuck in a job you don't care for."

Kinsley heard a note of regret in her voice. "What are you talking about?" she asked.

"It doesn't matter," her mother said, brushing aside her question.

"It does," Kinsley pressed. "Are you unhappy with your job?"

"It's just that, it's just…" Her mother hesitated again. "I've been working at the library all these years, but it wasn't what I wanted to do when I started out."

This was news to Kinsley. "What did you really want to do?"

"What I really wanted to be was a skydiver, but there's not many employment opportunities for that." Her mother chuckled at her own joke. "But seriously, I always wanted to do more painting."

Their house was decorated with a variety of her mother's paintings, something she had dabbled in for years. "I never knew you wanted to become serious about that."

"Well, I did, but my mother talked me out of it. She said there was no future in the arts. I knew she was right, but there are many times I wished I had followed my dream. I see a little bit of the same thing in you, with your photography. Don't get pushed into a place you think you need to be."

Kinsley thought of Elliot's taunt, when he accused her of wanting to work for Jill because her business was higher-end than Drake's and his mother's. As hard as it was for her to admit it, there was a glimmer of truth in his accusation.

"Thanks for your words of wisdom," Kinsley said. "And thanks so much for the call."

"Anytime, my dear. You know that your father and I love you. He sends his greetings, by the way."

"Say hi back," Kinsley said.

Her mother ended the call, and Kinsley stared at the screen a moment, looking at the picture that came up. It was a photograph she'd taken of a cardinal perched in a tree, his head up, looking to the sky. One of the many thousands of pictures she had stored on her computer. Some of them she had printed and framed, hanging them beside her mother's oil paintings.

Her mother's words ran through her head, gathering together all the uncertainties she had been feeling the last few weeks, reshaping and arranging them.

Was she doing the same thing she accused Elliot of? Being involved in something to prove herself to someone else rather than forging ahead and being her own person?

Thoughts of Elliot made her heart clench again.

He was becoming more and more important to her, and she found, right now, she wasn't willing to let their last conversation between them truly be their last.

She fixed her makeup, tucked her shirt in, combed her hair, then made her way downstairs and out the door to where the crew, she assumed, was still cleaning up.

She followed the voices, and when she came around the barn to where the tent had been, there was a vast and empty space, the grass trampled down from the night before. Cash and Hope were running around the arch, which was still set up. A few flowerpots still flanked it, the others set out in front of the barn where everyone was gathered, sitting on straw bales that they had dragged out onto the grass. The same straw bales she presumed, she and Elliot sat on last night.

She noticed Mason and Tricia, Zach, Carmen and Brent, and Nathan and his wife as well as a few other people she didn't recognize. Friends of the family, she assumed.

"And there she is, the woman of the hour," Tricia called out, waving her over. "Come and join us. We're celebrating with leftovers."

She noticed the blanket spread out in front of them, with paper plates of food scattered on it.

"So where's Elliot?" Tricia asked as Kinsley lowered herself gingerly onto one of the bales.

"I don't know. Last I saw him he was headed to the cabin he's staying in. He didn't come back here?"

"That's weird. He said he was going looking for you, to ask you to join us," Tricia said, wiping her mouth with a leftover wedding napkin.

The low growl of an engine broke into the peace of the moment. Kinsley looked up to see Elliot's distinctive cherry-red truck leaving the yard, tires spinning, throwing out a cloud of dust.

"Where's he going in such a hurry?" Zach asked, frowning as he got to his feet, as if to see better.

"Who knows with Elliot," Tricia said with a heavy sigh.

Kinsley swallowed down a lump in her throat. Swallowed down the faint glimmer of hope she had held that they might find a way to get through this.

Once again he was running away. But this time she sensed he was leaving for good and that was the end of it all.

CHAPTER 16

ack on the road again, Elliot thought, heading out from yet another motel room.

He tossed his gear in the back of his truck, climbed in the driver's seat, and heaved out a sigh as he stared sightlessly at the motel in front of him.

Elliot had been driving for days now, not sure where he was going, only sure he had to keep moving. To stop thinking.

After he'd left the ranch on Saturday, he'd driven down to Boyle to attend the rest of the rodeo he'd missed because of Kane and Faith's wedding. He hung out with the cowboys, listened to their boasts and busts. Relived their rides with them. The next day he watched the slack go-rounds and the last round of the cowboys who would be his competition in the next rodeo.

He spent one more night with the guys then hit the road again.

Monday rolled into Tuesday, which rolled into today.

Tomorrow he would have an all-day road trip to get to Armstrong, British Columbia. After that it was back to the rodeo in Olds. The Hanna Pro Rodeo after that if he still needed to chase Cody King, his chief competitor.

He backed out of the motel, spun his steering wheel, and headed down the road again.

Driving and more driving.

No matter how fast he drove, he couldn't outrun Kinsley's words. They played like an insistent drumbeat in his head over and over again.

"I'm saying you don't have to make a choice. You have to make a decision. For yourself and your own life."

He had decided, he told himself. It was a plan he had been working on for the last couple years. He was actually getting somewhere.

But despite his self-talk the doubts that had been hounding him the last couple of weeks taunted him, hissing accusations at him. Questioning his choices.

He slammed his hand on the steering wheel, wishing the doubts away. But he couldn't get rid of them. They spoke to the emptiness that had crowded into his life the past year. A feeling of senseless chasing. Choosing chaos because it was easier than the alternative.

Wondering what kind of person he really was. Would beating Dennis at his own game prove that he wasn't his father's son? That Dennis's blood didn't run through his veins? That his father's temperament wasn't his?

And what about Kinsley? When he was with her, he felt as if everything was right in his world. As if he had traveled a long ways and finally come home.

And yet, she had her own complications. She was making her own bad choices. He didn't know why she thought she had any right to lecture him about his choices when her motives for the decisions she was making were so obviously messed up.

Maybe they just weren't meant to be. Maybe those brief

moments of connection was them trying to fill the lonely places in their lives.

But even as he thought that, a part of him couldn't believe it. Despite her constant questioning of his motives, he felt so right with her. She wouldn't ask if she didn't care, he realized.

He switched the radio on, needing to hear other voices. Needing to drown out all the questions hounding him, twisting him in knots and going nowhere.

He soon realized the radio was tuned to a local Christian music station. Zach must've been the last one to use his truck. He was about to switch the station when the words of the song that was playing caught his attention.

"Why do we seek salvation in the ones who cannot give,
why don't we devote ourselves to the One who makes us live.
Our Father is our Savior,
And He will give us life."

Elliot recognized the song as a favorite of Grace's. She used to hum it while she was working.

He remembered sitting with Grace after an especially bad visit with Dennis. He was still hurting physically and emotionally. He was angry that he couldn't stay with them all the time, and Grace was upset as well. He remembered crying and telling her that he didn't have a father, he had a monster.

Grace soothed his pain, held him close, and once he finished crying, she told him he had many fathers. That Zach was his father as well. That Zach loved him like a son. But, she said, this is the best part.

You have a perfect Father. A Father who watches over you and takes care of you. A Father whose love will never fade or grow old.

Her words had been puzzling at first, but as he spent time in church and in youth group, the notion of God as his Father had slowly become part of his life.

"You have an earthly father and a heavenly Father who only want what's best for you. Why don't you think of them more?"

Elliot heard Kinsley's words again, a counterpoint to the song still playing on the radio.

Yearning surged through him, and he gave directions to his Bluetooth to make a call.

The phone rang and rang, and Elliot wondered if he would answer. Then a familiar voice came through the truck speakers.

"Hey, Elliot."

"Hey, Zach."

A moment of silence followed his reply. "Where are you, Son?"

Elliot fought down an abrupt stab of pain at his father's words. "On the road. Driving."

"When's the next rodeo?"

"In a few days. I'm headed there now."

"You okay?"

Elliot knew he meant physically. Injuries were a part of rodeo life, but they were often the difference between first and second place. Between being able to carry on or having to quit.

He heaved out a sigh, staring at the highway rolling ahead of him, the scenery as stunning as ever.

"Actually, I'm not."

Zach waited a moment as if giving the comment some weight. Recognizing the shift into another conversation.

"Talk to me, Son."

Son. That word again.

"I'm tired. I'm chasing this...this thing. But I feel like the closer I get, the less it matters."

"Dreams can be like that," Zach said. "They can take over and consume you so much that you sometimes can't see the long game. Only what's right in front of you."

"And for me that's always been the next rodeo and the one after that and the one after that." He pulled to the side of the road and stopped the truck. From where he was parked he could look over the sweep of the valley that held the Bar U Ranch, a historic site that was, at one time, one of the biggest ranches in Canada.

A legacy that was now faded away. He didn't even know who had owned it before it became a historic site, nor did he care. It didn't matter. Life moved on. People didn't care about how prosperous it was. That was in the past.

"It's been your focus for a long time, that's for sure," Zach said.

Elliot sighed, leaning back against the seat, suddenly, utterly weary.

"Will it be worth it? If I win?"

This was followed by a beat of silence. "Son, that's up to you," Zach finally said. "This has been your battle. Your focus. You know why you do it."

"That's the trouble. I don't know anymore. Kinsley...Kinsley said I was trying to please the wrong father. What do you think?"

Another pause.

"I think she may be onto something. She's a pretty smart girl."

He could hear the disappointment lacing his father's voice.

"She is. She's amazing."

"She was sad when you left so abruptly."

His father's comment created both hope and guilt.

"I'm sorry. I shouldn't have done that. She was...she was making me think about things I wasn't sure of. Doubting decisions I've been making for a long time."

"You've made a lot of sacrifices for this, haven't you?"

Yes, and I made one more when I walked away from Kinsley.

"Did you ever care about my run for the CFR?"

"All I've ever wanted was for you to be happy, to be content, to find peace and rest in God's love. How that happens is up to you. However, I do think you've leaned too heavily on your father's opinion."

"You've never spoken against Dennis," Elliot said.

"He's still in your life. And you care about what he thinks. Your mother and I never wanted to confuse you. To make you choose."

How selfless this man was. And how wise.

"I'm sorry... I'm sorry I never called you Dad."

"You have two fathers. I understand."

"I'm glad I have you in my life," Elliot said, rubbing his forehead, trying to arrange the thoughts that had been swirling around the past few days. "I've always been thankful for what you gave me. The home you provided. I...I love you, Dad."

"And I love you, Elliot." The sincerity in his father's words was almost his undoing. "And I've only ever wanted what was best for you."

"Should I keep going?"

Zach's sigh echoed through the speakers. "That's a question only you can answer. If it means enough to you, you'll keep going. If it doesn't..." Zach let the comment fade away and Elliot mentally filled in the rest.

If it doesn't, you'll stop.

"Either way, I'll be praying for you to your heavenly Father. A Father who loves you even more than I ever can."

Elliot smiled at the reference. Again, the same one Kinsley had made.

"Thanks for that, Dad. That means more than you can know."

"And I feel like I need to tell you that there will always be a place for you here. On the ranch. Always."

"Are you saying—"

"I'm saying I would love nothing more than to have my sons

working together. Here. At Tall Timber. But again, that's your choice."

Elliot held the words close, feeling like he had to tuck them away for safekeeping. Pull them out when he dared think of the implications of his dad's offer.

"You think about that," his dad said, "but in the meantime, drive safe, Son. Be safe. Know that I love you."

"I love you too, Dad."

They said goodbye and Elliot sat a moment, letting his father's words wash over him. Letting them settle into the empty and lonely parts of his life that he tried to fill with constant movement.

Forgive me, Lord, he prayed, not sure he could manage more.He massaged the back of his neck. Tight again. Stress again.

He needed to talk to Kinsley.

But when he dialed her number, she didn't answer. He tried again, but again no answer. Was she ignoring him?

Leave it. You don't deserve to talk to her.

However, even as those words ran through his mind, he knew he couldn't just leave things the way they were. He had left so abruptly. Maybe there was a chance for them yet.

He pulled out his wallet and took out Jill's card he had grabbed off the table when they were setting up for the wedding. He wasn't sure why he'd taken it. But now he had it. He glanced at the address, plugged it into his GPS, and grimaced. Just as he figured. Right in downtown Calgary.

Oh well, nothing for it.

He spun his truck around as a woman's flat and dispassionate voice told him he had to drive east to Highway 2, which he already knew. While he drove, he prayed. Disjointed and uncertain prayers, but conversation with his Father.

It took him less than the time it said on the GPS to get to Jill's business. But his next challenge was finding a parking space. He fought down his frustration as he drove around, finally parking in a spot that was probably illegal, but he didn't care. He was on a mission.

Ten minutes later he strode down a carpeted hallway, trying not to feel intimidated by the decor, the smells, and the silence. He glanced down at the card again then finally found the door with the same logo on it. Swirly and pretty and very weddingish, he thought as he pushed the door open.

More sweet smells assaulted him. Flowers spilling out of glass vases sitting on vintage-looking cupboards and fancy but uncomfortable-looking chairs filled the open space. And a chandelier hung from the ceiling. If Elliot wasn't intimidated before, he certainly was now.

"Can I help you?" A young woman, wearing a black silk shirt and white skirt came from one of the side rooms. Her hair was pulled back in the same style Kinsley used to wear. Obviously a wedding planner uniform, he thought.

"I'm looking for Kinsley Janas. I understand she is working here?"

The girl frowned, looking behind her as Jill came into the room.

"Hello, Jill," he said, sucking in a nervous breath as he faced the smiling woman. All the way here he had rehearsed his speech to Kinsley. Planned what he wanted to say. He didn't figure on having to run the employee gauntlet to get to her. "I'm hoping I can talk to Kinsley."

Jill's friendly expression grew sour again. The five-lemon look.

"Kinsley isn't here."

"Well, can you tell me when she will be?"

"I have no idea," Jill said, folding her arms over her chest in a defensive gesture. "She doesn't work here."

The atmosphere in the room had gone down a few degrees. Elliot almost shivered.

"She turned down a very generous offer from me. Even though I was willing to overlook some of the mistakes she had made with your brother's wedding."

Elliot watched her mouth move, trying to take in what she was saying. When it finally registered, it was his turn to frown. "She's not working here," he repeated, realizing he sounded like the hick he was in his cowboy boots, jeans, twill shirt, and cowboy hat.

"I believe we already covered that." Jill lifted her chin, looking even more sour.

"So where is she?"

"I have absolutely no idea. All she said was that she decided to follow her dream and that she had an in on buying some business in the town close to where the wedding was. Rockyview, I believe?"

Elliot felt a rush of confused joy.

Kinsley was in Rockyview. Right now. Buying a business.

"Okay, then I know exactly where I need to go." He flashed a smile at Jill, winked at the other woman, spun on his heel, and strode out of there as fast as he could.

He didn't even care that his truck had been ticketed. None of that mattered.

Right now he had to get to Rockyview.

⎯⎯◯⎯⎯

"I think you'll do good with the business." Jeff looked around the studio and then back at Kinsley. "It's in a good location. You've got Scrap Happy beside you and the bookstore across the street. Carmen's Coffeehouse is just around the corner. Mug Shots, another popular coffee place down the street. Lots of eyeballs on the place. I just got tired of it. I could give you a deal on the lights, backgrounds, and modifiers if you want them. I won't be using them." Jeff looked morose, and for a moment Kinsley felt sorry for him.

Until she remembered how he had let Faith hang too long, creating so much tension for her.

"I'll have to think about that," she said, looking around. There was a lot of equipment stashed in the studio. Some of it looked fairly old.

"No one else wants it, and I won't get much for it if I try to sell it." He sighed as he sat down on a nearby carpet-covered box. "I heard you got the job taking the family pictures at the church."

"I did."

"If you want some advice, you'll want the strobes and umbrellas."

"I have some speed lights."

Jeff made a face, waggling his hand. "Strobe lights give you better coverage. Faster. With families you'll have kids, and they move. A lot."

Kinsley bit her lip, considering. Though she had done some family shoots, and some indoors, they had always been casual shots. Which was exactly how the clients wanted them. But this would probably entail more formal shots.

"And you'll need to move quick," he added. "You'll be working with time slots and appointments. Cranky kids."

"Sounds like you know something about this," Kinsley said, restraining a sudden burst of anxiety.

"I did it a number of years ago." He shrugged and heaved out a sigh, looking so doleful Kinsley wondered what she had gotten herself into. "But, if I'm around, I might be able to help out."

"That'd be nice." She looked over the equipment again, mentally doing the math. She had set money set aside to buy into Jill's business. The same money she had saved up to buy into Drake and his mother's business.

Was it enough?

"How much do you want for it all?"

Jeff wrinkled his forehead, as if thinking, scratching his chin. "Tell you what I can do. I'll let you try everything. See how much you'll use, and then we can name a price. I'll be reasonable."

"You've been fair so far," she said. "I think that's a good deal."

"Excellent. I'll draw something up. Where will you be staying?"

"I'm staying at the Hidden Creek Inn, but why don't you bring it to me at the bank? It's right in town, and I'll be starting my job there tomorrow."

He was about to say something when his cell phone rang. He gave her an apologetic glance. "Sorry. I have to take this. It's the real estate agent."

Kinsley nodded as he left the studio to go into the adjoining office. Jeff was not only selling his business, he was selling his house and moving into an apartment. Downsizing his life, he told her with a wry smile.

Kinsley sat down on a stool to give her hip a rest, swiveling as she looked around.

The quiet enveloped her, and for the first time in days, she wasn't hustling, talking, or planning.

Things had moved quickly for her the past few days.

After Elliot left, she couldn't stick around the ranch as Tricia had offered. Her heart was aching, and she felt as if her world had come apart.

She drove back to the city, thinking, crying, thinking some more, and praying.

Though her confrontation with Elliot was supposed to be about him, she knew she was being hypocritical, just as Elliot had all but said. That she was doing the same thing she accused him of. Doing the wrong thing for the wrong reasons.

When she discovered that Jeff was thinking of selling his

business, she took a huge gamble and approached him. To her surprise he jumped on the opportunity. He had called her while she was in Calgary, and she made some snap decisions.

Jill was disappointed when Kinsley turned down the opportunity to work with her and tried to make her feel guilty about missing out on the, in Jill's words, "once-in-a-lifetime opportunity."

But Jill's words had the opposite effect. If anything, they were a wake-up call to Kinsley, warning her what working with Jill would be like.

She thought of Elliot's initial reaction to Jill and, as always, thinking of him was like a stab to her heart.

You'll get over it, she told herself, closing her eyes.

But, as usual, doing so only brought Elliot's picture to mind. The way his eyes sparkled when he laughed, how his hair curled, and how soft it was when she slid her fingers through it—

Stop. Stop.

She clenched her fists, fighting the waves of sorrow that memories of Elliot gave her. *The pain will go away,* she told herself. It had before.

But even as she clung to that reassurance, deep in her heart she knew it wasn't true. Elliot had wound his way into her heart so quick and so deep. His humor, the way they connected, how he helped her with her fear of horses. All this combined to make her realize how much he meant to her. How much she missed him now.

Why had she pushed him so hard? Why had it mattered so much?

The questions that had roiled through her mind the past few days held the same vestige of regret. But as she relived their conversation, as she considered it from all angles, she knew she was right to let him go.

Just as she was right to let go of what she thought she should do and do what she wanted to do.

Yes, photography would only be part-time for now, hence the job at the bank. But she sensed she could do well if she applied herself. The job doing the church photo directory was an answer to a prayer she hadn't even dared utter.

This would work, she told herself as she looked around the studio, taking in some of the photos that Jeff had framed and pinned to the walls. If he could make a go of it, despite his lack of enthusiasm, she surely could.

She would be living close to Faith. She and Tricia had gotten to know each other well. The community was a good place.

Sure, she might have to see Elliot from time to time, but given the direction he was headed, she doubted he would be back in Rockyview much.

She pulled in another deep breath and with it a prayer for peace. It would all come together. She had to trust God had brought her to this place, had given her this opportunity, and that she now had to use it well.

She just wished her heart would stop aching.

"Okay. That's all done," Jeff said as he came back into the studio. "Sorry about the interruption."

"Not a problem," Kinsley said, standing up. "Everything okay?"

"Yeah. I think I have a buyer for the house, so that's good."

"Nice. Glad to hear that."

"Like I said, I'll get something together for you and bring it to the bank." Jeff fidgeted a moment, and Kinsley sensed he had other things to take care of.

"Thanks for your time," she said, shaking his hand. "And I'm excited about the business."

Jeff looked around the studio, a melancholy smile on his face. "Lots of memories captured here." Then he shrugged. "But I know when it's time to move on. I'm looking forward to traveling. Doing more nature photography." He nodded, as if underlining that resolve when his cell phone rang again.

"See you tomorrow then," Kinsley said.

She took one more look around, trying to imagine herself working here. Capturing memories.

She took in a trembling breath, stilled the doubts that could still clutch at her, and walked to the front door.

As she stepped outside, she was momentarily blinded. The studio had been darker, and it took her a few seconds to adjust to the light. She blinked a few times and then, just as she was about to walk to her car she heard her name being called.

And her poor, overworked and bruised heart leapt in her chest.

Please, Lord, she prayed as she turned to face Elliot.

He looked as tired as she felt, she thought, as she drew in a long, slow breath, trying to still her pounding heart.

"Hey," was all she could manage. She swallowed, then swallowed again.

"Hey yourself." He not only looked tired, he sounded tired. He wore an old jean jacket, but his head was bare.

"What...why..." She stumbled over her words, annoyed that all it took was one look at him and she was reduced to this stumbling idiocy. She straightened her shoulders and lifted her chin, determined not to let him get to her. "What are you doing here?" she finally asked.

"Looking for you."

He only spoke three words, but they deflated her anger.

"Why?"

"You were right."

His words sifted through all the pain she had endured the past few days, creating a flare of longing. Their eyes held and hope quivered in her soul. Could it be?

"Elliot. What you doin' here?"

The slurred and angry voice broke into the moment, shattering it, echoing down the street.

A man strode across the road toward Elliot and Kinsley.

"You ain't s'posed to be here," the man shouted, waving his arms, his eyes wild. "You're s'posed to be in Armstrong. Pro circuit rodeo."

Kinsley felt herself recoil at the anger in the man's face, in his posture, his voice.

Elliot closed his eyes, as if praying for patience, then gave Kinsley a humorless smile.

"Kinsley, meet Dennis."

Ice slipped through her veins as she looked at the raging man with a battered cowboy hat, worn plaid shirt, and torn blue jeans. His craggy face was full of broken veins, his skin like old, cracked leather. He had a look about him that made Kinsley move just a little closer to Elliot.

"You best get goin', mister," Dennis shouted, now standing directly in front of Elliot. He lifted his hand and poked a bony finger into Elliot's chest.

Elliot grabbed his father's hand and pushed it aside. "Don't ever do that again," he said, his voice even, controlled. But Kinsley heard the edge in it.

"Why ain't you gone?" Dennis yelled.

"I'm not going," Elliot said, taking a step closer to Kinsley, standing right beside her now, as if to protect her. "I'm done."

"What? Whaddya mean, done?"

"I'm not competing. I'm finished with the rodeo."

Kinsley heard his words, but they wouldn't register.

"You're finished?" she asked, trying to make this all fit.

Elliot's expression shifted to softness as he gave her a careful smile. "Yeah. I did a lot of thinking the past few days."

"You should be thinkin' 'bout how you're gettin' to the CFR," Dennis said, his hands resting on his hips as he swayed back and forth.

Kinsley caught a whiff of rancid alcohol.

Elliot heaved out a sigh and turned back to Dennis. "I'm not going. I don't care about the CFR. It means nothing to me."

His father blinked slowly, then a sinister smile crept over his lips. "You realize what this means?"

"Yes. Nothing."

"It means everything," Dennis slurred. "It means you'll never win that title. You can never say you went to the CFR. You can never say you beat your old man."

Elliot said nothing for a beat, simply staring at his father. Then he laughed.

"I already have."

"What you mean by that? You've never been better than me."

"I know I have," Elliot said. "You can have your CFR title, you can have your winnings, your buckles, and your glory. I don't want any part of it."

"Yes you do. You need this."

"I never did. I don't know why you care. But it doesn't matter anymore. Because you don't matter anymore."

Dennis sputtered, staring at him as if he couldn't understand a word Elliot said.

Elliot took Kinsley's hand. "I don't know about you, but I want to get outta here."

Kinsley nodded, and without a backward glance, they left.

Dennis called out to them, yelling at Elliot. But Elliot kept his face ahead, his jaw set, as they walked away.

"Where are we going?" Kinsley asked.

"There's a path along the river," Elliot said. "Let's go."

As they walked, Dennis yelled after them, his voice growing more faint with each step they took.

Kinsley could hardly believe what she had just heard. A hundred questions tumbled through her head, but she waited.

"Just head down here." Elliot pointed to a side street that

angled down. She could hear the river splashing over rocks, the sound growing louder as they walked downhill.

A few moments later they were in a parking lot. A few cars and trucks were parked there and in the distance Kinsley could hear a dog barking.

"We'll go this way," Elliot said, pointing to an even, paved path that led off the parking lot.

Kinsley felt as if she were in a dream. As if she would wake up and none of this would be real.

The path curved, and ahead of them was a bench that looked out over the river, its back to the path.

They walked to the bench and Kinsley sat down, hugging her purse, as if protecting herself.

Elliot dropped onto the bench beside her, glancing over his shoulder as if to make sure Dennis didn't follow them.

"I'm so sorry about that," he said, shifting his arm to rest across the back of the bench. "I didn't know he was in town. Just bad luck."

Kinsley nodded, watching the water catching bits of sun, spangling it back at them, dancing over the river bed. She inhaled slowly, centering herself.

"Did you mean what you said?" she asked finally. "About quitting the rodeo?"

"I did."

Kinsley looked at him, puzzled. "Why?"

He leveled her an incredulous look. "Really? You laid out every reason I should the last time we talked. If you want to call it that. And now you're asking me why I took your advice?"

Kinsley nodded, not sure what to make of his questions.

"You were right," he said finally. "I was doing the wrong thing for the wrong reason." He heaved out a sigh, taking his arm away, leaning forward, his elbows resting on his knees as he stared ahead. "Like you said, I was trying to beat my dad at his own game. Trying to prove something I never needed to prove."

He angled his head to one side to look at her, his eyes piercing. "I may have my ghosts and my shadows, but I know one thing for sure. I don't want anything to do with the things Dennis has done. I don't know how much of his character I got from him. That used to scare me. I guess I always thought if I did what he did, but did it better, I'd show him I'm better than him. But I know now that I've had a better example of fatherhood, and I've been taught how to make good choices. And I choose to quit trying to prove something to Dennis that I was really trying to prove to myself."

His words rang with a sincerity that gave Kinsley goose bumps as did the intensity of his look.

"I'm glad to hear that," she said. "I'm so glad."

He straightened up and smiled at her. "Me too."

They were quiet a moment, allowing his words to rest between them.

"How did you know how to find me?" she asked. Part of her wanted to throw herself in his arms, but it felt as if there were something hanging between them yet. Something that needed to be cleared up.

"Jill told me," he said. "And I have to say I'm glad you decided not to work for her."

"You went to see her?"

"I thought that's where you would be," Elliot said. "I needed to talk to you. But you weren't there. She told me you had come back to Rockyview." He shifted a little closer to her, taking her hands in his, squeezing them gently. "So why did you come back here?"

"You aren't the only who can follow advice, you know. And you're not the only one who needed to be told to shift plans. I'm buying Jeff's photography business. I won't be able to do it full-time right off the bat, so I got a job at the bank. It's just part-time, but it should work out." She stopped, getting distracted by how Elliot's thumbs were tracing small circles over the backs of her hands, sending delightful shivers dancing up and down her spine.

"Well, that makes my heart glad," Elliot said.

Again silence drifted between them, again their eyes caught and held.

"So what happens now?" Kinsley asked.

"I'd like to leave that up to you," Elliot said. "I'm willing to follow your lead."

"That's a new angle for you," Kinsley said, her lips shifting into a smile.

She squeezed his hands then leaned close and pressed her lips to his. Suddenly his arms were around her, holding her tightly against him while his mouth moved over hers, creating a thrill deep inside of her that spread, filling her, creating a yearning for more.

The kiss went on and on, and yet, when he pulled away, she felt as if it hadn't gone on long enough.

He leaned his forehead against hers, his eyes closed. His hands resting on her waist.

"You mixed me up so much," he said, his voice quiet. "I was so turned around, I didn't know what I needed or wanted anymore. But then a song on the radio reminded me. Reminded me that I was looking in the wrong place, looking to the wrong thing to save me. That only God can give me life. And I realized that I've been blessed to be a part of a family and a community given to me by God."

He drew back, his hands cradling her face. "I'm so thankful for what you showed me," he said. "So thankful that you reminded me that I have two fathers who love me dearly."

Kinsley smiled, looking away from him to the river flowing below their feet, the same river she had fallen into. The same river he had ridden his horse across. "Even though our first meeting wasn't the best," she said, smiling at the memory.

"It wasn't exactly the best first impression," Elliot said. "But don't forget, you were the one that was trespassing."

"I wasn't really trespassing," Kinsley protested, then caught the glint in his eye and the lift of his lips. She decided to play along. "You do realize that the river is not private property. I had every right to be there."

"I can tell you're gonna be a lot of fun to argue with," Elliot said.

"So you're going to stick around long enough to find out?" Kinsley asked.

Elliot grew serious at that, his hands lowering back to hers again. "I talked to Zach... Dad," he said, his voice growing serious. "Dad told me there's a place for me on the ranch. I think I'm going to take him up on that."

Kinsley felt like her heart was going to burst in her chest, and then as if she wasn't happy enough, Elliot lifted her hand to his mouth and brushed a gentle kiss over her knuckles. He took a deep breath, biting his lip. He looked uneasy, and Kinsley wandered what he was going to say next.

"Kinsley, I may not be the best person, and I haven't made the best decisions in the past, but I'm hoping to make better decisions in the future. Starting now." He sucked in another breath, his hands squeezing hers so tightly she thought her knuckles were going to break. "Kinsley, I love you so much. I don't want to live my life like I did the last few days. I don't want you out of my life at all. I want to marry you, I want to have kids with you, I want us to be together for the rest of our lives."

Kinsley's heart trembled, and she had to swallow down a knot of tears. She pulled in a trembling breath. "I love you too. I missed you so much too," she said, her voice breaking. "I don't want to be apart from you either."

He swept her close, in a crushing embrace, his hungry lips seeking and finding hers.

When they drew away they were breathless, but they were smiling.

"I'm glad you said yes," Elliot said. "I have to confess I was a little worried. I'm sorry I don't have a ring and everything. I wanted to do it right, but I couldn't wait."

"I've already had the romantic proposal," Kinsley said, her mind ticking back to the elaborate production Drake had made out of his offer of marriage. Candles, music, flowers. "But this means a lot more to me than anything that happened before."

"I want us to set a date right now," Elliot said. "I don't want to wait too long. You need to know I'm committed to this."

Kinsley chuckled at his intensity, love for him pouring through her. "I could pull out my clipboard and pencil you in."

Elliot chuckled. "Nice to know I'm gonna end up just another notation on your calendar."

"You should be so fortunate," Kinsley said, laughing.

"Okay, looks like we have things to do." Elliot stood up and pulled her to her feet. "And before we do anything else, were going to go find a jewelry shop in town. I got money burning a hole in my pocket and a ring I want to buy right now."

"I'm game for that," Kinsley said.

He slipped his arm around her waist and together they walked down the path, toward town.

Toward their future.

* * *

And now Elliot has found his soul-mate even though she came in a way he never expected.

As well, if you're wondering about Lucas, who showed up at the wedding via a Face-Time call, his story is coming up next. Here's a taste of what to expect:

. . .

Chapter One - The Cowboy Returns

He was coming home.

After three tours, long months of tension, pain and disappointment, healing and hurt, seeking a ragged peace, Lucas Groves' life as a soldier was over.

Now he had come full circle and was coming back home to Rockyview.

He made the last turn off the road onto the driveway lined with poplar and aspen trees, a few yellow, gold and orange leaves still clinging to the now-bare branches. Rockyview County was between fall and winter, that waiting time.

He sighed as he followed the gentle curve of the road, left-over leaves fluttering down from the trees onto his Jeep, like small welcome-home gifts.

Coming here was a way to give himself some closure. Some space. A time for reflection.

Time to make a decision about this place and the ranch-land connected to it.

He and his parents had only lived on this yard, in this house for a year before his life was torn apart. The place held few happy memories, but it had been his since he turned twenty-five. These were the stipulations his parents had put in their will, never thinking they would leave behind a nine-year-old as an orphan when the kayak they had been in tipped and trapped them, drowning them both.

Lucas tossed off the old, worn memories. That was many years ago and since his parents died, his foster father Zach rented the land. Lucas had put the house with its Granny suite in the hands of a property manager who took care of the renters and managed the finances.

As a result Lucas had a healthy nest egg, a valuable ranch he was contemplating selling so he could move on to the next part of his life.

Which was?

Again, he pulled himself back to the present. There was no rush to decide right now.

As he made the final turn, he crested a hill and slowed a moment, allowing himself a smile as he looked at the ranch-style home spread out along a copse of trees, a creek flowing beside it. From there his eyes drifted upward to the mountains standing sentinel over the small ranch.

The Rockies had been there for thousands of years; they would be there long after he died, watching over this country and the changes that tiny humans created.

He stopped, hands resting on the steering wheel as he let the sight of those rugged peaks fill his soul. The five-day drive here had shown him much of the beauty of this country. He drove through thick forests, lakes and the rocks of the Canadian Shield. Then the prairies with their vast sweep and a horizon that seemed to fall below the road. But as soon as he saw that faint blue ridge ahead, he couldn't drive fast enough. Couldn't get to this valley quick enough.

All those years sweating it out in full battle rattle as he worked with Iraqi security forces on tactical missions, dodging bullets from the Daesh, dust swirling up from Griffons, memories of the mountains would ground him.

When things got too hard, his mind sifted back through his memories. Horseback riding with Elliot, Kane and Tricia up in the cool mountain air. Baling hay, moving cattle.

He even scavenged through his winter memories when the heat was especially unbearable. Snowboarding with his buddies on the local ski-hill, a sport disdained by his uber cowboy brothers. Taking the sleds out up into the hills, snow spraying out from the tracks, risking frost-bite as they tore through mountain valleys and along frozen creeks.

Now, through no choice of his, he was back.

He reached up to his face, letting his fingers run along the scar that ran from the corner of one eye toward his ear. The

CAROLYNE AARSEN

injury that caused his medical discharge. Limited vision in one eye had become his one-way ticket out of the forces and out of the army. He could have fought it. Pushed for a desk job but he was soldiered out. The dream that had pulled him through basic training, a tour in the Ukraine then two in Iraq had sucked the life out of him. His counselor had told him he'd been lucky to have avoided, so far, the extreme end of PTSD. The bad dreams were subsiding, the memories shifting.

He knew it would be years before he could put his war experiences in their proper place in his life. He'd always been thankful for the faith instilled in him by Grace and Zach Tye. The quiet trust in a God that knew who Lucas was and, in all the mess of the world, knew where he was.

Curbing the memories that could still hold him hostage, Lucas put the Jeep into gear and cruised down the hill to the house.

Two cars were parked on the gravel pad by the garage and he assumed one belonged to his grandmother, the other probably to a visiting friend. A year ago the people who had been renting the house moved out and his grandmother had e-mailed him in Iraq, asking if she could move back to Rockyview and back into her old home.

Despite the lack of a strong connection between them, he felt he couldn't say no to his maternal grandmother so now Glenda was staying here. And, he had found out from conversations with Zach, that she'd recently had hip surgery and was recuperating. Glenda had hired a private nurse, however, to care for her so that responsibility wouldn't fall on Lucas.

Not that he would have taken it on. He and Glenda had a complex and diffident relationship. He had limited expectations from the woman who didn't want to take care of her orphaned grandson. A birthday card and a cheque every year, a text message even less often and, when he was in the hospital, a phone call.

Thankfully Glenda her own locked off apartment containing a small kitchen, dining area, living room and bedroom and her own entrance.

Lucas assumed that was where she was staying, which left the larger, spacious house for him.

He parked his truck beside the cars and as he got out, he paused, listening to the utter quiet that pressed in on him, almost creating a pressure on ears assaulted by the steady noise of his vehicle and, before that, every city he'd visited.

He'd forgotten the complete stillness of this place. Though it was merely a stopover, he knew being here would help him on the final stages of healing, of moving into a new part of his life.

A faint breeze sifted through the trees, sending another shower of coloured leaves, carrying with it the earthy smell of fall. He inhaled it in, letting the familiar damp earth scent blended with dying apples from the trees behind the house settle into his soul, creating the usual feeling of melancholy that this season brought out.

Though it was the end of November, there was still no snow on the ground. Unusual for this place nestled so close to the mountains. Which probably gave Kane, Zach and Elliot lots of time to get the hay hauled home and bring the cows down from the upper pastures, safely corralling them in the huge yards on the Tall Timber Ranch.

Tomorrow, he promised himself. Tomorrow he would head over to the ranch and share a meal. Catch up. Spend some time in his other home.

But for now, despite his scattered relationship with his grandmother he figured he better say hello and at least get settled in.

He grabbed the duffel bag he'd been using the past few months from the back of the Jeep.

Slinging it over his shoulder, he strode toward the private

entrance of the suite and rapped on the door realizing his mistake.

Of course, Glenda wouldn't come; she just had surgery. But when he tried the handle, it was locked.

His grandmother was probably staying in the main house.

So he strode over to the other entrance rustling up a few dead leaves that had fluttered from the whispering trees above. The flowerbeds flanking the sidewalk had been raked and the shrubs crowding under the bay window of the house's living room had been trimmed in preparation for winter.

Glenda had clearly been taking care of the place before her surgery.

He pushed open the large front door, no need to knock here, tossing his bag on the floor of the tiled entrance. As he did a memory slithered into his mind. His mother's voice calling out to him to slow down, his father's laughter.

And right behind it a flash of light, the sound of gunfire.

The disconnect was disorienting, and he stopped himself, releasing the memories of the past few years. Then he slowly breathed in an out, centering himself.

Praying.

His counselor told him the after effects would ease with time and deliberation and to remind himself he was safe now. Another breath and a reminder that he was home.

"Glenda, are you here?" He glanced into the living room to the left, but that space only held the furniture leftover from his parents. The sight was like a gentle touch to an old bruise. A melancholy pain that didn't cut as much as it had the first time he'd seen it after his parent's death. His grandmother, who had been living next door, hadn't bothered to get it cleared out as the people renting the house were happy enough to have furniture supplied.

The beat of footsteps on the hardwood floor caught his attention as he entered the family room to the right of the main entrance. He doubted the quick, light steps belonged to his grandmother. Probably the nurse she said she had hired.

And as he came face to face with a petite woman, her light brown hair pulled back in a loose ponytail and her large gray eyes staring at him with confusion, icy fingers clenched his heart.

"What are you...how..." he couldn't get the words out as he stared at Summer Auger the one woman who could still make his heart beat faster. The one woman who had held his heart then tossed it aside.

At one time they were supposed to be married and living in this house.

And now she was staying here.

And she was pregnant.

* * * *

The Cowboy's Return is up now available.

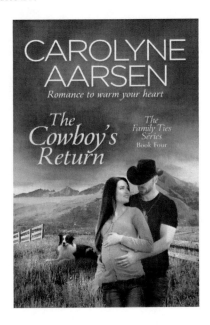

As well, if you enjoyed Taming the Cowboy, I'd love if you could let other people know by leaving a review. Reviews keep me writing. Reviews keep me motivated. Reviews keep me on my toes.

Go to the Amazon website to let me and other readers know what you thought of the story.

Thanks so much and I hope you like spending time in Rockyview county. It's a place I'll be coming back to a number of times in the future so stay tuned.

FAMILY TIES

Introducing a new series called

FAMILY TIES

Four siblings trying to finding their way back to family and faith

A COWBOY'S REUNION

He's still reeling from the breakup. She's ashamed of what she did. Can a chance reunion mend the fence, or are some hearts forever broken? If you like second chance stories, buried passions, and big country settings, then you'll love this emotional novel.

THE COWBOY'S FAMILY

She's desperate. He's loyal. Will a dark lie hold them back from finding love on the ranch? If you like determined heroines, charming cowboys, and family dramas, then you'll love this heartfelt novel.

TAMING THE COWBOY

A saddle bronc trying to prove himself worthy to a father who never loved him. A wedding planner whose ex-fiancee was too busy chasing his own dreams to think of hers. Two people, completely wrong for each other who yet need each other in ways they never realized. Can they let go of their own plans to find a way to heal together?

THE COWBOY'S RETURN

He enlisted in the military, leaving his one true love behind.

She gave herself to a lesser man and paid a terrible price.

In their hometown of Rockyview, they can choose to come together or say a final goodbye...

SWEET HEARTS OF SWEET CREEK

Escape to Sweet Creek to discover redemption, forgiveness and romance.

#1 HOMECOMING

Will past bitterness blind her to future love?

#2 - HER HEARTS PROMISE

When the man she once loved reveals a hidden truth about the past, Nadine has to choose between justice and love.

#3 - CLOSE TO HIS HEART

Can love triumph over tragedy?

#4 - DIVIDED HEARTS

To embrace a second chance at love, they'll need to discover the truths of the past and the possibilities of the future...

#5 - A HERO AT HEART

If you like rekindled chemistry, family drama, and small, beautiful towns, then you'll love this story of heart and heroism.

#6 - A MOTHER'S HEART

If you like matchmaking daughters, heartfelt stories of mending broken homes, and fixer-upper romance, then this story of second chances is just right for you.

In this series you'll get to know the residents of this town set in the Kootenay mountains and surrounded by ranch land and populated with interesting characters.

Nadine Laidlaw, a newspaper reporter, who can't seem to get rid of her meddling, matchmaking Grandmother and Clint Fletcher, her new boss, who is a reminder of all she wants to forget.

Tess Kruger whose pain has sent her back to her hometown of Sweet Creek trying to find redemption. When her ex-fiancee, Jace Scholte shows up and she's forced to work with him on a fundraiser she struggles with her old feelings for him and the secret she can never tell him.

Cory Luciuk is working her way through life, waitressing at the Riverside Cafe. And then the man who broke her heart and tainted her past shows up again.

Kelsey Swain, a widow with a small boy has seen her share of sorrow when her husband died. She now runs the Riverside Cafe, struggling to get it off the ground. Then his ex-partner comes back to Sweet Creek and with him a reminder of what she lost.

The series is complete and ready to be binge read at your leisure!!!

THE HOLMES CROSSING SERIES

The Only Best Place is the first book in the Holmes Crossing Series.

#1 THE ONLY BEST PLACE

One mistake jeopardized their relationship. Will surrendering her dreams to save their marriage destroy her?

#2 ALL IN ONE PLACE

She has sass, spunk and a haunting secret.

#3 THIS PLACE

Her secret could destroy their second chance at love

#4 A SILENCE IN THE HEART

Can a little boy, an injured kitten and a concerned vet with his own past pain, break down the walls of Tracy's heart?

#5 ANY MAN OF MINE

Living with three brothers has made Danielle tired of guys and cowboys. She wants a man. But is she making the right choice?

#6 A PLACE IN HER HEART